Tails of the Wolf

by

C. R. EISENBACK

DORRANCE
PUBLISHING CO
EST. 1920
PITTSBURGH, PENNSYLVANIA 15238

Dorrance Publishing Co
585 Alpha Drive
Pittsburgh, PA 15238
Visit our website at *www.dorrancebookstore.com*

ISBN: 978-1-6386-7204-3
ESIBN: 978-1-6386-7733-8

Tails of the Wolf

Contents

Chapter 1

The Chameleon

As the sun set across the desert, a shadowy figure appears. It has been many years now since the world fell apart due to an unknown disaster. The Great Disaster, as it is known to those who survived, left humanity crippled, killing hundreds of thousands. This forced the survivors to adapt to a new harsher environment.

Most people who survived the Great Disaster merely tried to pick up their lives from what they could remember of the old world. But it wasn't always so easy to do, for there were many who would use the people's fears to get what they wanted. In this world, there are no heroes or saviors for the people to believe in. Evil men with evil desires are all that remains.

As for this man, his desires are neither good nor evil; they are merely his own. He was of a medium build with light brown hair and dark brown eyes. Under his long, dark gray jacket strapped to his legs he had a pair of M9 pistols and a sword by his side. On his right shoulder was a large bag, and in his left hand was a smaller bag. As the man walked, he could see a town far in the distance.

In this time, when people gathered in large groups, they would form new towns and villages. To a wanderer like this man, towns were the best places to gather the supplies they needed or anything else they were looking for.

As he entered the town, he noticed that the people would look away or would go inside their homes as he passed. This was nothing new to this man, because people often feared strangers who came into their town.

As the man walked down the street, he looked over the town taking into account all the buildings, people, and the items sold in the various shops and stands. Beside the homes, there were many other buildings, which were inns and taverns. The stranger also saw a schoolhouse and a blacksmith with a stable beside it. Just outside the town he also saw acres of farmland ready for harvest.

Written on one of the signs in bright lettering were the words "Chameleon's Head Tavern". The sign itself had a chameleon on it with a mug in his hand. Taverns and bars were normally cheaper places to eat and drink. Some would even have a few rooms to rent, being cheaper than the more expensive inns. Also, they are perfect places for gathering information about anything you're looking for or wanted.

The tavern's main room was large and already filled with many of the locals. From the look of the men, they were most likely farm hands and laborers. Everyone had strong builds and tanned skin with sunburned necks. They sat around shabby wooden tables nursing their drinks; a group of men were even in the back playing a game of cards.

Several young women in short skirts and skimpy tops walked around serving drinks to the men. The stranger knew by the way the men fondled the serving girls that it wasn't just the food and drink that they served here.

After entering the tavern, the stranger walked across the well-worn wooden floor up to the bar. As he sat down on one of the many wooden stools, the heavy-set bartender moved over to serve him.

"Welcome to Hellsdome, stranger. What could I get for you lad?" the bartender said speaking in a deep Scottish ascent.

"What do you have?" the stranger asked.

"Well we have some scotch, whiskey, or beer that we make ourselves," he said listing off the drinks. "So, what will it be?"

"I will take the beer," the stranger said.

The bartender reached down under the bar and pulled out a small glass. He poured a light brown liquid from a large bottle and put the glass on the bar.

"That will be one can sir," the bartender said.

There is no currency or money in the world anymore. All transactions are done merely through trade, and canned goods are the most popular item for trade. So, the people use canned goods as a sort of value of how much food or water they wanted.

The stranger bent down and opened the large bag by his side. Inside the bag could be seen around fifty or more cans. When the bartender looked over the bar, he shuddered at the site.

"Ammm," he started. "Is there any thing else you need, a room, a woman, a man, drugs, or anything else at all?"

"Just a room," the stranger said, not looking at the bartender.

"Well we have several different rooms available.

We have a basic room for five cans, but you should know you may share the room with four other people. We also have private rooms. Ten cans will get you a room with just a bed, or for fifteen cans you can get a room with a sink and a tub. But you must fill the sink and the tub by hand." "Or you can get our best room for twenty cans. In this room, you will get a nice bed, a full mirror, a sink, a tub with indoor plumbing, and electricity, very rare."

The stranger sat there as if in a deep thought.

"Which one would you like, sir?" the bartender asked.

"I think I will take the best room you have," the stranger said as if he were coming out of a trance.

"Very good, sir," the bartender said, "that will be twenty cans, please."

The stranger turned again back to the large bag of cans and began to pull them out one by one. As the stranger did this, the bartender watched as each can was being placed on the bar one after another.

"Can I have your name, sir?" the bartender asked.

At this, the stranger looked up from his task and peered into the eyes of the bartender. The bartender, seeing this look, began to shudder.

"F-for my records," said the bartender shuddering. You could hear the fear in his voice. "Unless you would rather no one know your name, sir?"

"No, it's fine," the stranger said. "It's Matrix."

The noise once so loud turned silent with fear as those words were spoken. Matrix looked around, and he saw that everyone was looking at him with fear in their eyes. As he placed the last can on the bar, he saw that the bartender had even taken a couple of steps back as well.

"Not *the* Matrix, right?" the bartender asked in a shaky voice. "Not the man that they call the Wolf, right?"

Matrix looked up at the bartender and in a clear voice said only one word, "Yes!"

Several men jumped from their seats and ran out the door. While the others seemed to be transfixed in their chairs and even though their minds told them to run their legs could not move. The girls too stood as if they were petrified.

This is the effect of this man's name; it made men turn to stone, women scream in fear, and children run and hide at the sound of it. It is the name of fear; it is the name of the devil.

"I cannot believe that I am in the same room as The Wolf Matrix," the bartender said, the fear rising in his voice. "I mean, I have heard story after story about you, sir. They say that you move and fight likes a wolf and that when you get angry you even transform into one. They also say that you never leave a town without killing at least fifty men."

"So, is that what they are saying about me these days?" Matrix said taking a drink from his glass.

"Yes, sir, Mr. Matrix, sir!" the bartender said.

"Well, is this going to become a problem?" Matrix said looking over his glass.

"Oh! No, sir Mr. Matrix!" the bartender stuttered.

"Good! And it's Matrix!" he said.

"What, sir?"

"It is just Matrix. Not Mister!"

"So, what brings you to our town Mist... ah, Matrix?" the bartender asked with fear rising once more in his voice.

"I am just passing through, that is all," he said he emptied his glass and pointed to the bartender to fill it again. "I am not looking for any trouble. Are you going to make trouble for me?"

"Oh, no, sir," the bartender said almost dropping the bottle in his hand.

"Good, because I was looking forward to a good night's sleep tonight, and there is nothing worse for that than someone trying to kill you in your sleep. You agree?" Matrix said looking at the bartender.

"Oh, ah yes, sir!" the bartender said laughing. "But don't you worry, sir, for I will see to it personally that you won't be disturbed."

"And if I am, I will hold you responsible!" Matrix said as he stared into the bartender's face. "And what they try to do to me, I well do to you too. Do I make myself clear?"

"C-crystal clear, sir," the bartender said, his voice disappearing into a small whisper.

The bartender sat there in silence for a moment and then went back to serving the other people in the tavern that didn't flee in terror at the sound of Matrix's name. The men as well had gone back to their own drinks and to their everyday lives, but still stayed ready to run away at the first sign of trouble.

The bartender then, at a gesture from Matrix, refilled his glass once more and then tried busying himself cleaning up the bar. At this moment, he thought it to be the best time to ask the question that was on his mind.

"Ah.... Matrix, ah... sir," he started.

At the sound of his voice, still shaking with fear, Matrix put the glass down and sat there waiting for him to get to his point so that he could get back to his own drink.

"Ah... Would you be so kind to ah," the bartender said his voice still shaking even more so now that Matrix was looking right at him with a look of growing impatience. "I mean it would be a great honor to me if you were to tell me the true story of one of your many adventures... Ah, please!"

Matrix looked at him as if he were speaking a foreign tongue. "You want me to tell you the truth about my life?" Matrix reiterated.

"Ah... yes," said the bartender.

"And what would you do with this story that I tell?" Matrix asked.

"I will tell all who wish to hear the truth about Matrix and his adventures!" the bartender said.

"For a price, of course," Matrix asked.

"Well ah... No! No! I would tell the story for," the bartender cleared his throat. "Free!"

"Ha, ha," Matrix laughed. "What are you talking about? Nothing, and I mean nothing, in this world is free. Everything has its price. So, don't try to fool me. It is one of the things my father told me about this world. Nothing in this world is free. But it did not matter to my father. My father could talk his way in or out of anything, depending on the situation. Yes, my old man was some negotiator. And he was in good shape too, so if the going got tough, we could get away from trouble too. He was a little taller than I am, but our eyes and hair were the same. He was a great man." Matrix paused for a moment as if remembering something terrible that had happened to him.

"And what about your mother?" the bartender asked, an attempt to break the uncomfortable silence that was in the air.

"What?" Matrix said shaking off the feeling of those painful memories.

"Your mother?" the bartender said again. "Who was she?"

"I don't know," Matrix said. "She died in the Great Disaster. I was around six months old when it happened. So I can't really remember her or of the old world in which she and everyone used to live in. My father tried several times to tell me about her, but it was never enough for me. And in the end a dream is all I have of her."

Matrix put his glass down and saw that the bartender was looking at him with the strangest face that Matrix had ever seen. It was as if Matrix had confused him with the story. But he knew where he had lost him in his story, so he waited for the bartender to say something.

The bartender saw this and slowly started up the conversation. "Ah. What do you mean by a dream is all you have of her?"

Matrix smiled, disturbing the bartender more than Matrix's eyes or his name.

"What I mean is," Matrix said, "that I have had a dream with my mother in it. It is one of the only things I can remember clearly about my childhood. For as far back as I can remember I have had this dream. Every so often the dream would come back to me, as if my mind does not wish me to forget it."

Chapter 2

The Butterfly

My dream starts with me sleeping on the floor. The ground itself wasn't hard like concrete but soft. Opening my eyes, I found myself lying on a soft shag rug; it was so comfortable that I could have just lied there all day.

Just then something grabbed my attention. It was a butterfly that flew over my head. It must have come in through the open glass door that was on my left.

I thought that this little thing was the most wonderful thing that I had ever seen. I followed the butterfly wherever it went. I watched as the butterfly flew over to a mirror that had been placed on the floor.

When I made it over to the mirror, I tried to catch the butterfly, missing it; I had caught a good look of myself in the mirror. It is in this moment that I knew that I was a little child in this dream, around six months old.

I turned away from the mirror to chase after the butterfly again. It was now heading back to the open door to escape the six-month-old beneath it. But it was not going to lose me that easy.

So, I followed it out the door onto a concrete floor. I looked up to see where the butterfly was. Within several steps I found myself up against a railing of metal bars.

I discover I was on a balcony. Looking down I could see the people on the street. I then cast my eyes skyward to find the butterfly, but it was already on the next floor above me. Disappointed, I turn my head back into the room that I had just come out of.

There were two people inside the room looking at me. They had been watching me this whole time. I could not see who they were because the sun was in my eyes, making it so it was hard to see them clearly. I felt that we were close, but I did not know how. All I knew is that they were the only ones who could help me now.

I tried to tell them what I wanted, without using words. I then turned my head back to see were the butterfly was, but it had flown away, and I could not find it again. But something new caught my attention.

It wasn't a butterfly or another bug, but a bright green light. It was like a flash from a camera, but it looked like it was alive, for it looked as if it were moving towards me. I looked back at the people in the other room, and in the green light I could see my father and my mother's faces.

The dream continued with me waking up on the concrete floor. I picked myself up and moved over to be where I last saw my mother and father. I made it to the spot where my parents were, and for the first time I could see my mother's face clearly.

She had a beautiful face, deep blue eyes, light blond hair, and I would say that she was a little shorter than my father. My mother was lying as if she were asleep, but no matter how hard I tried to wake her she wouldn't wake.

It was then I noticed that she was propped up on a pair of legs and that two massive arms were holding her around her waist. It was my father. He was holding her tight; with tears in his eyes he was rocking her back and forth. And at this site of my father and mother together and with tears in my eyes I cried out, "Mommy!"

With a start, I would wake up, always with tears in my eyes and sweat on my head. As I said, my father was the one who raised me as a child, but he did not know about my dream at all. I didn't think it was necessary to tell him about it. So, I pretended that it didn't it happen, but the dream just would not leave me alone.

It got so bad that when I was eight, at the end of my dream when I cried out for my mother, I woke both my father and me.

"What is it, son?" my father said.

"Oh," I started, "it was just a dream. That's all, Dad."

"Well to me it looks like it's more than a dream to you," he said seeing the expression on my face.

My father was good at identifying different facial expressions and knowing what they meant. It was a big help in his negotiations but made hiding something from him hard. For now, my face was saying to him that that dream was not your everyday dream, and that it was very disturbing to me. And of course, he was right.

"So why don't you just tell me about this dream," he said to me. "You never know, it may help to talk about it."

So I told him. He always seemed to have a way to get me to tell him what was on my mind. After I had told him the whole dream, he just sat there in silence, deep in thought. And as I looked hard at him, I could see what appeared to be tears in his eyes. He was crying, but I did not know why. It was just a dream, or so I thought.

"Dad," I said trying to break the silence in the air. "Are you okay?"

At my question, he looked up at me and shook his head. "No, I am not, my son," he said still with tears in his eyes. "For that dream of yours is not just a dream; it is in fact exactly what happened on that day."

"You mean that my dream is really a memory," I said looking at him.

"Yes!" my father said. "The fact that you described your mother perfectly is proof enough. That dream is a memory of that day, but the dream is not perfect, for there is more you need to know. First, I must ask you to forgive me; the things I am going to tell you should have been told to you."

So, my father started talking about events that happened after the realization of my mother's death. And I learned more about who my mother was, and about my family. For I had not seen anybody who was related to me except for my father, but that was the same for everyone.

I know now that after the Disaster, my father tried to grab things that could help me know my mother, but it was too late. For we had just moved to a bigger place and the more valuable stuff was at our old home.

We all know the first moments after the Great Disaster were chaos! That is all it was. Homes were pillaged, valuables were stolen, and anything that was worthless was destroyed, and that was the fate of anything that showed my mother.

"When it was all said and done, I said that I would raise you as best I could," my father said with fresh tears in his eyes. "And I told myself that I would teach you all you needed to know. As a teacher, your mother believed that education was the key to survival. I know she would want you to know how to read, to write, do math, know your history, and all the other things that I have taught you. This is what your mother would have wanted for you.

"But the one thing you should have known from the beginning, I held it back. More because it was still hard for me to bring it up. I hid that by saying you were too young to fully understand what I was saying. For that I am sorry. But now you know everything, my son. I hope you can find some comfort in my words."

At that we both went back to sleep for it was still very late.

My heart was still racing when I tried to get back to sleep. Everything that my father had told me was still on my mind, and I could not quiet my thoughts. And the thought of my mother brought tears back into my eyes, and I could not stop them. So in the end I had cried myself to sleep that night, and the dream seemed to leave me. I was glad for that, for I could not bear to see my mother after what my father had told to me.

Chapter 3

The Fox

After a while, life returned to normal, and the dream was the last thing on either of our minds. We lived a simple life, always on the move. Most people were just looking for a sign of civilization and trying to stay out of any political disputes.

There were many like my father and I, people who were neither with the Government Party or the Anarchist Party. The Government Party, we all know, was the accumulation of what remained of the world's government officials, such as world leaders, judges, lawyers, and military men and women.

The Anarchist Party, on the other hand, consisted of all the people who thought that the government had failed to do anything to stop the Great Disaster. They thought that the government shouldn't have another chance to destroy the world. And of course, the two parties fought over the way the world should be run.

So, fights broke out, and both the Government and the Anarchist were fighting and killing one and other. In doing so, it made those who did not wish to get involved in either party to wander all over to find a place of peace. For many, they found a place that they could be content with; even if it was not perfect, they would find a way to make do with what they got.

But like so many other people, my father and I did not settle in one place. Instead we traveled the world looking for our own nirvana. But where we were going, or what we were looking for I didn't know, for my father never talked about what he was looking for.

So, we just traveled the world going from town to town doing the best we could to survive. But as with most people in this world, we found that it was hard to do.

Like when we one day we came to a small town by a river in the east. It was like any other town that we had ever been to, with small homes on both sides of a road. In front of some of the homes were small stands set up for trading of goods for the travelers who came through the town.

My father would go to all the stands and talk to all the people to see what the people in the town were willing to trade and find a place to sleep for the night. As for me, I was looking around the town for anything strange or dangerous to us. This is something that we did whenever we came into a town or village.

On the first glance of the town, it seemed to be like any other town we had ever been to, but as I had seen in other towns before, that meant nothing. It only meant that the town was quiet for now, but if we didn't watch what we did here, we would be in big trouble. Then again sometimes trouble just finds you know matter what you do.

As I looked over the town, I noticed five men were walking down the street. If not for the way they were walking I would not have noticed them. Four of the men were walking behind the fifth man in a two-by-two formation. This to me said that the man in front was a man of some importance, so either he was the leader of the town or a leader of the local gang in this area.

Though the look of the man suggested the second. For one, he did not look like a town elder; he was far too young to have been given that honor. Although a gang leader, on the other hand, he does not need age, or wisdom, just strength and a power to command. For them it was the strongest led and the weak followed.

Either way we needed to watch out for this man and try to stay out of his way, but that would prove to be the hardest thing to do.

The looks on the people's faces confirmed what I first believed. Even at my young age I had seen that look a hundred times. Fear! The fear of death, the death that this man deals or by those he commands.

The merchant's eyes also saw the five men coming into the town and seemed to wish to get out of site. But my father was not letting him leave without getting a good deal.

"Ten cans!" the merchant said in a sharper and hurried tone what he may have wanted.

But that was not what my father had wanted.

"You must be joking! This stuff is hardly worth five let alone ten cans," my father said as if the offer were an insult.

"What do you mean they're not worth ten?" the merchant said sounding uptight about my father's actuation.

"I mean this equipment is all battered and worm," My father said picking up an old blade that looked like a climbing tool. "I don't think this thing could last one day on a serious climb, and you want 10 cans, no way."

The merchant said looking seriously discussed with my father, "These pieces are in fine condition, as good as they get in this world.

"Yes, maybe but not good enough for 10 cans. I say it is worth 6 cans but no more," my father said.

"No!" the merchant said. "Nine cans."

"Seven!" my father said not faulting for one moment.

"Eight cans," the merchant said, his eyes turning to look at the five men walking closer to us.

His eyes told me much. That these men were not friendly and our merchant friend wanted to finish his business and get off the street.

"All right," the merchant said, "seven it is. Just take it and go now before."

"Is there a problem here?" a strange voice asked behind us.

The three of us quickly turned to face the voice; it was the gang leader with his four bodyguards. I could see now the man in front was the tallest of the five, and even my father had to look up a little to see him. He also seemed thin; at first glance his face looked very kind, but an evil look was in his eyes. Those eyes told me what I thought about him was wrong; he was worse.

The four guys behind him were completely different than him. They were far larger than him. Their arms were like boulders, and each of the men's faces showed their respect for this man.

"No," said the Merchant, looking distressed at the sight of the men.

"Yes, we are just doing some business here," my father said looking right into the tall man's eyes. "And it does not involve you."

The five men around us seemed to flinch at these words. Only I, my father, and the tall man acted as if this statement was a natural thing to say.

"Maybe it is, and maybe it isn't," said the tall man. "But that does not matter. All that does matter is for you to understand how things work around here."

"And how do things work here?" my father asked.

"It simple," the tall man said. "All you have to do is to do what I say, and you will be just fine."

"And who are you sir?" my father asked.

"Oh where are my manners," said the tall man. "My name is Blaze, and you are?"

"You may call me BJ," my father said, "and this is my son Junior."

"It is nice to meet you both," Blaze said, and as he did, he had nodded his head.

My father and I mimicked his motion, but I had refrained myself from lowering my eyes from his. I was determined to watch this man always. My father however seemed not to be taking this man or the four men behind him serious. He just remained calm and polite always. I didn't understand why, but I thought that at least I would be ready for anything that may happen, whatever may happen. I was wrong.

Both Blaze and my father just stood there looking at each other like they were waiting for the other to make the first move in a great game. It was my father who broke the silence on that road first when it came apparent that Blaze seemed to have nothing else to say.

"Well then," my father said holding out his hand to Blaze, "if there is nothing else, I think my son and I will get our things and be off."

Blaze did not take my father's afford hand but started up the conversation once more.

"I'm afraid you and your son cannot leave," Blaze said taking a step forward, and with him the four men behind him followed.

"And why is that?" My father was not backing down at the oncoming of the five men.

"Well there is the small matter of a traveling tax that all travelers must pay when entering our town," Blaze said seemingly surprised that my father did not back up at the site of the five men.

"Well of course," my father said looking surprisingly happy at this, which threw both me and Blaze for a loop, "and how much will that be?"

Blaze regained his composer and then said, "What do you have of value?"

"We have very little of anything," my father said. "But what we do have is about twenty pounds of bear meat to trade."

"Bear meat eh," Blaze said looking overwhelmed.

"Yes, sir," my father said, "just killed today by my boy here."

At these words two things happened. One, I got a big hearty slap on the shoulder by my father, and Blaze turned to me in amazement. And why not? After all, I was only ten years old. Not many ten-year-olds could go up against a full-grown bear by himself.

"He must be quite the hunter," Blaze said looking right into my eyes. "He also seems to have a fighting spirit as well."

"Yes, he does indeed," my father said almost laughing at these words, "but then again who doesn't these days."

There was a small pause where the two men just sat there thinking on what was said. When the pause was disturbed, it was again my father who spoke first. "Now then," he said gathering his thoughts, "how much is this traveling tax of yours?"

"Mm... about ten pounds of your bear meat would be enough," Blaze said.

"Very well, if that is the tax, I will pay it," and my father reached into the bag at his feet and pulled out two large bundles of meat and gave it to one of the four who stood behind Blaze.

"Well then," Blaze said. "Well I guess that concludes our business, and I hope you come and visit us again in Oxhelm."

And with that Blaze inclined his head again and proceeded down the street. My eyes followed him and his escort until they were all out of sight.

Chapter 4

The Weasel

"You two don't know how lucky you are," a voice sounded from behind us.

It was the merchant, but now his face had changed. It was as if someone had just lifted a blade out from under his throat.

"You seem to be relieved to see him go," I said.

"You would be too, boy, if you knew Blaze as well as I do," the merchant said. "Blaze is a brutal man and is completely in control of this town. If I were you, I would leave this town now."

"But we just got here," my father said, "and besides, we were hoping to get a good night's sleep in a nice bed for a change."

"After what just happened, I would think you two would just leave now," the merchant said.

"We don't scare very easily," my father said. "Besides, we had given him all of his so-called taxes. Why else would he have to bother us?"

"Because you are here," the merchant said. "Blaze takes everything that comes into his reach, and now he has you two."

"But why would he want us?" I said. "I mean he doesn't even know us."

"Yes!" my father said. "How can he use us if he does not even know what use we can be to him? So why would he want to keep us here?"

"You are both still young," the merchant said. "You both still can do physical labor. That is only until Blaze finds out what other talents you have to offer him."

"He seems to be a very impressive man," my father said, "and it seems he gets what he wants and does what he wants."

"It is not that getting what he wants," the merchant said. "It more that he just takes what he wants. We here are no more than just slaves."

"But you don't look like a slave," I said taking another good look around the town. "I mean I see no guards to keep you here. Why not just run away?"

"What you see here in the town is only an illusion," the merchant said. "This whole town is a prison, and he is the warden."

"But as my son has just said, there seems to be no guards," my father said. "So, tell us what is really keeping you all here."

At this the merchant laughed and began to look around.

"Look down the street. See the two men in the red and green shirts," the merchant said.

Both my father and I looked in the direction he had pointed to. Indeed, there were two men standing near the entrance of the town. At first glance they looked like any other townsfolk in the town.

"So, what about them," my father said turning back to the merchant.

"They work for Blaze," the merchant said. "They are the ones who keep us here. They try to stay unnoticed by the people in the town so they can move freely without being noticed."

"The best way to keep an eye on the sheep is not to be the sheepdog," my father said, "but for the dog to be in sheep's clothing, eh."

"Well it seems you have some great intelligence," the merchant said. "It is precisely why Blaze has them here for."

"So, they are here to spy on the people and tell Blaze what they see and hear," I said taking another look at the two men. "Blaze's eyes and ears."

"Exactly," said the merchant.

"But wouldn't they be more efficient if no one knew who they were?" my father said also gazing once more at the two men.

"Well to most people in the town they are unknown," the merchant said. "I only know because I once saw those two men dragging another man away for trying to escape. I don't know how many others are working for Blaze, but I am sure there are more than those two."

"So, Blaze keeps any number of these watchdogs here to keep an eye on the people of this town and all those who came into the town," my father said.

"Yes, and that is why you two should leave right now," the merchant said. "If he comes to think that you can be something of use to him, he will force you both to work for him."

"Maybe, but we both are still tired and a good night's sleep in a nice bed would be a wonderful change," my father said. "If you are unable or unwilling to give us a place to sleep then I will find someone who will."

"Fine, I will give you a place to stay for the night," the merchant said, "and in the morning I will even give you several days' supplies and equipment."

"And how much will this cost us?" my father asked.

"Nothing," the merchant said.

"Nothing," my father repeated. "Nothing in this world is free, and yet you want to give us a place to sleep, supplies, and equipment. What is the catch?"

"No catch," the merchant said. "I just don't think you will be able to pay for anything."

"And why not?" I said. "You think we will not pay you for your services?"

"No, young one," the merchant said. "I know you can pay for my services; I just don't think you to will survive the night."

"So, you think that Blaze will try something tonight?" my father said.

"That's right," the Merchant said.

"And what if we do survive the night?" my father asked. "Then what will happen to your generosity you are showing us?"

"Nothing," the merchant said. "If you and your son actually make it through the night, my deal remains the same. You get everything for free like we agreed. No strings attached."

"Will I guess we have no other choice," my father said. "Show us the way to the room kind, sir?"

The room turned out to be a small cabin that was behind the merchant's own home. It only had one large room in the cabin. The cabin had a small wood stove, a small sink, and two very small beds in the far end.

"So, this is your room you are going to rent us?" my father asked.

"Yes!" the merchant said. "It's small, but it will keep you out of the way."

"Out of the way?" I asked.

"Out of my way of course," the merchant said.

"What are you afraid of? If Blaze comes for us, do you think he will go after you to as well?" my father asked.

"No!" the merchant said. "What I am saying is that I am not going to let him try to do harm to me. If Blaze wants you, he will come for you and he won't care how or who gets in between you and him."

"Does Blaze really scare everyone that bad?" I asked.

"You have seen Blaze with your own eyes, little one," the merchant said. "Don't you find him intimidating?"

"I thought he was an impressive person," I said, "but I don't think he was intimidating. I don't think he can do a thing by himself."

"He doesn't have to," the merchant said. "His men do all the dirty work. And they are who I am afraid of."

"Well hopefully we won't have to meet anyone of them," my father said.

"You can do whatever you want," the merchant said, "and I will do whatever I have to as well."

He left the cabin with a look that told me he believed that we were as good as dead. But we were not going to let his feelings disturb us. So, we started to prepare our nightly meal and then went to bed.

It felt as if I had only just fallen asleep when a crash rang through the cabin. I awoke suddenly and looked about to find the sources of the noise, but instead I found fire. I could still see the shattered remains of the bomb on the ground. The fire blazed into life and started to spread rapidly.

"We have to get out of here," my father screamed.

As if I needed to be told, but the problem was that the fire had already blocked the door.

"How do we get out, Father?" I said taking stock of are situation. "The door is blocked by fire."

My father grabbed the bed sheets and dumped them into the bowl of water we had on the stove. Once damp, my father threw the sheets over my head.

"Keep the sheet tight around you," my father said.

He then threw the other sheet around him, and then we ran as fast as we could into the flames in the direction of the window. As we approached the flames, I closed my eyes and brought the sheet closer, covering my face.

I felt the flames licking my body and heard a large crash as my father and I smashed through the window. We hit the ground hard and rolled out of the sheets.

When I looked up, I found myself looking at Blaze's face. Not just Blaze, but a band of his men. They were all dressed in black leather and had mad looks in their eyes. They were carrying all different kinds of weapons in their hands. Swords, daggers, whips, clubs, and many other weapons lay by their sides.

It was Blaze who helped me to my feet while one of his goons helped my father. Once on my feet, I returned to my father's side not liking the touch or the look of Blaze.

"Well it seems that everyone is okay here," Blaze said looking very innocent. "We saw the smoke from the fire and came to see what had happened. We are all glad to see you are both alright."

"I'm sure you are," my father said in the same innocent voice Blaze was using, "and we are grateful for the assistance that you were going to give us."

"You are quite welcome," Blaze said with a mock bow, "but perhaps I can help you after all. I would be greatly honored if you two will stay with me in my home. I have plenty of room to accommodate you both."

As he said this, two of his men came around and stood behind us with their backs to the burning cabin. My father and I looked at the two men behind us and then at each other.

"Well I guess, we don't have any other place to go," my father said, considering Blaze's eyes. "We will be happy to take you up on your offer."

And at that we started out, walking in a two-by-two formation with two of Blaze's men in front of my father and me while two of his men were behind us. Blaze then came up behind them and the rest followed behind him.

The street, as we walked, was empty of life. No one could be seen outside, but I could still see shadows moving behind the windows. The townsfolk were aware of what was happening within their town but were not about to be seen by Blaze or by his men.

Chapter 5

The Dog

Matrix paused for a moment and took a long drink from his glass. As Matrix did this, the bartender took the chance to ask a question of Matrix.

"So, Blaze lit the cabin on fire to get rid of you two?" the bartender said reaching down to fill Matrix's glass.

"So, you also figured that out just by my narrative," Matrix said. "Well you are as quick as my father and I were then. For us both thought the same thing."

Matrix took another drink from his glass, finishing it in one swig. The bartender poured another glass, with a look like a child waiting for candy to drop into their hand.

"So, what happen after that?" The bartender said waiting patiently for the story to resume.

"Don't worry," Matrix said, "we have plenty of time for the story, but first how about some food. I am very hungry right now."

"Oh, certainly, sir," the bartender said hurrying to prepare a meal for the legendary man.

The bartender was quite good. He quickly lit a fire on the stove behind him and put a skillet on the flames. He then picked up a can from under the bar and opened it. He first examined the content of the can; it looked like dog food covered in gravy. The bartender sniffed the meat to ensure that it was safe to eat.

He then emptied the meat into the skillet and began to stir it with spatula. The bartender started to pull down different spices and herbs from the shelf above his head. White wine and added things like salt, pepper, barley, and many other spices that Matrix could not see. The smell from the skillet was overwhelming. The bartender threw his concoction onto a plate and served it to Matrix.

Matrix bolted down the meal. Matrix was amazed by the meal. It tasted like nothing he had ever had.

"Now that was the best thing I ever had," Matrix said, "but you're not interested in my comments of your cooking. You are more interested in my story. So where were we? Oh yes I remember."

My father and I were being escorted to Blaze's home. His home was a mansion. It was huge; it was three windows high and seven windows long.

We walked along the path leading to the front entrance. The entrance to the mansion was a large dark cherry double door. Two guards stood in front of the door under the great stone archway. As we approached, the two guards straightened and opened the doors.

As we passed through the doorway, I was amazed by the size of the great hall. A small home could have fit inside it. There were doors on both side of us, and two sets of stairs that led up all the way up to the third floor.

My father and I were pushed towards the stairs. At the bottom of the stairs, we were separated from each other. My father went up the right-hand stairs flanked by two guards, while I was forced up the left-hand stairs with my two guards behind me as well. I saw Blaze enter the first door on the left on the ground floor accompanied by his four bodyguards.

Meanwhile my father and I continued up the stairs until we reached the second-floor landing. At the second floor, we parted ways once more; my father went right, and I went left. They seemed bent on keeping us as far away as they could.

I watched as my father was thrown in to one of the rooms, just before one of the guards opened the door to my room. I was then shoved into the room. Hitting the floor, I turned around to get up. I watched as the door was closed and heard the door was locked.

I ran to the door and feverishly tried the door, beating it with my fists and feet until my hands ached with pain. I then slumped in front of the door to rest and to give my hands time to stop throbbing. After I had rested long enough, I stood up and began to explore my surroundings.

In the dim moonlight, I could see that there was a large four-poster bed with two side tables and a small dresser by the door. Both the dresser and the side tables were empty. I also found that the bed had clean sheets on it. No matter how Blaze came off at the cabin, he seems to want to treat us as honored guests.

My eyes then traced the moonlight to the two windows set on either side of the bed. I turned to the window next to me and opened it. I was surprised to see it open without difficulty. At first, I thought that Blaze had become careless, but my joy was short-lived when my hand reached out to touch cold steel. Just outside the windows bars had been mounted.

"Well, I guest I won't be getting out this way," I said to myself, "at least not without a tool of some kind.

I then decided that any further exploration could be done in the morning. So, I quickly removed my shoes and my shirt and slipped under the clean sheets and was soon fast asleep.

The new day dawned revealing nothing new to my surroundings. In the light of day, I could see that all the furniture had been nailed to the floor. I could also now see there were two doors on the right-hand side of the room.

I opened the first door to find a walk-in closet. I soon found out that Blaze's precautions had found its way in here too. For the bar that was used to hang clothing was gone as well.

The door beside the closet led into a bathroom. The bathroom was decorated differently than the bedroom. It had been painted like that of an underwater cave. Both the walls and ceiling had the look of stone. The floor, however, was like walking on polished glass, and it shined like glass as well.

Even the fixture son the sink and the shower had a feeling of stone. I turned the handle of the sink, but no water came out.

"I guess Blaze is not going to give us that many comforts," I said to myself, "as if I need such comforts in the first place."

I was pulled from my thoughts by a knock on the door. But before I could say anything or prepare myself to do anything, the door banged open.

In the doorway, there were three men; the first two had broad shoulders, and in their hands they carried crossbows. As they entered, they stood to one side of the door and raised their crossbows to me. They said nothing just stood there as the third man entered.

The third man was taller than the other two and was dressed in finer clothing. On his side, he had a long sword and a knife on his chest. As he walked in, the two other men stood up even taller in respect for the taller man. I could sense that this man commanded great authority.

"You are to come with me!" the tall man said. "My Master would consider it an honor if you would join him for breakfast."

"Very well," I said keeping my voice as courteous as possible.

At that, the taller man beckoned me to follow him. As I passed the doorway, the two guards with the crossbows followed us, closing the door behind them.

As we walked along the landing, I saw that my father was being escorted down as well. When we got close to them, I could make out my father's escorts.

The man in front was much like the man in front of me, but a little shorter and broader. On his side, he carried a mace. Behind my father were two men with crossbows in their hands too.

No one said a word as we headed down to the first floor. We turned to the right and headed for the door that I saw Blaze went into yesterday.

When we entered the doorway, we found ourselves in a large dining room. In it was a long table with three chairs set on the other side of the room. At the table we separated each taking one side of the table.

We sat down in the two chairs on the side leaving the chair at the head of the table open. As we sat down, the four guards with the crossbows stepped back behind us keeping ten spaces between each other and us.

While this was happening, the two men who led us in had left the dining room, leaving my father, our four guards, and me alone.

No one seemed to want to break the long silence that followed their departure. As the silence stretched, both my mind and eyes began to wander around. I found myself looking for the same old signs, looking at the ways in and out of the room. I soon found that the door that we came in through was not the only door. There seemed to be another door.

My eyes then turned to the ceiling to see the large chandeliers. As I stared up into it, I noticed that it looked like hundreds of tiny icicles.

I was just about to start a conversation with my father when the door at the far end of the room opened. As I looked down at the table, I saw that it was Blaze, and with him came his bodyguards following behind him.

The two men, who escorted my father and me to the dining room, detached themselves from the others and came toward us. They forced my father and I to stand as Blaze approached us.

"It's so nice of you two to join me this morning," Blaze said to my father.

"We are honored to join you, Blaze!" my father said in mock pleasantry.

"Indeed," I said in the same mocking tone.

Blaze seemed satisfied with our response and moved on to his chair. He sat at the head of the table with my father and me beside of him and his bodyguards behind him.

"Please, my friends, sit," Blaze said gesturing to our chairs.

"We our very glad that you have taken us in to your home," my father said sitting down.

"I hope you two have enjoyed your commendations?" Blaze said.

"They are very comfortable," my father said keeping his mocking tone.

"Yes!" I said, trying to please Blaze. "We rarely sleep in such comfort."

"I am pleased to hear that," Blaze said.

"Yes, and you will also be pleased to know that we will be leaving as soon as we have gathered supplies," my father said being as forceful as he dared.

"Oh no, I don't think so!" Blaze said.

"What do you mean by that?" my father said.

"Let us discuss your future later," Blaze said raising a hand as to brush the question aside. "For now, let us eat."

Blaze clapped his hands, and the doors to the kitchens opened and out came several servants with trays of food in their hands. I noticed that as the servants walked about the dining hall, they never walked behind Blaze. They would instead walk to the far end of the table before coming up and placing food on the table.

It seems to me that Blaze didn't let just anyone walk behind him. Indeed, when we walked to his home, my father and I walked in front of him. It's seemed that the four men behind him right now were the only men he indeed trusted to stand behind him.

This theory was further proven when a child on her way back to the kitchen tripped and fell behind Blaze's chair. Before the child could pick herself up, one of Blaze's bodyguards was at her side, his knife in his hand. But before he went further, Blaze raised a hand. The bodyguard put a way the knife and helped her up and sent her on her way.

"Your guards seem a little jumpy," my father said seeing the same thing I just did.

"It is more that my guards and I have had many bad experiences from back-stabbing by those who were thought to be allies," Blaze said.

"So, is that why we are so far from the door?" I said with an air of interest. "You do not trust us. You think that when we leave, we will try to kill you?"

"You son has a quick mind," Blaze said looking at my father, before returning to face me. "You are right, little one. None may walk behind me but the four men behind me now. And only them because they have proven themselves time and again. But enough of this; let us eat."

We started to eat, my father and I carefully eating only what we saw Blaze eat first.

"You need not worry!" Blaze said noticing our behavior. "I have not poisoned the food. It is safe to eat."

"I am to assume that you have other reasons for inviting us to your home, and to this wonderful breakfast," my father said poking a strawberry and putting it into his mouth.

"Indeed," Blaze said.

"So, what is it that you want from us?" I said looking curiously.

"What I want is simply," Blaze said, "you!"

"Me!" I said surprised.

"Not just you, but your father as well," Blaze said. "Both you and your father have skills that I want, and I *get* what I want."

"And you want us to work for you?" my father said.

"No! You don't get it. You *are* working for me!" Blaze said.

"What, you're going to force us to work for you?" my father said.

"I told you I always get what I want," Blaze said.

"And what is it you want from us?" I asked thinking I had nothing he wanted.

"Your skills are what I want from you, child," Blaze said. "Yours and the skills of your father."

"What skills do we have that you want?" my father asked with a look of intrigue.

"Your gift with words for one, and your son's skills with a bow," Blaze said. "I don't know many men who can kill a full-sized bear, let alone a child of your age. Your father, on the other hand, can seem to be able to make others to do what he wants, or to get what he wants with ease."

"But so can you!" I said with an air of defiance.

"Yes, I can, child," Blaze said, "but you father can do it without fear. He does not need to make people afraid of him to get what he wants. I do. I need him to use his skills to improve my station with these people."

"To improve your station," my father asked.

"As I am sure you noticed, the people in this town have not quite accepted me as their leader," Blaze said. "What I want from you is to make them accept me as their true leader."

"You want to smooth out your flaws and make you into some sort of saint," my father said looking at Blaze as if it were impossible.

"You are very wise as well," Blaze said. "But you sound as if it is impossible."

"The people of this town are not total idiots," my father said. "They know what you are, and nothing I say can make you look any better."

"Are you saying that you are useless to me?" As Blaze said this, his bodyguards put their hands on their weapons. The men behind my father and I raised their bows as well.

"Well I always did love a good challenge," my father said.

"Good! Then it is settled then," Blaze said gesturing to his men to stand at ease. "Then you should take the time today to get used to my home. Tomorrow we can discuss how best to use your gift. Until then feel free to explore my home and the grounds around it, but I must ask you not to leave the grounds themselves. My men will show you around and watch over you always. You will be safe in their hands; I assure you of that."

"We thank you for your concern," my father said.

As he said this, we stood up and made our way to the doors, our guards following behind us.

Chapter 6

The Otter

Our time at Blaze's mansion passed slowly. Our bodyguards always accompanied my father and me. Only in our rooms were we free from them.

Our day always started and ended the same. We would get up, eat with Blaze in the dining room. My father and I were then split up; I would go off with the other hunters, while my father stayed with Blaze and his "advisers".

I soon found out that many of Blaze's men were like my father and me. Blaze seemed to have a talent of finding those who have talents he can use, and only a rare few seemed to share Blaze's thirst for fear in the people.

I begin to talk to the others who like me were being forced to work for Blaze. I found out that several of them were travelers like my father and I, while others had lived in the town before Blaze had arrived.

With their help, I could learn what happened to this town. It seems that the town was very different. It was quiet and peaceful, that was before Blaze came with his gang.

He took over quickly; the people did not put up much of a fight. Blaze and his small group of men had dominated the townsfolk easily and had continued to do so ever since.

No one knew much about Blaze before he came here. Some say that he was once part of the Anarchists Party and that he was a key member of the eastern faction. It seemed that after the Anarchists Party won against the Government Party, the members of the Anarchists Party went their own ways.

It seems the Anarchists Party went into chaos even after the Government had been defeated. Blaze went his own way taking as many men who would follow him. It was on Blaze's travels that Blaze came onto this town. The townsfolk knew nothing of fighting, nor did they possess any weapons. This made Blaze's job of taking over the town easier.

All Blaze needed to do was to come into town in force, kill a few people, and the people started to beg him to stop. Fear has been Blaze's greatest weapon. Now it seems that he wants the people to love him for what he did.

From the discussion between my father and Blaze over all our meal times, my father was not having much success at making Blaze into hero.

"Well, how is it going?" Blaze asked one night at dinner.

"Not so good," my father said. "The people are as hard to persuade as I had thought.

But I have not given up," my father said seeing the look on Blaze's face.

"Good!" Blaze said. "And how are you getting along?" he said looking at me.

"I am adjusting!" I said.

"I am sure that the other hunters are all finding your experience and talent useful," Blaze said.

"Yes! But many of the others think that I am just a kid," I said.

"Well I guess they will just take longer to adjust to you," Blaze said.

"Well, we can only hope that they do," my father said.

"You sound as conniving as when you talked about your task," Blaze said.

"Well, as I said, people don't change so easily or quickly as you think or as you want," my father said.

"Well, you know the mind of the people better than me," Blaze said. "Are you saying that you can't make the people do what you want?"

"You make it sound as if I manipulate people's minds," my father said.

"Isn't that what you do?" Blaze said.

"No!" my father said. "All I do is show people the better way to act or to live, but they always have a choice to agree or disagree with me."

"Choices are all we have in the end; that is what my father always said to me," I said.

"But here now there is only one choice, whatever I said," Blaze said.

"Then you are far worse than I thought; to take away choice in this world is unforgivable," my father said, his voice without a trace of fear.

Blaze just laughed at this statement. "But my way works well, don't it," Blaze said. "After all, you and your son have also given up your choice."

I lay in bed after dinner thinking as I had often done before going to sleep. My thought this night was on what was just discussed. The fact is that my father and I had been forced to be here by Blaze. Blaze had said he wanted my father's talents and my own.

But why was I in this room? Why was I living here at all? Why wasn't I in the hut where all the other hunters under Blaze's control lived? The answer was because of my father. Blaze wanted to keep my father on his side, and the way to do that is to keep me nearby.

Though how much longer will Blaze keep me here for my father's sake? If my father continues to make no progresses with the people of the town, Blaze may start to use me to convince my father to try harder to do his job or something me might happen to me. And if I knew my father as well as I thought, he was thinking the same thing.

It was just too bad we were unable to talk about this together. For Blaze had made sure that except when we were in our room, we were always followed by his men so we would not able to talk freely.

I got up, thinking hard on the problem, and walked into the bathroom to the sink. Blaze was kind enough to turn on the power and water to our rooms. But whatever the real reason for this, I didn't care because for the first time in my life, I was using plumbing and electricity. Indeed, on the first day the plumbing and electricity was turned on, I went overboard with it turning the light on and off, flushing the toilet, and turning the water in the sink and shower on and off as well.

But I have passed the point and now just considering the water, my mind is racing with the same thought: "how to get out of here." We needed to get out of here, but as far as I could see, there was no way out. I went back to my bed and fell a sleep.

At breakfast the next day, Blaze's had given both my father and I the day off. We had spent the time walking the grounds, talking about our separate experiences since arriving at Blaze's.

"So how are you really doing," my father said.

"Ok!" I said walking around the courtyard. "The other hunters are taking to me faster then I would think."

"How many other hunters are there?" my father asked.

"Around twenty," I said.

"And how many are with Blaze?" my father asked.

"At least twelve," I said. "But no one knows who. They are supposing to remain hidden from us and keep an eye on the hunters. Keep them from running or rebelling."

"So, there are only eight hunters who are even trustworthy," my father said.

"Yes! And it's hard to figure out who is a hunter and who is a hunter guard," I said. "Blaze has hidden them very well. They act, eat, sleep, and shit just like the rest of the hunters."

"Yes, I believe that Blaze would have them to be as convincing as possible," my father said. "Blaze is not the type to make that kind of mistake. I even bet that Blaze's other men don't even know who they are. That way when the hunters get bullied by the other men, they get treated the same way."

"That would make sense," I said. "If they were treated differently than the rest of us, we would be able to figure out who they are."

We started around the hunters' encampment and looking back, we found that two guards were still behind us just nearly in hearing.

"And what of the task that Blaze gave you to do?" I said lowering my voice to a whisper. "And how long do you think it will take before Blaze starts to 'persuade' you to hurry up?"

"Well, as I have said to Blaze, the people are not too willing to believe that Blaze has any good intentions," my father said but seemed to want to forget the second question.

"You are avoiding my second question, Dad," I said. "Are you afraid of the answer, or how I will react to that answer?"

My father just walked quietly looking though the cage of the hunters' encampment.

"Junior, it is not that I don't think you are capable of handling the truth," my father begins. "I just want to protect you from danger."

"But the best way to do that, I think, would be to tell me everything there is to know, Father, and not hide things from me," I said pleading with my father.

"You are properly right my son," my father said.

"So how long until Blaze uses me to get you to make you do what he wants faster?" I asked

"If I know Blaze as well as I think I do, about a week," my father said grimly.

"That soon, you think," I said looking at my father.

"If not sooner, yes," my father said. "To be totally frank, I'm surprised that he has waited this long to do anything at all."

"He probably didn't want to risk turning you into a bigger enemy," I said.

"You surprise me sometimes, my son," my father said looking at me. "Your mind seems to work in some way as many people in this world do. And Blaze is right to fear me becoming an enemy, for I could get the people in to a position to oppose him."

"Is that what you have been doing all this time?" I asked.

"I would if not for the fact that Blaze never leaves me alone when I am in town," my father said. "And it is hard to talk to people with Blaze's men there. The people seem to be just as afraid of his men as well as him."

"So how do we get out of here, Dad?" I asked lowering my voice so our guards could not hear.

But before my father could respond to my question, we saw Blaze walking toward us.

"Ah, there you two are," Blaze said as he approached us. "I am afraid I need to cut your time together short."

"Why!" I asked.

"My servants are becoming restless, and I need your Father to help keep them in control," Blaze said turning to my father.

"Fine!" my father said with a hint of malice in his voice. "I will see you at dinner, Jr., okay?"

"Okay, Dad!" I said.

"You may go into town if you want, but my guards will stay with you at all times," Blaze said.

I watched my father and Blaze head back to the mansion flanked by Blaze's personal guards. As they walked away, my mind wondered why Blaze had given me the leave to go into town. Perhaps he thought that going into town would make up for cutting my time with my father short.

Whatever the reason was, I didn't really care much about it. So, I turned my back on the mansion and headed into town.

It had been several days since I was last in the town. Although the town had not physically changed, the place did seem different. The people looked afraid of me, or at least afraid the two men behind me.

I spent the day in town walking around and talking to the townsfolk. By time I was forced to head back to the mansion, I had not made any progress with the people. But with Blaze's men behind me the whole time, I shouldn't expect much to happen.

When I reached the mansion, I found both my father and Blaze already at the table. They were in deep conversation.

"I am telling you, you cannot change how people see you," my father said. "And that is if there is even a chance to change their opinion."

"You have said this before," Blaze said, "but you also said that you could do it. Was that a lie?"

At a gesture from Blaze, the two guards behind me reacted. One grabbed me by the neck and put a blade to my throat, while the other guard aimed his bow at my father.

"Wait! Blaze, no!" my father said.

"So, you now know how I negotiate, don't you," Blaze said. "So is what I am asking you impossible or possible?"

"Yes, I can do it. Just don't hurt my son," my father said pleading with Blaze.

"Very well," Blaze said, and at another gesture the two men relaxed. "But remember I am in control of everything here."

At these words, I reacted; I don't even know why I did it. Somehow I knocked down my two guards and got one of their crossbows and fired it Blaze. The arrow flew though the air-hitting Blaze on the right shoulder. Before I could reload the bow, one of Blaze's guards had hit me in the stomach with the butt of his sword.

As I lay there in pain, I felt an edge of a sword in the back of my neck. I turned my head to see what was going on and found the same guard who hit me had his sword on me. I could see Blaze slowly coming around the table with one of his guards following him. The other two guards were holding my father, who was trying to get to me.

"Should I kill him, Master?" the guard holding me down asked.

Blaze stopped right in front of me. He then looked down at me then back to my father then back to me.

"No! I went him alive for now," Blaze said as if making up his mind. "Take him to the dungeons."

I felt something hit me in the back of my head and knew no more.

When I awoke sometime later, it was like my eyes were still shut it was that dark. I tried to look around to but found that the darkness was everywhere. There was not even a small crack of light which could be seen.

I stood up and began to explore my cell. It was a square about ten paces in all direction. There were no windows in this place, but halfway down one wall my hand touched something cold like medal. The door itself was thick, by the sound of the echo; it was at least three inches deep. I couldn't see any way out unless someone lets me out; I sat down in one of the corners and waited.

I lost all sense of time in that cell. All that time I felt so hungry; the small amount of food that was pushed under the door never seem to be enough.

The days in that darkness seemed to never end. Then one day, I heard loud noises outside the door. It sounded like a fight was going on outside. I could hear screams and yells of pain outside.

Then a new sound came from the door, the sound of a key entering the lock and the door being unlocked.

As the door creeped open, the light blinded me from being so long in absolute darkness. A shadowy figure walked into the cell. I could not see him for my eyes were still blinded by the light. But I knew who he was when the figure took me in his arms and held me.

"Everything will be all right now, son!" my father said in my ear.

"Father," I said my voice cracking as I spoke.

"Yes, it's me!" my father said. "You are safe now. Come, let's get out of here."

And with that, I walked out of that cell with my father beside me. As we walked, he told me of everything that had happened since I was put in the dungeon.

It seems that the people heard of my little revolt against Blaze and that it had hardened the people to fight back. They stormed the mansion killing the guards. Even the hunters joined the fight, after killing all those who served Blaze.

Not all of Blaze's men died in this fight; many had joined the townsfolk to fight Blaze and liberated the town. Blaze had elected to fight the townsfolk and died at their hands.

My father, who was and is a peace-loving man, was not part in the fighting but indeed was the cause of it. In the end, my father was there when Blaze faced his end, showing him who was responsible for the destruction of his world.

My father also told me that he had forced Blaze, with his dying breath, to tell him where I was being held. With a few volunteers, he came down to find me.

Chapter 7

The Owl

"So, what happen after that, lad?" the bartender said as Matrix took a drink from his glass.

"Patience, my friend," Matrix said. "The night is still young, and I have much to say. But if I were to tell you all the adventures, I'm afraid we will be here until next spring. And I can tell you, we had many more adventures getting in and out of trouble, sometimes by the skin of our teeth."

Six years after the time we spent in Blaze's home, we found ourselves in a different village. My father had always seemed to be searching for something. What that was, I never knew, but my father always seemed determined to find it. We had traveled to many places, but each one never seemed to be what my father was looking for.

But that would change one day when we came across small village. I could see the attraction to this place. The village itself was in a large valley, surrounded by tall mountains. On the eastern end of the village was a large forest, which was full of wild game, and there was a large pond on the western end.

Even the mountain's path that my father and I were on was hard to find. It was really a stroke of fate that we had found the path.

At first sight of the village, my father's face glowed with emotion. We stared at that scene for several moments before my father turned to face me.

"My son, I have found what I have been searching for all this time," my father said. "All this time I have been looking for a place that we could live in peace, a place where you and I will no longer have to fear the people around us. It is truly a shame that we hadn't found this place sooner. For you have now seen more of this new world in these last sixteen years I would not have wished you to see. But now we can try to live a normal life without the pain and suffering of this new world. Do you understand?"

To be truthful, I couldn't understand. All I knew was my father wanted to take me away from the only life I knew, to live a quiet life. All this time we had lived on the move and at times on the run from one danger to another. But now we had a chance to live a better life, and I was willing to give it a try. After all, my father had never led us astray so far.

I nodded at my father and we started down to the village.

As walked into the village, I saw that the village had a real plan of defense. Most of the towns and villages I had seen had been designed in a way that each home was made to act as a barrier to keep bandits out. And in these towns, there was normally one way in or out of the town for added protection.

The homes themselves were as different to many of the other villages and towns as well. They looked fresh and new like the people of the village built their homes themselves. Where the other towns I had seen had used the building from the old world for their homes, those homes were built with new materials.

We walked though the village looking from side to side in hopes to find some sign of who led these people. Most times people choose the eldest and wisest to lead them. These Elders would sometimes find themselves in a large home as a symbol of their position. The Elder of this village must live a simple life like the rest of the village.

As we wandered though the village, we could feel the villagers' eyes on us. Many of the eyes we felt were the same eyes we had felt in every other village or town we had entered. But there were other eyes on us that would be different; they were not the same looks of fear and mistrust but of interest and curiosity. But the villagers were keeping their distances.

My father managed to stop a boy as he ran by and asked him were the village Elder's home was. The boy seemed scared by us, but after looking over us, he then pointed to home at the end of a lane. My father thanked the boy and in payment gave him a large can of unmarked food.

We followed the direction that the boy pointed. The house was not like other elders' homes I have seen. It was just as plain as the other homes in the village, but it seemed older like it was from the old world.

My father moved to the door and knocked on it. We only had to wait for a moment before the door opened. In the doorway was an elderly old man. He was slightly hunched and had gray hair from the top of his head to the tips of his long beard.

"So, what do I owe the pleasure to have guests at my door?" The old man said in a voice that sounded aged and wise.

"Great Elder, my son and I have traveled far and wide," my father said bowing to the Elder. "In all our travels, we have never set eyes on a place like this."

"Is that so," the Elder said with a grin. "Is our village really something wonderful?"

"Yes, it is, oh great Elder," my father begins again. "For us who have only seen misery and pain, this village is paradise."

"Paradise, is that what you see here?" the Elder said. "If a paradise is what our village is to you then you will understand that we can't let you stay without knowing who you are and what you can do for us."

"We do know we must prove our worth to your village and are willing to wait if we need to," my father said.

"But what can you give to us?" the Elder said look us up and down.

"Well, sir, my son here is a truly gifted hunter," my father said gesturing to me.

"Is he now?" the Elder said looking as impressed by this news like everyone else my father told. "That is an impressive feat for one so young."

"Yes! It is a feat only my son could do," my father said.

"And what about you, young man? What can you do for us?" Elder said.

"I have knowledge to give, books and papers that I have used to teach my son all he knows, and I can teach the children in your village the same," my father said pulling out a large book of history from the bag of books he carried.

"Ah! Knowledge is indeed something of true value to us," the Elder said stroking his beard.

"But you said that this is what you have become in this world, what you were in the old world," the Elder said. "I can tell you were not a teacher in your old life."

My father smiled at this statement. "You see right through me," my father said. "No, I wasn't a teacher. I was a lawyer. I had the gift of speech. In this world, I have used it to our advantage."

"I'm sure you have," the Elder said. "And will you be using this gift on me?"

"No, sir?" my father said. "That would only hinder our chances to find a home here."

"Yes! Any tricks you do will indeed prevent your entry to this village," the Elder said. "But there is something I have been wondering for some time now?"

"And what is that, sir?" my father asked.

"Your son, does he not speak?" the Elder said grinning as he looked at me. "Or is he just an afraid to speak in front of an old man?"

I had to laugh at this statement. After all the terrible people in this world who only had seen me as an appendage to my father, it was good that someone saw me as an equal.

"Yes, sir, I can speak," I said to the Elder. "And I do speak to old men and women. But I only speak when I need and when I have something important to say."

"Indeed, you can," the Elder said laughing at my words. "And you can speak to an old man, too. But we have talked enough for today; you two must be tired. Please come in, I have several rooms you can use until the council of Elders can speak on this matter."

We thanked the Elder as we entered his home. He showed us upstairs to two very large rooms and told us good night.

The time spent in the Elder's home seemed to fly by. As it happens only in a small village like this, the news that we wanted to become a member of the community had spread throughout the whole village.

But the villagers did not seem to be outright against us; instead they seemed to be very welcoming. I had even managed to make some friends with the local children. This was the first time in my life that I ever had the chance to even get to play with kids my age and younger.

The kids seemed to be as interested in me, and I was starting to become interested in a new life in this village here. They had all heard that I was already a fantastic hunter and wanted me to show them my skills. But the other hunters wouldn't let me use any of their weapon. So I was left with only my knife, but I managed to entertain the village boys by showing a few knife tricks. I had even shown my accuracy by throwing my knife into the targets that the hunters used to practice with.

But that time was not all fun in games for us, for we were being questioned. The Elder wanted to know everything about our lives, all about our adventures and misdeeds, so that the council members could make their decision.

When it was time for their decision, my father and I headed to the Town Hall, where all the village council meetings were held. It was a large building; it looked as if it could have been a courthouse in the old world. As we walked into the council chambers, we could see all the members of the Elders sitting at the other end of the room.

As we walked up to the council members, we passed between the people of the village who were sitting in the row of chairs beside us. The council themselves were sitting at a half circle table looking out at the assembled villagers.

My father and I sat in the center of the half circle and looked into the eyes of the council members. There were five members on the Council of Elders, all between the ages of fifty and seventy. To my left was a gray-haired gentleman named Glendale who had fine wrinkles. His face was stern like that of a military man. In fact, I had heard that he had retired from the Marines after about five years, before the Great Disaster happened.

Beside Glendale a woman sat who still radiated beauty; her name was Jasmine. She was the youngest member of the council, so her face had not lost its beauty. Indeed, whenever she smiled her dark skin seemed glow like the moon over the night sky.

In the center of the table was the Grand Elder, whose hospitality my father and I had been enjoying. Sat in his chair looking around as if there was nothing more enjoyable than what he was doing right now. The people of the village called him only Grand Elder, but I had become accustomed to calling him by his real name, Augustus.

To left of the Grand Elder sat a woman who seemed to possess a face that was hard to read. It wasn't that she wasn't hard to look at; it was just that even in times of joy her face would look the same as when she was angry. Her name was Miss Masterson.

At the other end of the table sat a jolly old man with a short white beard with a mustache and short white hair. He was called Jack. Jack was a funny man, who loved to eat. This was apparent by his large gut.

As the Grand Elder started, the whole hall went quiet. He first looked around the hall at all the assembled villagers, then at his fellow Council members, and lastly at my father and me.

"My friends, we are here today to answer the question on whether or not the two before us can join our peaceful village," the Grand Elder said with his arms out wide as if to encompass the whole hall.

"And now," he said taking a breath, "before we tell you our decision, there are some who wish to speak more on this matter. Miss Masterson, the floor is yours."

"Thank you, Grand Elder," Miss Masterson said standing up as she did. "Council members, ladies and gentlemen, and of course our honored guests, welcome to this meeting of the Council. We all know why we are here, but I wish to speak to all about what these two men are offering in way of helping our village."

She paused for a moment to fix her glasses and then looked to my father as she began to speak again. "This gentleman here," she gesturing to my father, "he has come here to offer us something, that in this village is more valuable than food or fresh water: *knowledge*." She halted at this word to let what she said sink in.

"Yes, my friend, he has in his possession books and knowledge," Miss Masterson said. "And he had already agreed that he can stay to share all his knowledge and teach our children what he knows. To the mothers and fathers of this village who have tried their best to teach, this is indeed a gift for us. He will be able to teach our children better than any of us could. We know this because he had taught his son these lessons and he has learned well.

"But this young man's greatest talent can be found not in the classroom but in the wilderness," Miss Masterson said looking at me. "This young man has become a very accomplished hunter."

At this statement, Glendale made a gunning noise in his throat.

"Is there something you wish to add, Glendale, or were you just clearing out your throat there?" Jack said mockingly.

"No, I think he has something to say about the boy's skills as a hunter," Jasmine said.

"Well, is this true, Glendale? Do you have something to say on this matter?" the Grand Elder said interlocking his fingers.

"Well, I would like to remind the council that I oversee the hunters of this village, and this means I choose who can be a hunter or not," Glendale said in a military-like tone.

"No one here is denying that, Glendale," Jack said. "All Helen was saying was that the boy was a gifted hunter; that's all."

Miss Masterson looked affronted at the use of her first name but did not say anything.

"That is not my point!" Glendale said still in that same military tone.

"Then what is your problem," Jasmine said.

"Could it be jealousy towards the boy," Jack said looking from me to Glendale.

"No, that is not it at all, Jack," Glendale said. "It is just that the boy is too young to be a true hunter."

"Is that the only reason you fight his appointment?" the Grand Elder said. "For concern for the boy?"

"Yes, Grand Elder, it is!" Glendale said.

"Young in age the boy might be," the Grand Elder said, "but his sprit and experiences are older than even myself."

"But, Grand Elder, it is still my decision that the boy is too young for this," Glendale said. "And not even the council can overturn my decision."

"Very will, Glendale, if that your final decision then we will abide by it," the Grand Elder said. "Miss Masterson, is there anything else you would like to say on this matter?"

"No, Grand Elder," Miss Masterson said. "I am finished!"

"Very will then," the Grand Elder said standing up as he did. "Then all that is left to do is to tell you our verdict on this matter." He paused for a moment before continuing, "It is the decision of this council that you two may join our fair village."

A cheer rang out as the villagers screamed with joy about the decision made by the council. The Grand Elder waved for silence; it seemed that there was more he had to say.

"Now we must discuss a few more things before this meeting comes to a close," the Grand Elder said. "First things first we must find a place for these two to live. After all they cannot continue to stay in my home forever. As always Jack will see to their living arrangements. All those who wish to help prepare their home please speak to him.

"As for what tasks these two will perform while they live here is as follows. For the gentleman, here," the Grand Elder said looking at my father, "he will take up the position of teacher at the school. When this meeting is over, Miss Masterson will take you over to the school and show you around. Now that we have two qualified teachers, it will at least take off the strain on all those of you who have taken it upon yourself to teach our young ones."

"And as for this young man here," the Grand Elder said gesturing towards me, "it would be my wish that he becomes one of our hunters. But as we all heard here in this meeting, Glendale makes all hunter appointments and he will not make him a hunter. It is my wish that boy is only reasonably to be a child and do as all children do, play, go to school, and to do their chores."

Again, a cheer rang out from the villagers as the Grand Elder finished speaking. After the cheering had gone on for long enough, he signaled a hold to the cheers.

"I just have one more thing to say before this meeting comes to a close." The Grand Elder looked down at my father and me and said, "Welcome to our village, my new friends."

With that the meeting was over. My father stood up and walked over to Miss Masterson, who herself was just getting up as well. The two talked for a while and then walked out together. They were most likely on their way to the school.

Glendale also left the hall and without even a backwards glance at anyone or me. Jasmine stood and walked over to where I was sitting. She put her hand on my shoulder and kissed me on the check.

"Welcome to our village, young man," she said whispering in my ear.

I watched as she left the hall, my cheek glowing red as she walked away.

"I wouldn't put much in that kiss, boy," Jack said almost laughing as he said it. "She does that to everyone who enters our village. It is her way of welcoming newcomers."

"And what about Glendale," I said looking at his empty chair. "Is what happened in the meeting his way of welcoming newcomers?"

"No, I am afraid what happened in the meeting, no matter what he said, all it is is jealousy towards you," Jack said.

"Jealousy towards me? Why?" I asked looking puzzled.

"Glendale is an old military dog," Jack explained. "He is all about discipline and rules. He sees you as undisciplined and following your own rules. Demanding to join the hunters that he himself has trained, it is just something he does not understand.

But enough about that, why don't come with me and help me find a place for your home?" Jack said.

Having nothing better to do, I decided to go with Jack to find a place to build our home. Jack knew a lot about construction. In fact, in the old world he had his own construction company.

We looked all over the village before we settled on a spot on a hill, a little away from the village. At first, Jack did not think that the hill was the perfect location, but I told him it was fine because it was closest to the schoolhouse, which was in fact just down at the bottom of the hill.

"My father wouldn't want to walk though the whole village just to get to the school," I said to Jack ending the discussion.

"Very well, if you think this place is fine then I will get started on the blueprints of your home," Jack said waving goodbye as he headed back to the village to get his tools to start working on my home. "Why don't you go back to the Grand Elder's home and get some sleep," Jack cried back. "I will see you tomorrow to show you and your Father what I have come up with."

And with that he was gone. I stayed for a little while longer before I returned to the Grand Elder's home.

Chapter 8

The Ox

Time after the meeting, my father and I, as well as anyone who wanted, helped in the constriction of our home. This was the first time I had ever had a sense of community. Within a few weeks, our home had been fully built, even with fine detail.

By the villagers' count, Jack had outdone himself in its design. It has two stories and an attic. The only problem with the home was that we had nothing to put in it. Being on the road all the time, my father and I always had to travel as lightly as possible. So, this means that we did not carry much more than a few pots and pans with us at all times.

On the day our home was finished, a great celebration was held at the house. It was sort of like a housewarming party. Everyone in the village showed up for this party; even Glendale showed up for a short visit.

The celebration lasted all day and then through the night. Each man, woman, and child who came to our party came with gifts for us both. Soon our home had everything a good home needs including beds, dressers, and all other kinds of household needs.

The night ended with a great feast. The whole village was invited to the feast, which was held outside for all to attend.

Only when the children began to fall sleep during the celebration did it finally end. With sleepy children in their arms, the guests left for their homes. My father and I said our goodnight to all who attended before going inside.

The next day, life returned to the normal, or normal for a small village, my father and I going to the schoolhouse, him to teaching, and I to learning. The school was divided into two classes, with the boys and girls separated during class time. My father taught the boys while Miss Masterson taught the girls. Only on breaks did the boys and girls ever interact together.

After school, we would be left to our own. Within several weeks of this, I soon found myself missing my old life. I found that the village was far too quiet for me. I started to feel trapped in this village, and there was no way out for me.

I even found myself missing the hardship of the outside world. It was weird to find more comfort in chaos than in peace, but the uncertainty of the world outside made life more interesting. The village on the other hand was far too predictable.

I felt if I just had something more to do, my life would have more purpose. If only Glendale would let me go with the hunting party, my life would have some meaning in this new life. But the chances that Glendale would let me become a hunter now were small.

I soon found a way to overcome this feeling of longing. I would sneak off into either the woods or into the mountains near the village. These places were normally off limits to all but the hunters. They said that the animals were far too dangerous for the villagers and you shouldn't go in either place alone.

But the wildlife never bothered me, and I even managed to avoid contact with Glendale and the other hunters. The time I spent out of the village seemed to ease the feelings I was having.

My life in the village seemed to become easier in the months that followed. I was a little bit happier than I was before, but I still felt empty. My life here was more peaceful than I had ever known, but I was left without purpose.

In the wilderness outside the village, I had purpose. I was the hunter for both my father and I. Out there, I kept my father and me alive with the food I hunted.

But here, because of Glendale, the only thing I could do to help this village had been kept from me. It was his pride that kept Glendale from allowing me to become a hunter. To make it worse, I would have to wait until Glendale believed that I could be a hunter before he would even let me train with the other hunter recruits.

Four years! That's the how long for the hunters' training. Four years before I could return to being a hunter. That is if Glendale's pride didn't stop me from ever becoming a hunter again. If only there was a way I could show my skills to Glendale, maybe he would allow me to join now, but there was no way I could do it without getting into trouble.

I mean I could make a bow and some arrows and kill some game, but if the hunters saw signs of my kills, they would notice something and tell Glendale. Before I knew it, Glendale would figure out who it was and have me constantly watched. Not to mention that Glendale would see to it that I never became a hunter. Truly my only hope to become a hunter was to stay on Glendale's good side, and the only way to do that was to stay out of his way.

But my way to become a hunter soon came to me. I was in the forest just like any other day when I was on my way home when something stopped me on the path to the village. It was a King Snake, and a very large one. It was so large it could have wrapped itself around me twice.

The snake seemed to be agitated about something. I dared not get too close to it for fear that the snake would strike. So, I kept my distance from it as I tried to go around it. I soon found out that this was not going to happen; no matter what I did the snake would not let me pass.

It was now I remembered something that my father had said to me once. It was in one of his teachings; he told me that when the Great Disaster happened it had affected both humans and animals and even plants alike. But he had also said that the effects on humans were different than on the animals. It was only the humans who seemed to die in the Great Disaster, but the animals and plants didn't. They lived.

But they were affected but in a different way. The plants seemed to grow faster and become stronger, like they had lived for hundreds of years. The animals also grew but in numbers, but that was not all that had grown; more dangers did as well.

This is most likely why this snake was acting like this, and now I had to find a way to get around this problem. But the real problem was how? For no matter what I did, the snake coped my moves.

"Ok, little guy, I'm not going to hurt you," I said to the snake in a gentle tone.

As I said this, I slowly moved closer to the snake. I was planning to grab the snake's tail to gently remove it from my path. I had almost grabbed the tail when the snake struck out at my hand. I jumped back just in time just before the snake could bite me.

"Alright, pal, if you're not going to get out of my way then I am going to have to go through you," I said throwing my knife at the snake's head.

It lay there dead, and for a time I just sat there in silence over the death of the snake. It was the least I could do for the snake after killing it like I did. I have always had a deep respect for all creatures. Even for those I had to kill.

But now that it was dead, what should I do with it? The only thing I could do was to of course take the snake into the village. So, I slung the snake onto my shoulder and started for the village.

To say that the people of the village were surprised would be an understatement. To find out that I was in the forest was bad enough, but that I had killed a giant King Snake too, and with just a knife.

The news of my deed soon spread through the village. And it wasn't long before even Glendale was aware of what happened, and it was only a matter of time before I found myself in trouble with him.

"Well, you had an interesting day today, haven't you?" my father said. "I bet Glendale is a little uneasy to hear about what you did."

"So? I don't care what he thinks or what he is planning to do to me," I said without any feeling.

"You're just like your mother at times," my father said in a soft voice.

He always got like this whenever he spoke of my mother.

"She too never knew went to quit," my father begin to say. "She always challenged authority. You get that from her. Just be careful alright?"

"Don't worry, Dad, I will be alright." I said. "I can handle whatever Glendale can throw at me."

"Well I hope so," my father said, "for your sake."

I went to bed that night feeling freer than I had the whole time in the village. It was as if the hunt freed me from the quiet life in the village.

Then a loud bang rang through the house. I quickly got up and dressed before running downstairs to the door. I found my father at the door, and in the doorway was Glendale. He was standing in the doorway with a stern look on his face.

"So, what do we owe this pleasure, Glendale?" my father said inviting Glendale in.

Glendale did not move; he just stood in the door with that stern look on his face. His eyes turned from my father over to me on the steps.

"Well, Teacher," Glendale said speaking to my father but not taking his eyes off me. "To be truthful, I have come to talk to your son."

At this statement, my father turned to look at me as well. He gave me a 'I told you so' look. He then returned his attention to Glendale before speaking again.

"And what is it that you want with my son?" my father asked.

"You need not worry, Teacher," Glendale said his face as stern as ever. "I just wanted to ask if he wanted to come with us on the hunt. That is if the boy, I mean the young man still wishes to become, wishes to join us, that is."

"Sure!" I said with a look at my father. "That is if you want me to join the hunting party, Glendale."

At these words, my father stared at me while Glendale's eyes narrowed. But before anyone could say a thing, I had made my way to the door.

Glendale moved quietly through the village, but I could feel his hostility on me. We just walked in silence for several minutes before Glendale stopped and turned to me.

"Before we go any farther, there is something I want to say," Glendale said. "It was a very rash thing you did, boy."

"Maybe," I said. "But it was not like I had a choice."

"But you did choose; you chose to disobey my rules," Glendale said. "Rules are made to be followed; they are not to be bent whenever they don't suit you."

"You do not understand me, Glendale, and you never will," I said in a defiant tone. "That wilderness you speak of is, was my home for sixteen years. I am more at peace out there than I ever will be here."

"And that is your excuse for your defiance, so you could find peace," Glendale said. "You are a foolish child."

"You are wrong, Glendale. I am not a child," I said. "I have not been a child since I was two. I have never had the chance to be a child in this world. You are the only one here who sees me as a child. Even the Grand Elder sees that."

"Your skills as a hunter were never in question, boy," Glendale said. "Your maturity is what I am concerned with. You have never hunted in a group, never hunted with others. You yourself said that your father hated to hunt, hated to kill even for food so when you find yourself a natural hunter, he let you hunt.

If you want to be a hunter in this village, you need to work as a group and follow my orders," Glendale said in a gentle tone.

"What are you saying?" I said in an unsure tone. "Are going to let me join the hunters?"

"Only if you follow my orders from now on," Glendale said. "Do you think you can do that? Can you work as a team? Can you follow?"

"Sure thing, Glendale, I can follow," I said. "You'll see I can do anything you ask of me."

"Good!" Glendale said. "Then you better go to bed then. The first hunt is at dawn. Be ready before dawn you hear me?"

"I will be there, Glendale. Don't worry about that," I said.

Glendale then turned and walked away. I too turned and walked back to my house, though I moved with greater haste in my step.

My father was overjoyed when he heard the news, but somehow he was not surprised.

"Glendale's motives are anything but noble," my father said. "His reasons for letting you become a hunter are all politics. In doing so he can keep his power."

"What do you mean keep his power?" I said. "I thought that the council couldn't make decisions on who can be a hunter?"

"Yes, that is true," my father said. "But the council doesn't decide on whom their members are, and it's the people who tell the council who they would like to lead them."

"Well, I don't care for the reasons for Glendale letting me be a hunter," I said. "Just so long as I am a hunter that is all that matters to me."

"Nevertheless you should keep your distance from Glendale from now on," my father said. "Those in politics like Glendale will most likely do anything to stay in power."

"I will, Dad. Don't worry. I will be fine, "I said.

"I will not," my father said, "but still you should be careful from now on."

"Ok, Dad," I said.

"Well you should get some sleep," my father said. "You're going to have a long and difficult day tomorrow."

And at that we turned in for the night.

I woke up an hour before dawn the next day. I busied myself by preparing my things for the hunt. My father had woken up to see me off. As I left, he told me to be careful and to mind the others. Just the normal things fathers said to their children as they leave for the day.

The morning air was warm this day as I headed to the hunters' shack. The hunters' shack was the size of a small barn. Outside the shack were five hay targets. By the targets, the hunters were standing waiting for Glendale to arrive.

I just walked up to the shack just passing by the other hunters. As I did, the other hunters began talking in small whispers. What I could overhear, most seemed surprised to see me, but also eager. They had all heard about my exceptional hunting skills and were most likely wanting to see them in action.

I paid no mind as I leaned up against the shack. Everyone's eyes seemed to be on me as the time went by.

It was several minutes before Glendale showed up, several minutes of staring and muttering. But it stopped when Glendale finally showed up. His eyes looked around at all present before resting on me. As our eyes met, Glendale's eyes narrowed, but his tone was calm.

"Good morning!" Glendale said in a military-like tone. "As you all are aware by now, we have a new hunter among us. He is younger than the rest of us, but his skill as a hunter is great."

"But even though he is a natural born hunter, he has never hunted in a group like we do," Glendale said looking at the veteran hunters. "I will count on all of you to help him adapt to our way.

Now for your assignment," Glendale started again. "Daniel, Hans, you two are with me. Maddock, Luke, and Angelo will be with Ken. Jake, Dave, and Wade, you will take the new kid and show him the ropes.

"Wade is in charge so you will follow his orders as though they were my own, you hear me?" Glendale said looking at me. "Any questions? Good! Then you are dismissed."

Once more the hunters began to talk as they went around fetching weapons and gear. Wade came up to me and handed me a bow and a quiver of arrows.

"Here take this," Wade said. "I hope you know how to use them?"

Taking the bow and arrows, I notched an arrow to the bow and fired at the targets, a good fifteen feet away. The arrow hit the center of the bull's eye.

"This will do for now," I said. "I will make a bow of my own later."

"You are good," Wade said looking at the target. "I think this is going to be a great hunt today."

"So where are we going to be hunting?" I said looking around at the wilderness around the village.

"We will be hunting in the Quad three, today," Wade said.

"Quad three," I said with a puzzled look on my face.

"Yes, you see we have spilt the whole village into four areas," Wade explained. "If you were to think of the village as a circle with the council chambers at it center. Now if you draw a line connecting the north to the south and the east to the west and you will have four areas. Now starting from the north, you number the areas going clockwise. Northeast is quad one, southeast is quad two, southwest is quad three, and northwest is quad four."

"Ok! So, that would put us in the southwest corner of the woods, right?" I asked.

"That's right," Wade, said. "You catch on quick. So, unless you have some questions we will get going."

As we started for the woods, I learned that Jake and Dave were not much older than I. They had just become hunters one year ago. As for Wade he had been a hunter for years.

The woods were very quiet, the morning dew still on the grass. The sunlight streamed through the trees. Our group moved swiftly and quietly through the woods, but there seemed to be no sign of game.

But then as the sun came fully over the horizon, we saw it: deer tracks. By the tracks we could tell that it was a big one, most likely a buck. The tracks were heading to the west.

Wade said there was a small clearing just ahead with a stream running through it. The buck would most likely be there having a drink.

"This will be the best chance for us to act," I said to Wade.

"Are you kidding me?" Wade said. "There is no way to get close enough for the kill."

"You just leave that to me," I said notching an arrow to my bow. "I can make the shot."

And with that we set out for the clearing. As we made it to the edge of the clearing, we could see it. The buck was there at the stream drinking his fill.

Wade was right about the shot; only a very skilled marksman could make the shot. A skilled marksman just like me.

I set my sights down the shaft and prepared to fire. I fired just as the buck raised his head. The arrow zoomed though the air, piercing it into the buck's neck.

The others ran to the deer's body. Dave and Jake began preparing the buck for transport. As they worked, they chattered to each other.

"That was some shot," Wade said to me as I walked up to him. "A prefect shot, quick and clean."

"I don't like to make them suffer," I said to Wade looking down at the buck. "That is if I can help it. After all, it is bad enough that they are going to die so why should I make their last moments painful."

"Will, I guess that makes sense," Wade said as Dave and Jake finished preparing the deer for transport. "Tell me, did your father teach you that?"

"No! I taught myself that," I said.

"Well, I will say your skills as a hunter are far beyond mine," Wade said. "In fact, your skills could even be beyond Glendale's."

"That is what I have been saying all this time," I said watching Dave and Jake pick up the buck and putt it on their shoulders, on a pole. "It is just Glendale's pride that stopped me from becoming a hunter."

We moved back through the woods, Jake and Dave in front with the buck between them on the pole, and Wade and me in the rear. We made good time through the woods so by time the sun was fully up we had made it back to the village.

All the other hunting groups were there with their catches. As I looked around, I could see that their luck was not as good as ours. All they seemed to have caught were small, like rabbits, or other small animals.

All eyes were on us as we walked past. Dave and Jake took the buck to the place where it would be prepared. As for Wade and I, we just stood around with the other hunters.

As we waited, Wade entertained the others with the tale of my hunt. Wade had just finished the tale when Glendale came by. He was in the hut seeing to the cleaning and preparing of the meat. By the look on Glendale's face, he too knew about my buck.

"Well I see your first hunt with us seems to be a great success," Glendale said.

"That is an understatement," I said to Glendale.

The other hunters presented filch at my statement and stood ready to see what Glendale would do. He just shrugged as if what I said meant nothing to him.

"In any case, you do seem very capable to work as a team," Glendale said. "But even new guys can get lucky from time to time."

"Hey, Glendale, why don't you just leave me alone," I said in defiant voice.

"You insolent child," Glendale cried out. "You will learn some respect for me"

"Respect for you, ha!" I said. "You of all people should know that respect needs to be earned, not given."

Glendale turned and walked off to see to the preparations.

"Man, kid, you must have some guts to talk to Glendale like that," Wade said.

"Don't worry, Wade, I can handle Glendale," I said. "He is nothing compared with some of the guys I have dealt with outside this village."

"Someone worst than Glendale," Wade said. "I find that hard to imagine.

Well in any case, there is nothing left for us to do here so why don't you go home and get some rest," Wade said turning around to go about his other duties.

When I got home, I went to find my father. I soon found him in his study. He was busy planning his next day's lesson. He looked up from his work as I entered the room.

"And how was your day?" he asked with a smile on his face.

So I told him all that happened, though in the days to come he would be hearing about it repeatedly from the villagers.

Chapter 9

The Falcon

As time moved on, life in the village became far more enjoyable for me. Although Glendale was not having as good of a time as I was. My popularity as a hunter in the village had greatly increased, something Glendale was very much aware of.

But this was not something that Glendale was going to take lying down. I had become a threat to him, and he was thinking of ways to keep what he had.

Glendale's first plan was simple: undermine my hunts to undermine my popularity. But he would find that hard to do. For the next four weeks, Glendale had attempted this by sending me into areas that had seen little amounts of game on the last hunt.

Though this plan seemed simple, it was harder for Glendale perform. For it seemed that no matter where Glendale assigned my group, we would always come out on top. I never understood how my group always seemed to be in the right place at the right time.

Every time we came back from a hunt, Glendale would look at us with hate and disgust. Wade and the others in my group on the other hand were having the time of their lives. It seems that Wade's group was always the underdogs in the village.

It was one of the reasons why Wade was third in command in the hunters' ranks. But now thanks to me they were getting more notice then before.

Glendale did not take all this too well. In fact, Glendale became even worse about it. To have one person become bigger than the boss is bad, but to have a whole group become bigger, that was worse.

So, what does a person do who wants to hold on to all that he has? Split us up of course.

It was about eight weeks after I had become a hunter that Glendale came to us with an announcement. Three more men would be joining our hunting group. But what was the real surprise, being Glendale, was not placing them into one of the current hunting groups but a new one. He also said that the leader of this group was going to be me.

Some of the veteran hunters started to complain about the assignment. They felt that the assignment was being hastily done. Not only were three new recruits joining their ranks, which was strange, but to put them under an untrained leader like myself was something different.

Though many of the other older hunters were busy complaining, there were some who were not. Wade, Dave, Jake, and Glendale's second-in-command Ken were all as calm as could be. There was only one reason Ken would be so calm, because he was already aware of Glendale's plan.

All this was simply another of Glendale's plans to undermine me. He thought that the three rookies would hamper me. But he also had a second reason for doing this: to show everyone my place. He needed to show the village that he was my superior. To his disappointment, his plan did not work at all. Even with the newbies, my hunts were still very impressive.

As the years passed, not much changed. Glendale still seemed to think that I was some kind for threat to him. I had even tried to explain to him that I did not care for his job, nor that I wanted to have any possession of power. But Glendale didn't seem to believe me. He seemed to think that I was just saying that to put him off his guard.

No matter what Glendale thought the truth was, I never wished for that kind of power. In that way, I was like my father. He never desired to become a leader of any kind.

But even though I had Glendale still on my ass, I still managed to have a good time in the village. Our life in the village had soon become the most memorable time we had had in one place. It was certainly the longest time we had ever stayed in one place.

Though as we lived in that village, our lives finally became simple, became very peaceful. I had finally felt like I belonged. I had never felt like this before; always moving from place to place, I never had time to get comfortable. But this place soon became the home I never had or known, and the people had become the extended family I never knew.

My life here was happy. It felt like I could finally drop my guard a little. But never totally, for Glendale was always someone I had to be careful with. But the facts were that he was becoming someone I could deal with on a daily basis.

To be honest, I liked the fact that Glendale was always opposing me. It was a challenge for me. In my life, my father and I had faced many people like Glendale. Men for whom ambition was the only thing keeping them going; ambitions that we seemed to always be in the way of. It was like having the best part of my old life in my new life.

Not much changed in two years; my father was still teaching at the school. Glendale was still on my ass, and the village was flourishing. According to Jasmine who was in charge of the food and water for the village, the farmland was producing plentiful supplies of fruits and vegetables. And with my great hunting skills, the village would have plenty of meat to eat.

Indeed, the whole village was doing very well, and it looked like we would have many years of happiness. But in this world we live in today, we know that not all good things can go on forever. Misery always finds a way into our lives, but never in the same way as it came the last time. It is always changing just like the seasons.

For us it came on the Founding Day. It was the day that the entire village comes out to celebrate the day they founded this wonderful place. It was an all-day affair, one that started at first light and went on until midnight. During the celebration, the whole village would gather in the center of the village. There great food would be laid out for all to enjoy.

Villagers young and old would then dance and sing, tell stories of old and new, play games, and just be merry. My father and I were often asked now to tell about some of our adventures. These being the newest tales, the people would love to hear them over and over.

When night finally fell, everyone would sit down to four very large tables to eat a magnificent feast. A great fire would be made in the center of the tables, and several torches would be lit around the tables. Now, you would get a great sense of family.

It was now as well that the Grand Elder would say a few words. Normally these words talked about the village, speaking about the people, about the corps, or just some special event that happened this year. No matter what it was about, it always made me feel good, like we had accomplished something.

When the children's eyes started the droop, their mothers would take them to their beds and then return to the celebration. The talk and the feasting would continue until midnight. Tired and full of food and drink, the villagers would then retire to their beds themselves.

But this time something happened. A stranger came wandering into our village. We were just about to sit down and begin the feast went he came into our village. He was very ragged and looked as if he had not had a good meal in weeks. Indeed, the jumpsuit he wore seemed too big for him. It was also filthy covered in mud and dirt, with several rips and tears in the material.

His face was also a mess. His hair was very long, shadowing his eyes and falling to the middle of his back. He beard and mustache were very tangled and mangled, and beneath the hair his eyes looked dreadful. It was as if the man had considered the face of death many times only to be pushed aside like death did not wish to claim this man. As if he wished him to suffer more before death.

He seemed to have been drawn to the light of the fire, like a moth to the flame, for he drew closer to where we all sat. But before he got close enough to us to speak, the man collapsed on the ground. The Grand Elder and several others went to aid the man. He seemed to have been traveling long without food or water. The Grand Elder had ordered for water to be brought at once.

When the man had recovered enough, he was bought over to the tables where he could sit and get a good meal. He was helped by many men, for he seemed to have no strength left.

As everyone settled down to eat, the man seemed to have relaxed a bit. As the talk started up again, the stranger begin to eat. It seemed with each bite his strength seemed to grow.

The stranger was very quiet; he merely shook or nodded his head whenever someone talked to him. They soon grew tired of his silent replies and started to avoid speaking to him. As the conversations grew louder and wilder, I glanced at the stranger. For one moment, I thought I saw something in his eyes. It was there for only a moment, but his eyes looked malevolent.

But it could have just been the firelight shining on through his dead eyes. That is what I told myself. For no one else saw what I saw, and though I kept my eyes on him as much as I could, I did not see that look again.

After the feast ended, the villagers headed off to their homes and to their beds. As for the stranger, he would be enjoying the Grand Elder's hospitality.

As I left for my own bed, my eyes looked back at the Stranger. Maybe it was that look I thought I saw, but I was starting to get a bad feeling about this man. But there was nothing I could about it now; if I said anything about it, the others would just say I was being paranoid.

Only my father would believe me; having had experience with my feelings he would know they were normally right. But even with my father backing me, I doubt that the others would still believe. So, if I wanted to do anything about this stranger, I was going to have to find something to convince them that he wasn't trustworthy.

The next day I was going to watch the stranger like a hawk and see what he was up to.

I found it hard to go to sleep that night; my mind was racing. I found it hard to quiet my mind. My thoughts just kept going around about the stranger and my plan to follow him.

I had a dream that night. I was in a village much like this one but different somehow. I seemed to walk through the village as if on a purpose. I seemed to be heading to the center of the village where a figure stood. I couldn't see who the figure was for they some were in shadow.

Before I could get a good look at the shadowy figure, a fire had started around the whole village. The fire surrounded the shadowy figure, and soon the figure would be engulfed in the fire. A piercing scream shattered the silence and I awoke with a start.

I sat upright in bed shacking. That scream I heard was so real. A red light was streaming though my room. Looking out the window, I saw that half of the village was in flames. Looking up I found my father was in the doorway.

"Good, you are awake," my father said.

"What is going on, Dad?" I asked.

"I don't know," he said in a grave voice. "But I don't like it. Come on and bring your gun with you just in case."

I looked at my father with a questioning expression on my face. If my father wanted me to bring my gun, he must think something wrong.

I quickly got dressed and then pulled up a loose floor broad. I pulled out a small box from the floor and put it on the bed. Inside was one of the only guns my father and I had.

It was only a Taurus Gaucho .45 colt revolver, and my father had a Colt .38 Super. Normally we wouldn't use them because it was hard to find ammo for them.

I put the gun in my belt and grabbed my jacket and ran out the door. I quickly ran down towards the homes that were on fire; my father was just ahead of me. A small group had already assembled at the fires and had started a bucket brigade to try to put out the fires. But they seemed to be having no effect as another home began to burn.

But there was something wrong with this new fire. It did not seem to have been started from the outside by the other fires but from the inside. I quickly turned in the direction of the new fire to see why this happened.

As I reached it, my father was already there. The house was covered in fire, and I could see someone walking out of the inferno. It was the stranger covered in ash; in his left hand was a lighter, and in the right was a knife. It was small, not much bigger than a butter knife but not as sharp, and both the knife and his hand were covered in blood. But it were his eyes that disturbed me the most; in them was that some look of malevolence that I had seen in his eyes at the feast. I now knew that it was real, and that he was worse than I had ever thought.

"What have you done here?" my father said in a commanding voice pulling his gun form his belt.

"What have I done?" the stranger said, his voice cold and shadowy. "I have *killed*! I have *burned*!"

"But why," I asked looking deep into those cold eyes. "We have done nothing you. Why do you do this?"

"For the *blood*," the stranger said lifting his blood-covered hand to his face. "The *feel* of *blood* on my hand, the *sight* of it, the *smell* of it, the *taste* of it, it makes me feel *alive*!"

"You're mad!" my father said his eyes never leaving the stranger's eyes.

"*Mad*," the stranger said his eyes shining with anger. "They called me *mad* before. They said I was *sick*, *deranged*, a *danger* to myself and everyone around me."

"You are mad," my father said. "Junior, I need you to gather all the remanding villages and get them out of here. Take them to the north to the mountain's path."

"I won't leave you here alone, Father," I said.

"You will do as I say and now," my father said. "This man is mad, and if he gets a chance, he will kill us all! Now *go*!"

With one finally look at the stranger and then at my father, I did as my father commanded. Leaving the site of the fire, I began to lead the villagers to the northern edge of the village. It became harder to get some of the villagers to leave their homes, but fortunately Wade and some of the other hunters were there to help me. They had also seen what my father and I had seen in the stranger's eyes and knew the seriousness of the situation.

It took some time, but we finally managed to get all the people to the opening to the mountain path. The villagers all seemed very scared, but if they were more scared of the laid behind them or what lay before them. About half of the villagers that I found alive had never been outside the village, where the other half had not been outside the village for twenty to thirty years.

But a loud bang from behind settled any indecision. They began to run through the path spurred on by the gunshot. But my thought was not before me but behind. I turned to look down at the village.

"I am sure your father is all right," Wade said putting a hand on you shoulder. "Your father is a strong man."

"No, he is not!" I said moving away from Wade and heading back to the village.

"What are you doing?" Wade asked as I started to run back to the village.

"My father needs me," I said. "He cannot beat this man. My father hates violence; he was no match for this man, for he would have to kill him and that is something my father just cannot do."

And with that I headed off to the center of the village to where my father and the stranger were lasted seen. When I reached the center of the village, I had found that both my father and the stranger were gone.

The only sign left was their footprints and, "Blood!" But whose I did not know, and it pushed me to follow the footprints. There were two pairs, one running away and the other perusing. My first thought was that my father had forced the stranger to flee. But then why would my father chase him? If he forced the stranger to run, there would be no reason to follow.

"So, it must be my father running," I said to myself. "He must be trying to lead the stranger away from us. He must have shot the man to try to slow down the stranger. I have to find them and quick."

I headed off into the direction of the footprints. They were leading towards the south near the woods. I found them on the outskirts of the village. By the look of things, I had made it just in time, for my father was pinned to the wall of one of the houses. The stranger was over top of my father, his left hand grasping my father's gun hand while my father had the stranger's knife hand in his left hand.

They were fighting for superiority over each other. I was surprised to see that my father and the stranger seemed to be equally matched. But only the stranger had the willingness to finish this fight. I needed to do something before that happened.

I had to get the stranger off my father before I could do anything. If I were to fire my gun, the shot might hit my father. So, getting me father away from the stranger was the first thing I had to do.

I quickly grabbed the stranger's knife hand and forced it to the middle of his back. The stranger released my father's hand allowing my father to move in between the stranger and the wall. I then slammed the stranger up against the wall before he could make another move.

I then backed up with my father, my gun on the stranger. As the stranger slowly got over the shock of my surprise attack, my mind was racing trying to think what to do now. The stranger was turned around now rubbing his head; as he did my eyes saw where the blood I saw before was coming form. There was a large bullet wound in the stranger's left leg. It was bleeding very steadily, and it looked like it hurt badly. How the stranger was standing was was beyond me.

The stranger gave his head a violent shake, like a wet dog in the rain, before looking up at us. His eyes looked bloodshot. The angry look in his eyes had shifted to hatred. If he wasn't going to kill us before he was really going to kill us now.

"Well now I see the *puppy* has come back to save the *sire!*" the stranger said in that cold voice. "How very *touching,*"

"You stay back, you hear me!" I said shaking but my hand was strong.

"Ah, what are you going to do, little puppy, shoot me?" the stranger said breaking into a laugh. "Well I hope your shot is far better than your father's!" he said pointing at his bullet wound.

"You don't have the worry about that!" I said in a defiant tone.

"Junior!" my father said but didn't seem to be able to do more.

"You won't shoot me, boy!" the stranger said. "You who are the spitting image of your father. He don't have the nerve to kill me, and neither do *you!*"

"That is what you think," I said pulling the trigger.

The stranger fell to the ground; his blood spilled all over the ground. Not knowing if the stranger was dead or alive, my father and I left the site of the man's body. If he was dead it ends with us, but if he was alive then there was no reason to get close enough for him to finish whoever went to check.

We left in a hurry skirting the edge of the woods, trying to put as much distance between the dead or alive stranger and us. All of the sudden my father stopped on top of a hill that lay near the tree line of the woods.

"What's wrong, Dad?" I asked looking to see if the stranger was following.

"It's nothing," he said.

"There is something; tell me," I said.

"You know that I have done everything in my power to protect you form this world of violence," my father said his voice very serious.

"I know that, Father," I said, "and you have done a wonderful job."

"No, I haven't," my father began. "I have failed you. I have not protected you from this violent world, only introduced you to it."

"What do you mean?" I asked puzzled.

"What you did back there I mean," he said. "You shot that man back there. You have become as violent as anyone in this world, and for that I am sorry."

"I am not, Father," I said. "I am nothing like those people we have seen."

"But you are," he said. "But you are also different from them as well. If I am proud of one thing it is that you have not become like those others."

"Well!" a voice sounded form behind our backs.

We turned to find the stranger on his feet, his knife in his left hand for his right arm laid limp and useless. His whole right sleeve was covered in blood from the bullet wound in his shoulder. My bullet may have wounded him more than my father, but not enough to stop this man.

He must have had a very high pain threshold to keep moving like he was. Any normal man would have been in agony. They would be unable to move not even walk. Thus the stranger's movements were slow; the fact he was up to walking was amazing and a little frightening.

"You," I said in amazement. "I thought I killed you."

The stranger laughed as he came to a stop. "You kill me, boy? That is a good one! You may be a great hunter, boy, but a *killer* you are not! You do not have what it takes, boy! You are like your father—*weak!*"

"You're right; my son is not a killer, but it is not because he can't," my father said. "It's because of me that he has not become a killer like you. But my son is not weak only compassionate. Which is more than I can say about you!"

"*Compassion.*" The Stranger laughed. "Compassion is a true sign of *weakness!* Strength comes from being ruthless in *battle.*"

"I guess I was wrong," my father said. "Not even I can seem to avoid violence this time."

I looked at him with amazement. My father was never a violent man. For him to be forced to violence was serious. The real question is whether or not he could use violence.

The stranger seemed to have found the idea of my father fighting as a real joke.

"You are going to fight me?" The Stranger laughed. "You not a warrior; you are not even a hunter like your son. How do you expect to beat me?"

"I don't!" my father said, and as he did, he pushed me down the hill towards the wood.

In the same instant, my father did two things; he took the gun form my hand and gave me the necklace he always wore. When I hit the bottom of the hill, I looked up to see what was going on. My father had both guns in his hand shooting at the stranger. But the stranger managed to dodge the bullets somehow and got in close range, his injures hampering him little.

It was over in a flash. One moment my father was fighting the stranger, the next the Stranger had pierced my father's heart. The guns falling from his hands, my father fell to the ground dead. My father, the greatest man I had ever known, was gone forever.

But now was not the time to mourn over my father, not when there was a knife-wielding maniac on the loose. There was no time for it. I would have to make a run for it. Without a gun, there was no way for me to win. All I had was my knife, but it would do me no good for he was the superior in close quarters fighting.

Running was all I could do, but I had to head into the wood where I could hope to lose him. So, I ran into the woods first staying on the hunters' path then went off the path. I had hoped that going though the trees would slow down any pursuit of the stranger.

But it only seemed to make it clearer to me that I was indeed being followed by the stranger. I now heard footsteps and the breaking of twigs and branches. By the sound from behind I could tell he was moving fast. I needed to lose him before he caught up to me.

The only thing was that there was nowhere to hide. There were no hollows, large roots to hide under, or caves being so far from the mountains. Deeper and deeper into the woods I ran, going farther into the woods than any of the hunters have gone. The sound of the stranger in pursuit was all that could be heard. It was like the animals were afraid of the stranger.

The sun began to rise to the east illuminating the woods and the surrounding area. In the light I could see that the woods did not go on forever, but ended at a cliff side. Right up against the cliff was a small cottage or hut. It looked very old, most likely built in the old world, maybe used as a hunting lodger.

A sound from behind me told me that the stranger was close, and I was trapped; there was nowhere to go. I had no choice but to head into the hut and hope I could hide in there.

I had found the hut was not locked, but I found that there was not much in the hut at all. The hut wasn't even that big, only one large room. At first glance I did not see much furniture, or even a closet. But looking closer at the walls, there did seem to be another door of some kind.

The reason I did not see it before was because the door seemed to be part of the wall itself. The door was only opened a small crack being held open by something white.

Knowing that the stranger would be here any moment and that this seemed to be the only place I could hide, I hurried to the door. When I got near to it, I noticed what was holding the door open was a bone. Not just any bone but a human bone. It was a leg with the body still attached.

It looked the man fell as the door was closing and his leg got caught as it closed. How he died I could not say right now, but now was not the time with a menace after me. I quickly ducked inside the doorway removing the man's leg so to close the door.

I sat there in the darkness listening for any noises, but it was quiet. Then through the wall I could hear the faint sounds of footsteps. They first came toward the door, then started to move around the hut, before they moved away and died away. The stranger had come in the hut, looked around, and left most likely to go looking for me somewhere else.

I was safe for now, but I did not move. I did not go outside. I just sat there on the floor cradled in a ball. I lied there and began to weep.

Chapter 10

The Lamb

"I never image I would ever hear someone as strong as you admit having ever cried," the bartender said.

"Why is that so hard to believe?" Matrix said. "Even a cold-hearted killer cried as a babe. They may say they never have, but it is only a lie."

Matrix just sat there finishing his drink while the bartender just stood behind the bar. He waited for Matrix to continue the story, but Matrix did not seem to wish to continue the story.

"So!" the bartender said after Matrix remained quiet for a minute or two. "What did you do after that? Where did you going then? Who did you meet? Did you ever find that man again?"

"Do you think I am going to tell you everything tonight," Matrix said. "You forget I have been traveling for the last week and come here to rest."

"Oh, of course, sir," the bartender said. "Steven!"

A boy of sixteen came into the bar at the bartender's word. The boy who must be Steven was very thin for his age but also tall. He had golden blond hair and sky-blue eyes.

"Ah, there you are, Steven," the bartender said looking at Steven. "Take Mister Matrix's things to room five, right away."

"Yes, sir," Steven said in a small voice.

As Steven went to pick up Matrix's bag, Matrix picked it up himself.

"If you don't mind, I will carry my own bag," Matrix said.

"Very well, sir," the bartender said. "Steven, show Mister Matrix to his room."

"As you wish, sir," Steven said in that same small voice. "Please follow me, sir."

Steven led Matrix through door just off the bar. On the left side of the hall were doors leading to the different rooms the bartender talked about. There was also a stairwell on the right as they entered.

Matrix followed Steven down the hall passing four doors and stopping at the fifth door. At this door, Steven pulled out a key and unlocked the door and opened the door. He then turned and handed the key to Matrix.

"I hope you enjoy your night, sir," Steven said with a bow.

Matrix took the key from Steven and went in the room. The first thing Matrix saw on entering the room was that he wasn't alone. Sitting on the bed was a woman. She was very beautiful with long, dark black hair and green eyes. She was stretched out on the bed, like she was waiting for Matrix. She only had on very little clothes, but it was the eyes that Matrix saw. It was an eye that Matrix had seen many times before, the eyes of fear.

This woman was here not by choice; the bartender here sent her here to please Matrix. But Matrix was anything but pleased; this was not what he was looking for right now. All he wanted was sleep and nothing more.

"Hello, sir!" the woman said in a forced sexy voice. "How may I serve you tonight, sir?"

"You wish to serve me?" Matrix said.

She nodded her head, but it seemed half-heated, and Matrix knew she would rather be anywhere but here.

"You can best serve me," Matrix said, "by going home tonight and sleeping in your own bed. I don't need or want any company tonight."

"Is it that you do not find me attractive, sir?" the woman asked with a look of both offense and relief.

"No!" Matrix said. "You are a beauty among beauty, but I do not sleep with women by force or who have fear in their eyes, as you do. Eyes like yours lose their beauty when they are full of fear, and I won't have that in my bed."

Matrix then opened the door for her and waited for her to leave. Sliding off the bed, the woman made her way to the door. As she passed, Matrix she looked at him in his brown eyes. Her eyes were softer now, and a single tear fell down her cheek.

She then turned and walked out the door Matrix was holding and said good night. Bidding her a good night too, Matrix closed the door.

As Matrix sat on the bed, he thought back to the moment that their eyes met at the door. They had changed for the better, and Matrix could see the beauty in her eyes, but also he saw that she was pleased he had asked her to leave. Her eyes had said the one thing she did not say with her voice. Thank you!

Matrix stood up and walked over to the window. He just stood there looking out on the town. It was a quiet small town with a tiny river that flows beside the town, which was the reason the town was founded. Matrix had seen many villages and towns like this one. They were all the same.

Matrix then removed his jacket and laid it on the chair beside him. He then removed his sword, his knife, his guns, and his shoes. His guns he placed under his pillow; as for his sword, he left it next to the bed. Then he lied down on the bed and fell to sleep.

Matrix woke up to a beautiful morning. Matrix got up, bathed, and dressed before going down to the bar. Leaving both his jacket and his guns, Matrix walked down the hall locking his door on the way. With sword in hand, he went through the door into the bar.

Even this early in the morning, there were several people here at the bar. This place seemed to be the local hangout for most people. Matrix noticed that the people sitting here this morning were the same people that were here last night. Maybe they were hoping to hear more of Matrix's story.

Matrix walked back over to the bar and sat down. As Matrix sat, he placed his sword next to him up against the bar. Seeing Matrix at the bar, the bartender quietly went over to the bar to serve Matrix.

"Good morning, Matrix, sir," the bartender said serving Matrix a drink. "How was your night, sir?" A small smile started to grow on the bartender's face.

"My night was fine," Matrix, said taking a drink from his drink. "But next time I would prefer a mint on the pillow instead of a woman."

"Were you not satisfied her, sir?" the bartender said sounding as if he wanted to correct his mistake.

"No, she was a beautiful woman, but I told you that all I wanted was sleep and that I did not want to be disturbed," Matrix said, "even if the disturbance was a beautiful woman."

"I am sorry, Matrix, sir; it won't happen again unless you ask of course, sir," the bartender said.

"I hope so for your sake," Matrix said taking another drink.

The bartender went about preparing some food for Matrix. With the good cooking skills as before, the bartender soon placed a plate of food before Matrix. Matrix devoured his plate of food in no time at all. The bartender just stood there as Matrix ate. Matrix knew the bartender was waiting for Matrix to continue his story.

"So, let me think," Matrix said at last taking a sip from his glass. "So, my father was dead, the stranger, his murderer, gone, and me in a strange cave of some kind."

I don't know how long I was asleep but when I finally awoke, I looked around my surroundings. It took a while before I remembered what had happened. Feeling the need to do something and seeing that the door I came in from was not going to open, I went in deeper into the cave.

I soon found that the cave seemed to have been dug out by men for as I went deeper into the cave it went from a stone wall to metal. It looked as if this was once a natural cave that had been made larger by man, but for what I did not know.

The tunnel ended in a large chamber. The chamber reminded me of a military base. It was divided into several areas each area having its own purpose. Exploring the base, I soon found out that it had three floors, one above and one below. As I explored the base, I found many bodies all over the base.

The rooms above were mainly soldiers' barracks, but it also had a gym and a shower room. The ground floor had the briefing room, a room of offices, a motor pool, and a dump. On the basement floor, there was a sick room, a mess, a kitchen, stock room, power and water room, and an armory. Inside the armory was weapons galore; in the motor pool were the still vehicles and fuel. In the sick room, I found a full stock of medicine, and in the stock room there was enough food to feed ten men for years.

But I still didn't know what was this base was used for. In the offices, I found that the computers were still working, and so were the lights. I never had any experience with computers, but my father had told me all about them. Like when I used electricity back in Blaze's mansion, I started to play around with the computers. But I soon found out that I needed some sort of ID and password to access the files. No matter what I did, I could not break the code.

The computers were not the only things that were hard to access. The doors themselves were locked, but I found accessing them easy to enter. I soon found upon searching the soldiers some sort of identification device. It was small, about the size of my hand, and with a small screen on it. On examining the device closely, I found out first it was still working and it was showing this soldier's information. The doors themselves had a small plate by the door. Putting the M.I.D. up to the plates, I found that they would open for me.

I found more bodies of other soldiers as I went through the base. I began to gather the soldiers' remains and brought them down to the ground floor. Once I had brought down the last of the remains, I began going through their belongings. I then placed their remains into the dump.

Then using their dog tags, I made a sort of shrine to honor the soldiers in the briefing room. I was never very religious; my father focused more on my education than religion. But I have seen many villagers and townsfolk practicing the old religion and even some new religions in my travels.

But all the religions I have seen all gave respect to the dead. I had never prayed in my life, but I bowed my head and said a few words to the hanging dog tags. I went to the kitchen and had a good meal, then went up to the general's room and went to bed.

I spent the next week in the base looking through the hard copy files I could find. I pretty much read anything I could find in that place, but there wasn't much I could find out about the base. The most I found out about the place was this base was called The Shadow Matrix.

For days, I went over the files I could find, but I found not much on what this base was used for. I had figured that any of the files that I was looking for must be within the computers. I was hoping to find a passcode somewhere in the papers I found but had no luck.

But I was not about to give up. I needed to find out as much about this place as I could. Looking though the general's files and papers, I soon found several file cards with jumble of letters and numbers. Above the letters and numbers were written the words Login and Password.

I went down to the computer room the next day and entered the codes that I found. They worked, and I soon found that I had access to the files on the computer. I slowly went through the files, having never used a computer before now.

The first set of files, it looked like personal files. Checking the names on the computer with the names on the dog tags, I found that everyone who was posted here had died here.

The next thing I found was a file on the M.I.D. It showed everything about the M.I.D system including its features. The file also showed everyone who had a M.I.D. Besides the men and women in the base, there were two people who were not here, the head of the CIA and the joint chief of staff.

I had no idea where these men were or if they were even alive or dead. It didn't matter one way or the other if one of them was alive or not. With the access I had, it looked like I could do anything with the M.I.D. including adding or re-moving M.I.D.s from the system. So, I erased the other M.I.D. and added a new one in the same time.

I was halfway through spelling my name when I stopped to think. My life had changed since my father died, and now I needed to think about tomorrow. The fact is that I could not remain here forever. Not because of lack of food or water, but because I needed to get out of this place. As I had learned while I lived in the village, I could not stay in one place for too long. I needed more space, needed to go places, but more importantly, I needed to find that man and avenge my father's death.

It was this reason more than the others that stayed my head. I could not use my father's name if I were going to find that man and kill him. I would need a new name if I were going to take revenge on the stranger. I did not wish to kill using my father's name, so I would first need a new name, a new life. But what name?

As I sat there in that room, my mind wandering around trying to think of a name, my mind fell on the soldiers of the base. It was in that I had made my choice; I would call myself Matrix for now on.

I spent about two mouths at the Shadow Matrix base, looking over the all the files in the computer. I was very interested in this place and wanted to know all there was to know about it, and the people who were assigned here.

This base had many secrets, and I wanted to know them all. After two months of reading and studying, I finally felt that it was time to move on. I spent an entire day preparing for my departure, gathering weapons, food, water, and even fuel for I was planning to use one of the vehicles.

After looking over one of vehicles, I then went down to the armory. With a small sports bag in hand, I was looking around and I began to pull down weapons and put them in the bag. In the back of the armory there was a large back cabinet.

Inside the cabinet, I found several suits hangings. Taking one down, I looked at it. From what I read about these suits, it was the gear that the members of the Shadow Matrix would wear on their missions.

They were very well made both of Kevlar and metal plates. The suit was made to keep a person safe from bullets and even blades. Those, like all suits of armor, still have their weak points. But it still was better than to go out in just my own skin.

Putting on the suit, I found that it was very lightweight. I grabbed a pair of M9s from the wall and strapped them to my legs. I then walked out of the armory picking up my bag and my jacket that I found in one of the rooms.

My next stop was the stock room; with a large duffel bag I began to fill it with food. I also had filled up several cantinas and jugs with water. My last stop was the infirmary; the medicine here would be far more valuable than even food or fresh water. With all my supplies gathered, I went to the general's room and went to sleep.

The next morning was bright and hot, perfect weather to start a journey. Gathering my stuff, I headed down to the motor pool and headed out. It took me a while to learn how to drive, but I picked it up very fast.

First rays of light shined through the tunnel openings. The tunnel opened onto a small dirt road inside dense forest. Looking back, I watched as the tunnel opening closed before my eyes. The stone wall opening blended perfectly with the rest of the mountainside.

Turning my back on the Shadow Matrix, I headed out. Where? I do not know. But before I go anywhere, I had one thing to do first: the dead soldiers from the Shadow Matrix.

I traveled for several miles before I came across a large tree. It was here that I buried the Shadow Matrix soldiers. After the burial, I moved to the large tree and with my knife made a mark, one for every soldier who died in the Shadow Matrix. Once more I bowed my head in respect for the dead before I moved on. Where I was going, I did not know, but I did not even care.

Back in my vehicle, I looked back at the tree and at the graves. I will never be able to bury my father so this grave would have to do for him as will. With one final look at the grave, I turned to the east and drove off, saying good-bye to my father.

Chapter 11

The Goat

About a week after the burial, I had come on a small town. It was not much to look at. The little homes seemed run down. If not for the fact that there were people out on the streets, I would have thought it was deserted.

Those people seemed very friendly; they also seemed to be frightened. As if they were not sure to welcome me or run me out of town. But of course, the strange looks are normal for people like me. Even so, it was looking as if there was something more to there looks than plain suspicion.

"Evening, stranger."

Looking around I found a little old man in front of a small house. "Good evening, sir," I said walking up to the old man.

"Have you been traveling long, young man?" the old man asked.

"For an age and a half," I said with a smile.

"And how much longer do you have to go?" the old man asked

"To the ends of the Earth and back," I said.

"Well then why don't you come in; you can sleep in a warm bed tonight and head out again tomorrow," the old man said gesturing to the door of his home.

The old man's home was small but comfortable. The main room seemed to be both kitchen and dining room. To the side was a small sitting room, and in the back were the bedrooms.

"Sue, we have a guest," the old man said to the open air.

There came, from the back of the house, a young woman. She was very fair looking with long black hair and brown eyes.

"Who is this, Grandpa?" Sue asked.

"Just a wanderer looking for a good night's rests," the old man said.

"You're taking in another stranger into our home," Sue said.

"Sue, don't be rude," the old man said looking hard at his granddaughter. "He just needs food and rest and then he will be on his way."

"How can you be sure of that?" Sue said looking at me with an evil eye.

"I trust him," the old man said.

"You *trust* him," Sue said. "How can you trust him?"

"I trust his eyes, my dear," the old man said.

"Grandfather, you are far too trusting with people," Sue said.

"You don't have to worry," I said looking at Sue. "I do not plan on robbing you or to murder you in your bed. In fact, I will be happy to give you something for your trouble."

Opening the large bag on my back, I dumped about a quarter of my bag onto the large wooden table in the middle of the room.

"I think that this should do," I said looking at the old man then at Sue.

"There you have it, Sue," the old man said. "*Now*, will you show our friend here to his room?"

Sue seemed to be in a state of shock, either because of the amount I was willing to give or because of my generosity. She recovered quickly and started to lead me to the back of the house to the only spare room they had.

She said nothing as we walked to the back to the room. She didn't even speak as she opened the door to let me in the room. She just walked off without a word.

I moved into the room and threw my bags on the bed and turned to look out the window. My mind kept going over what Sue had said. Her words had proved that what I saw when I first came into the town was true. Those people have seen hardship at the hands of an outsider like me. Whether they were still facing it now, I could not say.

Walking back to the main room of the house, I found the old man in the sitting room smoking on a long pipe. He was just sitting there with his pipe in his mouth, his eyes looking out the window and a large amount of smoke over his head.

"Well now!" the old man said as I walked into the room. "Are you doing alright?"

"I am indeed, sir," I said taking a seat across from him. "You and your granddaughter have been more than kind to me."

"You say that even when my granddaughter insulted you when you first got here," the old man said with a small chuckle.

"It is all right, sir," I said. "I am used to far worse than that."

"I guess you right," the old man said. "But I am afraid that this is not normal. For you see, we in this town have been playing host to a band of ruffians."

The old man stood up and made his ways over to the window where he continued to stare out. It looked as if he were looking at a large house on a hill.

"They came here about two years ago," the old man continued. "They were just drifters looking for food and water. But when they got here, they found more than they needed. They found us."

"What do you mean by that?" I asked with a puzzled looked.

"I mean that they used us as much as our food and water," the old man said turning his back on the window and closing his eyes.

"That so they have been using your women for their pleasure," I said looking back at him. "And everyone else, for whatever else they want."

"Yes!" the old man said with sadness in his voice. "I don't even know why I am telling you this. This isn't your problem. Why should you care."

"The cruelty of this world is greater than one man can overcome," I said. "We all have our own lives to live, and our own problems to deal with."

"That is true," the old man said. "And that is why I won't ask you to help us or to do anything for us. You had your own life and you need to live you own, and we have ours."

"So, where did your granddaughter get to?" I asked looking around the house.

"Oh, she must have gone out to the fields," the old man said looking around himself. "She should be back any time now."

"Well, if you will excuse me, I think that I will go and get some rest," I said standing and heading in the direction of my rooms.

I had just climbed into bed when a noise came from outside. Looking out the window, I saw a large group of very massive men coming into the town. From the direction they were coming, they seemed to have come from the big house on the hill. These men must be ones the old man talked about. From what I could tell from the window, they seemed to be coming into town for food, water, and possibly entertainment.

I picked up my bags and made my way outside. The old man whose home I was in was talking to one of the men.

"Please, sir, the harvest is small this month," the old man said pleading to the man. "We have had very little rain, and there is barely any food for us."

"If you do not give us what we want then we will be forced to take what we want from you," the man said grinning as he said it.

"Now then," I said walking up to the group of men. "There is no need to take all these people's food for I have more than enough food to fed ten men for a month."

I threw my large bag of food to the feet of the men.

"Go a head, take the food, and leave these people alone, at least for now," I said turning my back on them and walking towards the house.

"You are giving us this food without trade," the leader of the men said.

I stopped and turned back around and looked at the man who spoke. "No, of course not, but what I want is just for you and your men to leave these people alone for at least one day. Just one day, so that I may rest before I head out tomorrow."

"But my men are bored and lonely," the leader said. "They need entertainment."

"Then why don't you teach them cribbage," I said, my hands moving to my sides.

The leader saw where my hand moved to my gun and knew he was outmatched. Neither of his men were carrying guns; it had been a long time since he needed to bring more than blunt weapons into town. I had the advantage; I could take them all out before they could get within striking distance.

"Very well," the leader said nodding to his men. "We will leave these people alone, for now."

And with that they left. I watched as they left before heading back to bed. I found Sue waiting outside the door to my room. She had a very business-like look on her face.

"I need to ask something of you," Sue asked.

"And what would that be?" I asked.

"I would like you for your help," Sue asked.

"You mean you would like me to fight those men," I said.

"Yes, I do!" Sue said looking at me hard. "I can pay you whatever you want."

"And what would that be?" I asked.

"Anything, anything you want," Sue said. "Food, water, a bed."

"I can get my own food and water," I said looking away from her. "As for the bed, I have already paid you for the use of it. Now, if there is nothing else, I would like to go to sleep."

"Wait, there is one more thing I could give you," Sue said walking up to me. "I will give you myself to do with as you please."

"How old are you, girl?" I asked not looking at her.

"I am nineteen, sir," Sue said her eyes red.

"And you wish to pay me to rid this town of those men with your body?" I said my eyes still closed.

"Yes, I will," Sue said tears now filling her eyes.

"No!" I replied.

"What?" Sue asked tears now running down her face.

"I said, no, I will not do it," I said.

"Why!" Sue said looking offended. "Am I unappealing to you?"

"Please, don't take offence," I said looking at her. "You are a fine woman, and I do not want to spoil you. Besides, I will not accept that form of payment."

"But we need help," Sue said tears flowing more freely. "We do not have the means to fight them. But you, you could do it. You have weapons; you can fight them."

"They are not my enemy. They are yours; you need to fight them," I said walking past her to my room.

"But we do not have the strength to fight them," Sue said crying into her hands.

"But, if I help you, you will never become stronger," I said opening the door.

"So, you will not help us, at all?" Sue said her face very red and fresh tears in her eyes.

"I have my own enemy to fight, my own battles. I cannot help everyone I meet, and you must deal with this yourself," I said closing the door.

As I lay in bed, I could still hear Sue crying in the room next to me. I fell asleep listening to her crying. My dreams were filled with crying women and men who all looked like the stranger.

I awoke very suddenly to a banging on my door. I could hear the old man saying something but was unable to hear clearly. Getting up I reached the door and opened to see the old man in a state of panic.

"What is wrong, old man?" I asked very puzzled by his look.

"It is Sue," he said panting. "She has left the house and has gone to the hill. I think her intent is to fight and kill the men up there."

"You saw her leave?" I asked gesturing the old man to sit down.

"I got up for the bathroom and just saw her walking out the door," the old man said calming down a little. "I went to the window to see what she was doing and saw her heading to the hill."

"What does she think she is going to do against them?" I said walking to the window where I had a good view of the hill and the big house on top of it.

"Well, I think she has taken one of your guns with her," the old man said.

"What!" I said turning to him.

"As she was running, I saw a small gun in her hand," the old man said looking shamed-faced. "We have no weapons in this town. Only you and the men up there have the only weapons here."

I pulled out my small bag and opened it on the bed. It did not take long to see the small .45 pistols were gone with some clips as well. She must have taken it before our little conflict outside my room.

"She had played a good act outside this door," I said, not talking to anyone at all. "Why didn't I see that? How could I not have noticed that?"

"Sue does not know what she is doing," the old man said now pleading with me. "She is young, and she has lost much. Her old sister was taken by those men two years ago; we have not seen her since. I can't lose Sue like I lost her sister. I do not have the right to ask you for this, but you are my only hope. Please do this for me, my friend."

"I will go and bring you granddaughter back so that I may reclaim what she has taken from me," I said grabbing my bag and leaving the room without a second look at the old man.

I ran out the door of the house and up to the hill. Ducking behind a large bush, I began to assess my options. I could see the front door from where I was. There were two guards standing by the door, but they were not the best guards in the world. They were fast asleep, several empty bottles at their feet.

Either these people have no worries about intruders, or they are the laziest men in this world. Either way, I was not going to let my guard down. I quickly and quietly moved around to the side of the house. I soon found a small door in the side of the house that was not guarded at all.

"How stupid can these people be?" I said looking around me. "One door being guarded by drunks and another not guarded at all. This may be easier than I thought."

I moved to the door very slowly, keeping my eyes open. I made it to the door to find that it was locked. I picked the door's lock and opened it to a small hallway.

Chapter 12

The Swan

The hallway was small, dark, and very empty. There seemed to be no one in sight. The hall was quiet; its walls looked battered and in disrepair.

There were many doors along the hall, all leading into what looked like servants' quarters. At the other end of the hall was anther door that led into the kitchen. There was no one in the kitchen, but I could hear voices coming from the door to my left. It sounded as if a large group was in the next room having some sort of celebration.

Turning away from noises, I headed towards the stairs to the upper floors. At the second-floor landing, I looked down the hall. At first, it looked as if the hall was deserted as the rest of the house.

The hall was not as deserted as I had first thought. A man was on the floor with his back against a door, a bottle still in his right hand. I thought that he might have been there in order to get away from the commotion of the dining hall. I was just about to move on when a loud bang came from the door.

"It would seem I have found the old man's granddaughter," I said.

The guard on the floor did not even react to the bang. It looked like he had drunk himself into a stupor.

"This will make things harder," I said looking at the guard as he slumbered on as the banging continued. "If I try to get by him, he may call for others. If he does, I will be forced to kill him, leaving bodies around, and they will know someone was here that should not be."

I moved out into the hall keeping a watchful eye on the guard. He did not move an inch as I walked closer to him and the door. I drew my weapons as I came right upon the guard.

As I came upon the guard, the door gave a violent shatter. The guard woke with a start and looked about bleary-eyed. Before his eyes could focus on me and raise an alarm, my weapon came down on his head knocking the guard out.

I then moved him to the side, keeping his bottle in hand. Once I knew he was not going to cause trouble for me, I used his keys to open the door.

The room became deadly quiet as I turned the key. As I entered the room, a shout caught my attention. I turned just in time to stop a board from cracking open my head.

"Oh, it's you," Sue said with a stunned expression on her face. "What are you doing here?"

"Why do you think I am here?" I said looking at her. "I am here for my weapons you stole."

"You are just here for you weapons?" Sue said.

"I told you before, I am not here to fight your battle," I said. "If you do not learn to stand on your own two feet, you will just be back to the same life if you don't."

"I tried that and look at where it got me!" Sue said.

"That is because you did not think before you acted," I said. You were far too rash. You only had two guns each having six shots each and no extra ammo. Stupid!"

"Oh, and I supposed you would have done better?" Sue said skeptically.

"Of course I could," I said with a mocking tone. "Who are you? You have never killed a thing. and you think you could take on these men? Foolish!"

"You're right," Sue said. "So, what are you going to do now? Are you just going to leave me here, or are you going to help me?"

"I should just let you sit here and rot," I said. "But I told your grandpa that I would try to help you."

"You're really going to help me out of here?" Sue said.

"I said I would, but afterwards I am leaving," I said.

"What do you mean? You still will not help us out?" Sue said looking shocked.

"No!" I replied. "I did not come here to save you. I came for myself and no one else.

Now is not the time for this," I said moving over to the window. "I am here now, and I am going to help."

Looking at the window, I found that it was sealed shut. I then started to look about the room for anything that could help us to escape. In the center of the room were several chains hanging from the ceiling.

"These will do nicely," I said pulling them down from the ceiling.

"What are you going to do with them?" Sue asked.

"You're going to use these to climb down to the ground and head back to town," I said to her.

"And what do I do after I get there?" She asked looking excited.

"Nothing," I said moving back to the window. "You are to go back to town and live your life as well as you can."

"But," Sue said but at a look from me she went silent.

Turning to face the window, I smashed the glass in. "You need to go, now," I said throwing the chain out the window. "Hurry, before someone comes to see what that noise was."

For once Sue did not argue and did as she was told. She quickly climbed onto the window and down the chain as fast as she could. As Sue climbed down the chain, I could hear footsteps coming close.

"Hurry," I yelled down to Sue. "They will be here soon."

As she climbed down, the door behind me burst opened; in the doorway stood three very drunk men. They each were swaying on their feet, a bottle in one hand and a weapon in the other.

"What's going on here?" the man in the center said. "Who are you? Where is the whore at?"

Letting go of the chain, I turned to face the three men. As the chain fell out the window, my hands went to my weapons.

"I am sorry to say, but the girl has left the building," I said taking a step forward. "But I am here for your entrainment."

"*You* let our whore go!" said the man on the right. "I guess we will just have some fun with you instead."

"Come on then, let's play," I said.

They came at me all at once, but their moves were very drunkenly. The three men attacked with their weapons out ready to fight. I went for my own blade ready to fend them off; even as drunk as they were, I still had to be careful.

The three men attacked with blood in their eyes and alcohol in their veins. They came at me, all at once. Ducking under the first strike, I followed with punch to his mouth. As he fell, the two others came at me with increased eagerness.

The other two came at me from both sides. I stepped to one side, and the two men crashed into each other. The smaller man fell to the ground and lied there unconscious. The larger man turned to face me again, leaving his friend on the floor.

He charged me, blind by rage moving over both his companions. He struck at my face with his knife. I blocked it with my own knife. I then countered with a hit to his stomach. The large man fell to the ground and stopped moving. Walking over the three men, I headed over to the door.

"Now to look for my weapons," I said opening the door, "but where should I go?"

Looking around the second floor, I found the weapons two doors down from where I was. Inside was a large group of weapons of all types. To my surprise, the smallest amounts of weapons were gun,; only eight guns and two of them were mine. After checking the other rooms on this floor, I headed back downstairs.

As I reached the kitchen, I noticed that the commotion from the dining hall seemed to have quieted down. Moving to the door, I slowly opened it and investigated the hall.

Inside the hall, I found it packed with sleeping men. The floors, the chairs, and even tables were covered with men. As I moved in between the slumbering men, I began to look around. While looking, I found five more guns and several more things of ammo.

After I searched every man for anything of use, I headed for the exit. Outside I found the four guards all out cold. I found two more guns on the guards. Putting the guns in my bag, I began my slow way back to the town.

As I came up onto the town, I found the whole town gathered in the center of the town. All the townsfolk seemed to be there, and by the sound of the gathering, they were making quiet uproar. As I approached the center of the town, I could hear what was being said.

"Why should we care what happens to some stranger?" yelled a man in the front of the group.

"He's right; why should we care if he gets killed," said a man in the back.

"But the stranger saved my life; we have to help him," Sue said looking down at all the people in front of her.

"But what can we do?" a woman asked. "We have no way to fight back."

"That's right!" someone said looking around at the townsfolk. "We do not have any weapons, but they have weapons and guns. How are we to fight them?"

"We have to try," Sue said. "We cannot just let them do what they want anymore."

Sue stopped her speech when she saw me walking into town. Went she stopped, the people turned around to see why. Everyone I saw had a shocked looked on their face.

"You're, you're alive," Sue said, her face white with shock. "How did you survive?"

"From there you mean?" I said pointing behind me and laughing. "I have seen men far worst than them in my life."

"But they all are very large men with guns," the man who first spoke said.

"Oh, you mean these guns?" I said throwing the bag to the ground.

As the bag hit the ground, the guns fell out of the bag.

"These are all the guns those men had," I said pointing at the guns on the ground. "And as for their size, it is no use if they're off their asses drunk."

All eyes were on me as I moved to the center of town and onto the platform that Sue was just speaking from.

"You people in this town need to wake up," I said looking around at everyone. "You all seem to think that someone is going to come here and save you from your problem. Foolish! You should all know by now that in this new world there are no heroes or saviors. If you want help you are going to have to learn to help yourself."

It was strange seeing all their eyes on me listening to all I had to say, and what was stranger, they were eager to hear more. With their eyes on me, I began to feel like my father. I had never thought I could ever speak to a crowd like my father could, but on that day, I proved that I was my father's son.

"You must stand and fight for your homes, learn to defend them from *all* who would want to take them from you again." And with that, I turned and headed back to my room.

Once I was back in my room, I started to gather up my things. When I was all ready to go, I headed back outside. To my surprise, I found that the all the townsfolk seemed to have been taking my words to heart and were all preparing themselves to fight. Only Sue was not helping to prepare the town for a battle. No, she was standing at the door waiting for me.

"So, you are leaving after all?" she said looking at the bags in my hands.

"I have already told you that this is your fight, not mine," I said opening my smaller bag and pulling out two boxes. "Just remember to bring ammo with you."

And with that I gave her the boxes and turned and headed out of town.

Chapter 13

The Dragon

"So, you just left those people to fend for them?" the bartender said looking a little surprised. "Why didn't you stay and help them to fight?"

"Because I wouldn't have been much help to them," Matrix said. "If I had stayed, they would not have learned as much. As my father always said, give a man a fish, feed him for a day, but teach a man to fish, feed him for a lifetime."

"So, do you know whatever happened to that town?" the bartender asked with some real interest.

"No!" Matrix said taking a drink. "I never went back to the town to check."

"Oh, right!" the bartender said.

"As for me, I went on my way not looking back, never looking back," Matrix said.

As I traveled, I found many more towns and villages just like the last one. But I also found towns and villages totally different to it. Like the one I found four weeks later.

I came upon one of the old cities; in it there didn't seem to be anyone there. Like most of the old cities, it looked deserted. The city itself looked as if it hadn't changed since the old days. The only true difference might have been the plant life growth. Vines, trees, and other plant life were overgrown, covering streets, walkways, and even buildings.

Walking the streets, I soon found the city was full of animal life. The Cities of Beasts is what the cities of old had come to be called.

Moving though the city, my eyes always looking for anything that might have been left of any value. But I soon found that not only was there not anything of value here at all, but I did find that there was still a presence of humans in the city.

I came upon a large chained fence, and on the other side of the gate were two men with bows and arrows in their hands. As I approached them, they raised their bows with arrows at me.

"Do not take another step," one of the men said.

I stopped and slowly went for my weapons. "I am only here for trade and for a place to sleep for a night."

"Very well," said the other men. "But you must leave you weapons here with us."

"All right," I said removing my guns and ejecting the clips.

One of the guards lowered his weapon and opened the gate. He then came to me and took my guns from me, all the while the other guard had his weapon on me the whole time.

"Are these all the weapons you have?" the guard asked looking me over.

"Yes! That is all I have." I said not wanting him to investigate my bag. "Oh! I do have a knife," I said as an afterthought. "Do you want that as well?"

"No!" said the second guard. "The laws of our land do allow men to carry a knife with them at all time."

"Thanks! Then that's all the weapons I have on me," I said hoping that they would not ask to look in the bags.

"All right, you may pass!" the guards said.

"What about my guns?" I asked as they closed the gate behind me.

"We will keep them safe for you!" the second guard said finally lowering his bow. "When you leave, you can have them back."

With that, I headed for a door right behind them. Inside, I found a gigantic space. This place must have been an old shopping mall at one point, but by the look of what I could see, it had not changed since then.

It looked as if the people just started their lives from where they left off. Many have opened stores or stands to sell their wares. It seemed that they had created a commerce town.

Looking around, I could see food was the common thing being sold. There were also other items being sold—tools, other supplies, and even old-world stuff that had no use in this new world. There was even an inn and several taverns and bars, but the shop I noticed was an armory.

This was easy to see for it looked out of place. Indeed, it was the only store that was selling weapons. There were no guns there, but there were swords, knifes, daggers, and other blunt weapons. Intrigued, I made my way to the little shop for a closer look at those weapons.

I noticed that no one looked in my direction as I headed toward the shop, but I knew everyone was aware of my destination and me. By the feel of this place, this shop was not very well liked or respected by the townsfolk. Everyone just seemed to pretend that it did not exist, but it also made it a lot easier for men like me to notice it.

The shopkeeper himself did not seem to mind how the others saw him or didn't see him. As the case may be. He was an old Asian man with a very thin beard and mustache. His white hair was pulled back into noble top not.

The shopkeeper's back was to me; the sound of metal on metal told me that he was at work on weapon.

"Is there something that I can do for you, son?" the shopkeeper said in a strong Asian accent.

"I was just admiring your work," I said looking at the weapons.

"So, you have an interest in bladed weapons?" the shopkeeper said.

"I have studied about them only," I said.

"Studied, how about used," he said turning to faces me.

"Only a knife but not a sword," I said. "You don't seem to be well liked here, do you," I said looking around once more.

"No, I'm not," the shopkeeper said looking behind me. "But it doesn't matter to me. I am going to do what I want and not care what everyone thinks or says about me."

"So, everyone here isn't into the whole weapons thing?" I said.

"Right, others seem to think my shop will attract the wrong kind of people," the shopkeeper said.

"And what kind is that?" I said looking around.

"Your kind, of course," the shopkeeper said. "Stranger and wanderers, the people think that any one of them may try to do us harm. But we need wanderers and strangers to sustain our lives here."

"So, it's a bit of a stalemate," I said with a laugh. "But if they're that afraid, why didn't they just kick you out?"

"My sister," the shopkeeper said. "My sister is our leader here."

"Oh! I see," I said, "so your sister keeps the others off your back!"

"Even if she does not approve," the shopkeeper said. "But family is family."

"I see," I said.

"But enough about that, what can I do for you?" the shopkeeper said becoming business-like suddenly.

"Well, let me see what you have," I said looking around his little shop. "Are those samurai swords back there?"

"Oh! Yes!" the shopkeeper said looking behind him at the swords hanging up. "Those are samurai swords, but they are not for sale. They are the swords of my father going back generations."

"Are you a samurai then?" I asked.

"In a way," the shopkeeper said. "I was trained in the ways of the samurai. My great, great, great, great grandfather was one of the last samurai in service to the emperor of Japan."

"That is some legacy to live up to, don't you think?" I said.

"It is not as hard as you might think," the shopkeeper said. "It is not living up to my family that is hard, but keeping the tradition going."

"What do you mean by that?" I said.

"I mean, I may be the last samurai in my family!" the shopkeeper said with sorrow in his eyes.

"Do you not have anyone to pass down your teachings?" I asked.

"No!" he said, his look of sorrow deepening. "All my children are dead. They all died in the Great Disaster."

"I'm sorry!" I said apologetically "I didn't know."

"Of course you didn't," the shopkeeper said. "But it is ok; I have had time to mourn for them all. As many of us have."

"What about your sister?" I asked curious.

"Oh, she was trained just like me in the way of the samurai," the shopkeeper said, "but she since has forsaken the samurai way."

"Why has she forsaken the way of the samurai?" I asked.

"She has come to believe it was people like me that caused the Great Disaster," the shopkeeper said.

"What people is she talking about exactly?" I asked.

"Warriors and soldiers," the shopkeeper said. "They are people who fight to protect what they believe in."

"So, people like us are the reason for the Great Disaster," I said.

"That is what she thinks, and nothing I say will ever convince her otherwise," the shopkeeper said.

"Warriors and soldiers do not start wars; all they do is fight the wars," I said. "The ones who started the war are the ones in power who simply want more power."

"You are very wise for someone so very young," the shopkeeper said. "You are right; my sister has forgotten what it is to be a samurai."

"And what is that, sir?" I asked.

"It is simply that a samurai is a protector of those they care for and believe in," the shopkeeper said.

"If you put it that way, it sounds as if your sister has not given to fighting at all," I said.

"Indeed, you are a smart young man," the shopkeeper said. "I only wish my sister could see it the way you see things."

"Well not all have seen what I have seen," I said. "In my young life, I have seen different men fighting in different ways. Some with violence, some with words, and some with actions like your sister."

"Yes, you're right, but she does not wish to see or believe it," the shopkeepers said. "Humans are beings who thrive on conflict, big or small; it does not matter."

"It is human nature I am afraid," I said. "It is not something that can be changed or erased; it is in our blood."

"Yes, but my sister still thinks that she can," the shopkeeper said. "But enough of this, what I can do for you today?"

"Well I did not know much about swords, at all," I said. "All I do know about them I learned from books my father had."

"It does not stop many others from buying and using them," the shopkeeper said. "You never know, you might be surprised."

"Well, I see you are not just a skilled samurai but also a skilled merchant," I said laughing.

He laughed as well. "I see you have noticed."

"My father was a smooth talker himself," I said.

"Was he now?" the shopkeeper asked. "So why not honor him by buying one of my swords?"

"You know, I think I will!" I said with a laugh. "But only if you were to give me your finest sword."

"My finest sword," the shopkeeper said. "Now, let me think!" The shopkeeper started looking around his little shop. "Ha! This is it! This is my finest blade I have made to date!" the shopkeeper said. "And for once I am not exaggerating. This is truly my finest sword I have ever made."

The sword he held had a dragonhead where the blade and the handle met. The dragonhead shined like silver. It was a very beautiful looking weapon.

"I made this blade several months ago," the shopkeeper said. "But the strangest thing was shaping the sword become."

"What do you mean by that?" I asked.

"The dragon," the shopkeeper said drawing the sword. "The dragon is a symbol of power to my family for hundred of years. We believe in it so much that we made the dragon as part of our family's crest."

And looking back at his family's swords, I could see that on the sheath of the swords a sliver chest of a dragon moving in a circle.

"So, does this mean that your family believes they have the strength from the dragon?" I asked.

"No!" the shopkeeper said sheathing the sword once more. "No, it means we were born from dragons and the spirit of the dragons lives in us."

"Is this really true?" I asked.

"Well, it is what my grandfather used to say," the shopkeeper said. "He would tell me the dragon's strength flows through our blood. It is this strength which makes our family the powerful warriors that we are."

"So, to you the dragon is more than just a symbol; it is the way you live your life," I said looking at the shopkeeper. "Is that, right?"

"Yes! This is true," the shopkeeper said. "The way of the dragon is the way of the warrior to my family, and so this sword must be used by a true warrior."

"A true warrior," I said puzzled. "And what is a true warrior?"

"A true warrior is someone who fights to protect someone else," the shopkeeper said. "He is someone who does not use the sword against the innocent."

"So, this is what it means to be a warrior," I said.

"Yes!" the shopkeeper said. "And I believe this sword was made just for you."

The shopkeeper handed me the sword handle first. As I took it in my hands, I suddenly felt as if a part of me had just reattached itself to me.

"This is quite a sword," I said with reverence for the sword. "It feels like this sword was made for me."

"This is just as a sword should feel to any swordsmen," the shopkeeper said. "A swordsman can use any sword to fight with, but a swordsman always fights best with his true sword, with the sword that feels like a part of him."

"So, you are saying this sword is my true sword?" I asked questionably.

"It would seem so," the shopkeeper said. "But if you take this sword, I must ask you never use it to slay the innocent. You must use it only against the wicked. Do you understand?"

I nodded, but to tell you the truth I was completely confused but I had to have this sword now. After holding it, I could not be parted with it.

"Very good," he said nodding. "Then I should have the sword sharpened and cleaned in time for your departure."

Taking the sword from me, the shopkeeper began working on the blade. Seeing it would take time until it was ready, I went off to look for a place to get something to eat and a place to sleep for the night.

It didn't take me long before I found a place to get something to eat. Sitting down, I quickly asked a woman for some food and for some water. As I waited, I noticed there was a man starring at me from across the way.

"Here you go, sir," the serving woman said. "That will be ten cans!"

Opening my bag, I quickly pulled ten cans out and put them on the table. The woman swept them up in her arms and left for the back of the tavern.

As the woman walked out, the man who was watching me started over to me. He was a tall man with bright blonde hair and deep blue eyes. As he walked, I could see he was the only man who seemed to be armed. He was wearing the same brown cloak the guards outside were wearing. This told me he must be an enforcer of some sort.

"Good evening," he said as he came to my table.

"If you say so," I said not wanting to deal with this man.

I could just know by the why he spoke that did not care much for the likes of me. So, I was not going to play around with this fake hospitality.

"My name is Frank Maxwell; I oversee our little enforcer group here," he said, angry at my disrespect for him.

"And why are you here," I said as the server came back with my food. "Have I done something wrong?"

"I just like to meet all the outsiders who come into our little town," Maxwell said sitting down without an invite. "It is a good way for me to find out about what is going on outside, and to see if there are any potential threats to our town."

Maxwell just sat there as I ate. It was obvious he was waiting for me to speak, but I didn't want him here in the first place, so I was not going to start a conversation with him.

"Excuse me, sir," Maxwell started again still in a nice tone, "but I did not get your name."

"That is because I haven't given it," I said not even looking up from my plate.

"And are you going to give me your name, sir?" Maxwell said his nice tone fading.

"No!" I said taking a drink.

"No?"

"No!"

"And why not, sir?"

"Because, sir, my name is not something you need to know."

"I think it is something I do need to know," Maxwell said. "After all, I oversee the well-being of this town, and I don't need people like you messing things up here."

"This is the second time someone has said, 'people like me'," I said. "What kind of person am I?"

"The kind of person who is always looking for trouble," Maxwell said.

"You're wrong!" I said pushing my bowl and cup away. "I have never in my life gone looking for trouble. No one ever looks for trouble; trouble can find people."

"And are you one of those people who trouble goes looking for?" Maxwell asked.

"Only on a bad day," I said standing up.

Leaving Maxwell at the table, I went looking for a place to spend the night. It didn't take me long to find a place; the whole town seemed to be nothing but taverns, shops, and inns.

"This is truly a commerce town," I said looking around.

"I will take that as a compliment," a woman's voice said.

"And you are?" I asked looking around to see who spoke.

"My name is June. I am Elder for this town," June said bowing to me.

"It is a pleasure to meet you," I said returning her blow.

"And you," June said. "But you have not given me your name, sir."

"Forgive me. You may call me Matrix," I said.

"Matrix, that is an interesting name," June said.

"It is just a means to identify me," I said. "That is all a name is to me."

"So, Mister Matrix, you are looking for a place to sleep for the night," June said.

"Well, I guess as the Town Elder you would know the best place to stay," I said.

"In fact, I do," she said. "You can stay at my inn. It just so happens I have a room available."

"Thank you!" I said blowing to her again.

"Please come this way," June said showing me the way.

"So, do you mind telling me why you are travailing for," she said as we walked.

"I am looking for someone," I said.

"Who?" she asked looking surprised.

"The man that killed my father," I said.

As we walked, I began to tell her everything that had happened. By the time we reached the room, her eyes were filled with tears. Wiping her eyes, she turned to me.

"Do you seek this man's death?"

"I do," I said turning back to her.

"And do you think killing him will bring your father back to you?"

"No!" I said turning away. "But it will bring me back."

"I don't understand."

"My father was not the only one who died that day," I said to her. "A part of me died with my father. When I kill this man, I can reclaim my old name and my old life. Though I may never ever be the same, but I won't be who I am now."

"I see," June, said. "And will my brother's sword aid you in your quest?"

"Yes, I believe so," I said.

"Well I cannot say I hope it will," June said.

"Yes! Your bother told me you dislike people like me," I said. "I am sure you would prefer that I did not kill this man, but I am afraid it is all I have to look forward to."

"Then I am sorry for you and sad as well," June said.

"As am I, but this is what I know I must do," I said.

Pulling out a key, she unlocked the door. Entering the room, I could see it was very small; only a small bed was in the whole room. There was not even a window; the only light came from a small candle on a table by the bed.

"You can stay here for the night, but I must ask you to leave by morning," June said, turning to me. "I do not wish for anyone with mind of vengeance here for too long."

"I understand," I said putting my bags down. "So, what do I owe you?"

"Twenty-five cans, and it is not up for negotiation," she said.

Opening my bag, I pulled out twenty-five cans and gave them to her. June gathered up the cans, said her farewells, and left the room. Once she was gone, I quickly stored my bags under the bed, removed my jacket and shoes, and got into bed.

The next morning, I got up, dressed, retrieved my bags, and left the room. I slowly walked down the hall and out to the common area. As I headed down to the exit, I did not look at the people, but I could feel their eyes on me the whole time.

When I finally made it to the exit, I found that there were several people there to see me off. There was the shopkeeper with my new sword in hand, June standing next to her bother, and Maxwell.

"Well, I didn't think I was going to get a big send-off like this," I said pulling my bags down.

"This isn't a send-off!" Maxwell said looking mad. "I am here on official business."

"As am I," added June in a softer tune.

"Whereas I am just here on business," the shopkeeper said handing me the sword.

"Here is your true sword, the Dragon's Edge. I have sharpened the blade to a fine edge," he said as I examined the blade. "Here, this will help keep the blade in excellent condition."

Sheathing the blade, I took the small bundle. Inside, I found tools for sharpening the blade as well as another thing for maintaining the blade.

"Thank you," I said bowing.

"Think nothing of it," he said returning my bow.

"That will be thirty-five cans, please," the shopkeeper snapped back with his hand out.

"You are still all business," I said laughing as I opened my bag and handed him the cans.

"For now, and for always," his said putting the cans in a bag laughing as well.

"Until we meet again, Master Samurai," I said bowing once more.

"Farewell, Young Warrior," the shopkeeper said bowing.

Placing the bundle in my small bag and putting the sword on my belt, I turned to June and Maxwell.

"Here!" Maxwell said handing my guns. "Take these and get out of this town now, and I hope I never see you again."

"So long to you too, Maxwell," I said taking the guns and grabbing my bags to leave.

"One more moment, please," June said stopping me.

"Yes?" I said turning to her.

"I may not approve of the way you wish to live, but I may have a way to aid you," she said looking up at me. "I have heard of a city to the north of here. They say they have records from the old world, and they may have information on the man you are searching for."

"Why should I care what they have?" I asked looking at her.

"Because I believe the man you are looking for could be in one of those records," June said.

"Why would you say this?" I said.

"You said the stranger was wearing an orange jumpsuit, right?" she asked.

I nodded.

"Well, did at anytime you notice the letters D.O.C. on him at all?" June asked.

I thought for several moments, my thought turning back to that day, back to the man I wished to kill.

"I think so!" I said. "Why?"

"Well because the letters D.O.C. are normally put on the prisoner's jumpsuits," she said. "If he was a prisoner, they will most likely have them in their records."

"How would knowing his past help me find him now?" I asked.

"If you know your enemy better, you may be able to predict what he may do next," June said.

"Maybe," I said walking by.

Chapter 14

The Wildcat

That night I camped out by a large cliff, north of the town. I was lying down in the back of the army hummer, thinking. My mind was racing, thinking about what June said. Maybe learning more about my enemy would help me find him faster. After all, I had not had a single clue about him.

"Find! I'll go and see what I can find," I said to the night air.

I continued north for several days, my eyes open for anything like a city. As I drove my mind wandered; I began to think about where I was going. June had called it a city, but I had never seen a city before, not counting the ruins of the cities of old. But a modern city, the thought of someone who could organize that many people and resources, was mind-boggling.

"Well I guess I will see it for myself, soon enough,"

Four days later I found the city. I could tell it was the city I was looking for because of the wall. The wall was at least twenty feet high, and around six square miles. Circling the wall, I could see there were only four ways in through four large doors. But it looked as if all four were closed; in fact I did not see any guards on the grounds, or even on top of the wall.

'What is with this place?' I thought to myself. 'Even the smallest village sets a watch, but I don't see anyone here at all.'

I would have to go up to one of the doors. I chose the southern entrance and banged on the large door. A shutter opened and a pair of eyes looked back at me.

"Who dares knock?" the eyes said.

"Just a weary traveler, looking for food and a place to sleep," I said looking tired.

"We do not give out free handouts here!" the eyes said. "Move along, now!"

"I am not looking for a handout," I said. "I am more than willing to trade of all I seek."

"We are in no need of trader neither!" the eyes said more forcefully. "Be off with you!"

"Please, I beg you," I said becoming dispirited. "I must be able to enter."

"No one may enter Lawmaker; that is the law!" the eyes said becoming enraged. "Leave, now!"

"What!" I said in shock. "You do not let anyone in?"

"All outsiders must remain on the outside and all insiders must remain in!" the eyes said.

"But how can you do that to your people?" I asked.

"It is the only way to keep order in our world!" the eyes said. "You, outsider, would destroy all that we have created if you had a chance! Now go!"

"No!" I said. "I wish to look through your records from the old world."

"How dare you!" the eyes said, the eyes widening. "No man may look upon the ancient records; it is forbidden! Leave now, or I will be forced to make you!"

"Then come out here and make me!" I said.

"No citizen may leave Lawmaker," the eyes said. "It is the law!"

"Then how are you going to make me?" I said.

The eyes said nothing and shut the shutter. With no way in, I started back to my vehicle and headed out once more. I noticed, both before and now, there was not another town or village even remotely near this grand city.

Normally, you could find a town or village at least a three days' walk away. Here, there was no town or village for at least six days away—at least that's what it looked like from the north, east, and south side of the city. The west side was different for there was a small village about a four days' walks with around a hundred people living there.

Hiding my vehicle outside of the village, I entered on my guard. As I entered, I noticed that the people here were not made uneasy by me. In fact, they seemed welcoming. The people would bow their heads to me, raise a hand in welcome, or give me a simple hello or good morning.

In all my years, I have never seen so much kindness. It was almost creepy.

"Good morning, stranger!" a man cried from behind me.

I turned to find an elderly man before me. He was a tall man with a dark and lined face with brown eyes, white short hair, and a smile on his face.

"Oh!" I said turning. "Good morning to you too, sir."

"By the look on your face, I dare say you have never had anyone greet you as I have," he said with his hand out.

"No, sir!" I said shaking his hand. "Most people are too afraid of men like me."

"Indeed, they are," he said, "but here we try to be more welcoming to the wanderers that wander into our village."

"Well, out of the two places I have been to this week, I have to say this place is a whole lot better," I said looking around.

"Where might that other place be?" he asked.

"Just the city of Lawmaker, four days east of here," I said pointing north.

"Well, there is your problem," the old man said. "No one may leave or enter Lawmaker, at anytime."

"So I heard," I said. "But if they are as strict as you say, why is your village so close to them?"

"You mean what benefits do we get being this close?" he said. "None!"

"Then why not leave?" I asked. "Why not find a village or town who is willing to start up trade between you?"

"Because many of us do not wish to leave our loved ones behind," he said turning in the direction of lawmaker.

"Do you mean what I think you mean?" I asked looking east as well.

"Yes! Most of us here once called Lawmaker our home," he said turning away. "That was of course long ago, back when times were different. When Lawmaker was a happier place, when the laws of the land were honest and pure much like they were in the old world. Back when I was the Grand Justice of Lawmaker."

"Hold on a minute!" I said with a shock. "You were the leader of that city?"

"Leader," he said. "I was the founder of that city, though back in the beginning it was only a small village. It was right after the war between the Government and the Anarchists had come to an end. My wife, Susan, and I were looking for a place to call our own, a peaceful place.

"In truth, my wife and I hoped the Anarchists Party would have been crushed by the Government. We hoped when they had, law and order would return. Sadly, this did not happen. Instead, it seems like chaos had taken over the world."

"So, we found our own place of order, a village that would follow the old laws of the old world." He stopped as if lost in thought. "We would have never imagined how much and how fast the village would grow. But I guess there were far more people than the two of us who wanted the same thing."

"Soon, our small village turned into a bustling town, then into a huge city. With the laws of the old world to guide us, we had our peace at last, but like everything else in this world, it did not last."

"What happened?" I asked fully into the story now.

"What happens every time?" he said. "Power corrupts!"

"This story is becoming far bigger than I thought," I said. "Though it would be easier to listen to it over a good meal."

"Very well then, I guess I will invite you to my home for a meal and I will finish my story," he said guiding me to his home. "By the way, my name Samuel, and you are, sir?"

"Matrix," I said as we walked.

"Matrix, that is a curious name," Samuel said, "and I am sure it has a story behind it as well, but first, a meal and the rest of my story."

Samuel's house was quite small, like the size of a hut, but was roomy inside. Inside, Samuel quickly placed some bread and cheeses on the table along with some fruits and a jug of beer.

"Now then, where was I," Samuel said. "Oh, yes, I remember. The corruption."

As we began to eat, Samuel restarted his story. "When I was the Grand Justice, everything was just perfect," Samuel said taking a bite of bread. "The people were happy; trade was good. At one time, there had been five other villages around us happy making trade between us. At the center of the five villages, Lawmaker became the place were all five villages came to trade.

"With all this prosperity, you think we had it made," Samuel said, "but there was one among us who feared the outside world. Marcus was a man who had lived in the outside world living in fear he would die, at any moment. He said to me once, 'Here in Lawmaker, for the first time in my life I feel safe.' Indeed, I could see this in his eyes.

"Soon, this young man found a life in Lawmaker," Samuel said taking a drink of beer. "He became a public servant and started to help the people of Lawmaker. He would say to me, 'I want to protect Lawmaker from those who would destroy it.'

"He became so involved with the law, studying every night," Samuel said. "The law became more like a religion to him; he was obsessed with it. He quickly rose in position and in the matter of three year became a powerful District Attorney for the city.

"You should have seen him in the court room," Samuel said standing and starting to walk around. "He had a passion for the law that I had never seen before. The only problem was he did not care for the innocent. He seems to believe the law was flawless. It matters not if they were innocent; he felt that if they were here in court, they must be guilty.

"It was as if he thought the justice system was infallible and to say one was innocent was an insult to the law," Samuel said. "If he had his way, all who came into that court room, no matter what the charge, he would have been found guilty.

"It was his eyes that showed his conviction to the law," Samuel said. "How they filled with joy when the guilty verdict was said, and how they looked when they were found innocent. It was as if the court itself had failed him."

"He felt betrayed by the very law he swore to protect?" I asked.

"Yes!" Samuel said sitting back down with his head in his hands. "But I truly did not think much of it. His passion for the law was truly something I had much respect for. So when he became Second Justice I didn't reject his appointment."

"As a justice, he showed the same conviction as he did as an attorney," Samuel said. "But soon his conviction was turning into an obsession. He was becoming blinded by the idea the law was perfect. He could not think that mistakes could happen.

"More and more, he would disagree with the other eight of us," Samuel said. "At first, it was only when we let a man or women go free; then when we agreed they were guilty he would disagree with the punishment. He would feel the punishment should be far worse. He seemed never satisfied, and he was beginning to despise us for this.

"It was not long before he began to plot our downfall," Samuel said. "You see in Lawmaker each of the nine justices is elected into office by the people. Though the Grand Justice is an elected position I never had to fight for it. Whenever the Grand Justice election came up, no one would ever run against me. To all in Lawmaker, I was the only Grand Justice.

"For Marcus to take my position, he would have to run against me," Samuel said. "Even he knew he could never beat me in an election. So, he needed to find another way to take my position. The only way he could do it was to destroy me first."

"His plan was simple: He first replaced the other seven justices with people who shared his ideas," Samuel said. "Then when it was eight to one, he would then discredit me. He would make me out to be a villain in the eyes of the people. Once the people were against me, he would have me removed me from office. Once out of office, he would then take my position, and to keep from returning to it, I was banished from the city of Lawmaker.

"It has been two years since Marcus became the new Grand Justice and increased the justices' time in office to life," Samuel said. "He built a wall, in the words of the new Grand Justice, 'To protect the people of Lawmaker'."

"But all he really did was maintain his control," I said.

"You're right," Samuel said. "He turned the city into a prison, and the people into prisoners. No one could ever enter or leave the city. His fear of losing his newfound power made him create new laws to keep the power and take power from the people."

"But I believe I have talked long enough," Samuel said sitting back down. "Now, it is time you tell me something, like why you are so interested in the city of Lawmaker anyway."

So, I told him my story. The hours passed slowly as I talked into night. It was nearly dawn when I had finished my story. Samuel didn't move or speak throughout my whole story. After I told my story, I just sat in silence waiting for Samuel to say something.

"So, you are searching for your father's killer in the present by considering his past," Samuel said rubbing his chin. "But can you be sure he even has a past to find?"

"I know it might be a long shot, but it is all I have to go on," I said looking up at the ceiling. "His outfit is all I have to go on. It is true he could have just found the prisoner's jumpsuit. That is why I need to see the records in Lawmaker."

"I know of the records you speak of," Samuel said putting his hands together. "But I am afraid there is no way to get to them now. The records are now considered sacred. No one may look on them except for the justices. I am sorry; there is no way to see those files."

"I'm sure I could get to those files if only I could get over that cursed wall," I said taking a drink for my glass. "The only question is how to do it. I have seen the wall there. I know a way to get in without blowing them up."

"But then you will have all of the enforcers on you before you get half a step," Samuel said.

There was no need for Samuel to tell me. It was the only reason I didn't use the entire explosive I had in my bag and in the hummer. I had to find another way in, a quiet way in, but how?

"I can see in your eyes you will not give up on seeing those files," Samuel said. "Instead of having you go and do something foolish, there is something I wish to tell you."

He stood and went over to the fireplace. He poked at the fire before he turned back around to me.

"I have not been truly honest with you," Samuel said putting his hands behind his back. "As I have said, the people in this village were citizen of Lawmaker; we all stayed here to be close to our families. But to be close is nothing like being next to one. It is our hope one day our families will be reunited together."

"But you have a giant wall before you and a mad justice in charge; how do you think you can get them back?" I said.

"All the people in this village were not banished from Lawmaker like I was," Samuel started. "Many of the townsfolk here have been removed from Lawmaker."

"*How!*" I said unable to control my voice.

"We go though the wall," Samuel said.

"But how do you go though the wall?" I said. "I walked around the wall; there was no way to get in without going though the gates."

"You're right," Samuel said. "Looking around the wall it would seem the wall looked solid. Then again, you didn't do a close inspection of every inch of the wall, did you?"

I thought for a moment before I shook my head.

"Well, if you did you may have found a way in," Samuel said. "You see, when the wall was being built, I had some secret openings placed in the wall."

"But I thought the wall was made after you were banished?" I asked thinking I had lost a key point in this story.

"Indeed!" Samuel said laughing. "But when Lawmaker had the wall made, they needed help from the other villages to aid in the contraction of it. After my banishment, I did not know what would happen to the people. So, when the wall was being built, I had asked those who were working on it to build the secret openings in the wall for me."

"They must have thought you were crazy for asking that," I said.

"You're right," Samuel said sitting down. "But after the wall was up and the doors were closed forever, they were glad they helped me. It's these openings which allow us to help get the people out."

"If you can get people out, it could be my way in, right?" I asked

"Yes!" Samuel said. "But there is so much we have to do before you go into Lawmaker. You will need some new clothes, and there are many things you will need to know before you go into Lawmaker. Are you ready?"

"Sure, why not!"

Chapter 15

The Panther

For two weeks, I lived in this small village, and the whole time I was learning about the laws of Lawmaker. There were many laws in Lawmaker, and I mean too many laws. There were laws against killing, against fighting, and even against talking about the city. And all these crimes had the same punishment—death!

I soon learned I had move, walk, talk, and act just right, for if I didn't, I could find myself dead. So, for two weeks the people of the town showed me how to become a citizen of Lawmaker.

When I was ready to enter the city of Lawmaker, Samuel, a few others, and I made ready to go.

"Are you sure you want to go though with this?" Samuel asked as I was getting ready to go.

"Yes!

My own clothes were in a large chest along with my guns, my knife, and my sword. Instead, I was wearing the clothes Samuel had given me. In Lawmaker, you were forced to wear uniforms, white for citizen, blue for enforcer, black for attorney, and red and gold for the justices.

The clothes themselves were more like a robe. There were white pants, white shirt, white shoes and socks, all under the white robe that went down to my feet. The robe even had a hood.

As I stood there looking at myself in the mirror, I had to say I looked strange. How I was dressed made me think of some sort of monk.

"Well, this is the point," Samuel said when I told him that. "When Marcus took over as Grand Justice, he turned the law from a practice into a sort of religion. This is the point of the uniform you are wearing now."

After I was dressed in my citizen robes, I followed Samuel out of the town. Once outside the town, we climbed into my hummer and drove to Lawmaker. I felt it would be easier to go in the hummer than to go on foot. So, it was Samuel, two others, and I from the town heading east to the city of Lawmaker.

It was about nightfall when we reached Lawmaker's wall. The wall before us looked blank; if there were a secret opening there was no way I would have seen it. But Samuel seemed to know what he was doing. He and the two men went right over to the wall. The three started banging their hands on the wall and listening.

In a matter of seconds, one of the two men beckoned everyone over to him. When I made it over to him, I found the two men moving a large block out of the wall. The block seemed to be moving as if it were on a hinge.

"Ok!" Samuel said speaking at last. "This is where we split up, my friend. Once on the other side of the wall, a man will find you. His name is Enigma; he will aid you anyway he can."

"How will I know him?" I asked.

"He will ask you, 'Who do you serve?' and you will answer, 'the true Grand Justice.' Do you got it?" Samuel said.

I nodded before heading to the opening. Bending down, I made my way through the opening. Once on the other side of the wall, I heard the block being put back into place. I was just standing there in the street, in the dark looking around at the dark homes.

The homes were built close together, and from what I could see, they were made of both stone and wood. Looking down the street, I could see there was no one out at this late hour. I knew from my lessons, the citizens of Lawmaker had a strict curfew so no one in white should even be out this late. It also meant I had to get off the street fast before I was caught.

I was just about to move to get off the street when the sound of footsteps could be heard. I did not know what to do. The approaching feet could be Enigma's, or they could belong to one of the enforcers. Samuel had told me the enforcers sometimes patrolled the street at night, looking for white roles.

I looked down the street in the direction of the footsteps; I tried to see who was coming. As the figure approached, I could see he was wearing a white robe even in the dim light. He was tall man with dark skin, a shaved head, with powerfully built arms and chest.

"What is a man like you are doing out at this late hour?" he said coming up to me.

"I could ask the same of you," I answered.

"I was just on my way home," he said. "And what about you, who did you serve?"

"I serve the true Grand Justice," I answered.

"Well, then you should come with me right now," Enigma said looking around as he said it.

I nodded. With Enigma in front, we made our way to a home on the main street of the city. Inside, I found the home to be small. There were only two rooms and a toilet in the whole house. The main room was the kitchen, dining room, and living room together, and there was the bedroom in the back.

"Well here you are," Enigma said lighting a candle on the table. "It may not be much, but it is all we white robes can have. The Law said if we have more, we will become greedy."

"It's fine," I said looking round the room.

"Well anyway this is your place," He said. "When you are told to go home, this is where you must go. On the table, here are your papers. You must have these papers on you always. Inside is your new identity; memorize it."

Picking up the packet of paper, I looked through the papers; inside the packet was a passport and a schedule.

"I got you a job in the Grand Courthouse," Enigma said heading back to the door. "Make sure you are there by third bell. Food will be at your door by first bell."

"Yes, I remember from my lessons," I said seeing him out.

"Be sure you do," he said opening the door. "I will return in one week if you are not imprisoned by; then I will help you out of the city."

"I understand," I said.

And with that Enigma left leaving me alone. Grabbing the candle, I headed back to the bedroom. The bed itself was nothing more than a cot with a few sheets and a thin blanket.

Sitting down on the bed, I placed the candle on the small side table. In the dim light, I looked though the papers Enigma had given me.

Once I had gone over them several times, I lied down and went to sleep.

The ringing of a bell woke me. I knew what it meant. In Lawmaker the bells were to mark the passage of time. The first bell means get up, second means go to work, third means start work, fourth is for the middle day meal, fifth is to return to work. The sixth is to return home, by seventh you should be in your home and stay there, by the eighth bell all lights in the city should be out. This schedule is strictly enforced.

Getting up, I headed to the front door. Outside the door, I found a basket. I found inside the basket was some porridge, some fruit, bread, and a bottle of milk. Back inside, I placed the basket on the table. I then went to the cabinet and pulled out a bowl, cup, and a spoon and put them on the table.

Sitting down, I ate my meal before getting ready for work. Thankfully Enigma had left me several other sets of clothes. So by the second bell, I was dressed and out the door.

I found myself in a mob of people heading in different directions. With my papers in my robe pocket, I headed to the Grand Courthouse. On the way to the Courthouse, I could see in the endless river of white robes there were also several of the blue robes on the side and within the white robes. The blue robed enforcers always watching the white robes.

As the group moved forward, we found ourselves passing through several checkpoints. At each checkpoint, I showed my papers to the guard. The guard would look at my papers then send me on my way. The guards didn't really look over the passport. There were just too many to do that, so they just looked at the name and where we worked.

I saw as I went through the checkpoint I found the crowd thinned out. By time I went though the last checkpoint, I found myself in a group of ten people. The guard at this checkpoint looked at my passport and sent me on to the Grand Courthouse, and for the first time, I found myself alone, a single white robe in a sea of blue.

I was now surrounded by enforcers, all going to and from the courthouse. They all passed me without looking in my direction. The outside of the courthouse looked much bigger than a normal courthouse I had ever seen. It looked more like an old cathedral than a courthouse. Everything about this place reminded me of a cathedral. From the grand stairs leading to the grand doors, I walked up to the huge statues surrounding the courthouse.

Looking up at one, I could not see its face for it was masked and hooded. I knew from my lessons they were the Nine Justices. The statues were all masked so that no man could look on the face of the justice itself.

Only the two guards at the top of the grand stairs noticed me. I handed my passport to one of the guards while the second guard was looking at me as if I had something to hide.

When the guard saw I was with management, he let me enter. Inside the Grand Courthouse was a large inter chamber. This was the entrance of the Grand Courthouse. There were several stairs both going upstairs to floors above and going down to the floors below.

I could see arrows on the walls of the courthouse. In the arrows were words which showed the way to wherever you were heading. Looking at the arrows, I found the one said management and headed in that direction.

The arrows led me to the stairs to the right. I saw that the stairs only went down, so I followed them down. Following the arrows, I came to door with the word management on it. Opening the door, I found myself in a small office; inside was a man sitting at a small desk.

When I came in, the man at the desk looked up at me. I could see he was young, in his mid-twenties; he had blond hair and blues eyes.

"Oh great, another new guy," he said rubbing his eyes. "How does the justice expect me to do my job if they keep replacing my people?"

I handed him my papers and stood there waiting. As he looked over my papers, I looked around the little office. I could see it was very simple much like the house I was living in. White-robed citizens were not allowed to own anything. Everything from their homes to their clothes were given by and owned by the city.

The reason for this idea was to keep theft down. Why steal something you already have?

"Well, your paperwork looks in order," the man said standing up.

"I am Stan, and I will be your supervisor," he said in a lackluster tone of voice. "Our job here is to service and maintain everything here in the Grand Courthouse. Your job here is basically is to keep the place as clean as possible. Your job will include washing floors, cleaning the courtroom, the cleaning for the justices' rooms, lawyers' rooms, and even the enforcers' rooms. All jobs must be done before the workday is finished or your rations will be docked. Entering any off-limit areas without escort will be punished severely. Do you have any questions?" Stan said.

"No!" I said sitting down.

"Good," Stan said sitting back down himself.

We just sat there waiting. We had to wait for the other workers to arrive. By the third bell, all had arrived, and we got right to work.

Leaving the office, the ten of us headed to a storeroom. Inside, we got all our cleaning items and headed back to the stairs.

Our group walked up the stairs past the entrance hall, up to the living quarters. The living quarters consisted of three floors, one for each class that lived in the courthouse. The top floor was for the justices, the floor below them was the lawyers and attorneys, and below them were the enforcers and guards. On each floor, there were bedrooms, studies, bathrooms, and a common room.

We started on the top floor. Once there, Stan gave us our assignments. He split us in groups of two, pairing everyone together. Then Stan told everyone which room they were to start with before everyone went his or her separate ways.

I found myself heading to the Grand Justice's room with Stan himself. He said he had to make sure I did the work right, so I was to work with him the whole day.

The first thing you see on entering the Grand Justice's room is the red and gold decor. The whole room was covered in red and gold, from carpet to the ceiling. After your eyes recovered, only then could I truly see the room and all that was in it.

I have never known luxury or great wealth, but even I knew the things in this room had great value to them. Furniture such as this would only be in rooms meant for royalty. The bed was a huge four-poster with red bedding and golden curtains. There were also several large dressers in the room stained red with gold nods.

If the furniture was huge, the room was gigantic; even with all the stuff in it, one could still move about freely.

We first started with removing the old sheets and remaking the bed with clean ones. With the bed done, we then started dusting. We made sure we cleaned everything, from the dressers to the walls. When the dusting was done, we cleaned the windows and mirrors. Finally, we cleaned the rug.

After the Grand Justice's bedroom was all cleaned, we went into his own personal bathroom. The bathroom itself looked to be about half the size of his bedroom. It had a full shower and a separate full tub. There was also a toilet and a full sink with mirror.

We got right to work picking up the Grand Justice's clothes from the floor by the shower first. Once his clothes were out of the way, we cleaned the shower, the tub, the toilet, the sink, mirror, and even the tiles on both the walls and the floor.

Once the Grand Justice's room was cleaned, we went on to the next room dumping the Grand Justice's clothes in a bag for cleaning later.

The next room we went next was of another justice. His room was much like the Grand Justice's room, but for some reason, it did not look as impressive. Maybe it was just because he was just a low ranking justice, and the Grand Justice was, well, the Grand Justice.

Once more, we cleaned the bedroom and changed sheets. Just like the Grand Justice, this justice also had a personal bathroom. After the bathroom was cleaned, we left the justice's chambers and headed down the hall.

We came to another group of rooms. These were the justice's studies. Each of the nine justices had a study for themselves. Again, I found Stan and I were heading for the Grand Justice's study.

The study was smaller than his bedroom. The walls were covered with bookshelves, all overflowing with books. On the right was an old wooden desk and chair, and the rug was a light gray.

While Stan started on the desk, I began working on the bookshelves. As I started to dust the shelves, my eyes wandered over the spines of the books. Reading the titles, I saw they were mostly books on law and government. They were not just on one type of government, but all forms of government.

There were also books on religion in the Grand Justice's library. Like the books on law and government, the book talked about every form of religion ever known by man. It was most likely this book gave the Grand Justice the idea for many of his new laws.

But the Grand Justice did not seem to be a man who was all work and no play. In his collection I had found many fiction books as well. Most of them seemed to have a courtroom theme to it. They depicted attorneys or judges having different adventures while solving a big case.

It would seem the Grand Justice, no matter what he may say to anyone else, seemed to long to have a grand adventure of his own. His own law and fears kept himself from having these adventures. But he could read story of *Tom Sawyer*, or *Moby Dick*, and *10,000 Leagues under the Sea*, all which were in the Grand Justice's liberty.

Once the room was dusted, the windows cleaned, and the rug vacuumed, we went on to the next study of a lesser justice. When all the studies were cleaned, we all headed down to the last room on the floor. It was the Grand Lounge.

The Grand Lounge was where the justices came to relax. It was a place for drinking and for smoking. A place where the justices could relax after a long day of ruining other people's lives.

The Grand Lounge was huge. It was so big the house I was living in right now could fit right inside it. The decorations were like the ones in the justices' bedrooms, red and gold. There was a long bar on one side of the room with hundreds of bottles, jugs, pitchers, and barrels of drinks.

I could only imagine what was in them all, but if I had a guess I would say they were filled with a little bit of everything, from beer to wine, either from the old world or made by those of the city, and all this to try and appease the unpredictable justices of the city.

The rest of the room was furnished with the finest chairs, couches, and tables. On several of the tables were boxes of cigarettes, cigars, and pipes with tobacco. There was also a record player in the corner by the window. Next to it was a cabinet filled with records. By the titles, they seemed to be classical music.

Once clean, we headed down to the floor below us to the attorneys' floor, the floors and the walls getting a good cleaning on the way down. As we entered, I could see there were more rooms then on the top floor.

As we cleaned, I found only the high-ranking attorneys had their own private bedrooms and the other low ranks had to share rooms. But both types of rooms had the same simple design to them. There was only one difference between the two types of rooms; the private rooms had their own bathroom. Everyone else used the communal washroom.

It was the same with the studies. Again, the higher ranked people had private studies while the lower ranked shared one larger study. Their Lounge was not as fancy as the justices, but it was still nice. There was a granite floor, a long bar with stools around it, and booths all along one side of the room. Over top of all the booths was a light hanging down off the ceiling, and in the corner, there was a jukebox. The music in the jukebox had a mixture of hard and soft music. There were more jazz records then anything else.

With the attorneys floor cleaned, our group went down to the enforcers' floor. One step onto this floor and you already felt a difference than the two floors above us. Where the justices' and the attorneys' floors felt comfortable, the enforcers' floor felt cooled, and I did not mean tempter wise.

I have had this feeling before. It was the same thing I felt every time I have been on an old military base. The enforcers themselves must act in the same way as military then cops.

Just like on a base, the floor plan on this floor was basic. The high ranked officers had their own rooms with small bathrooms. While the other men and women shared rooms in the barracks. One room would normally house up to ten men in a very cramped area. While the officers' quarters were not much bigger.

Next to the officers' quarters were the officers' studies. Just like all the other rooms, they were furnished with just the basics. Everything on this floor was just bland.

Also on this floor, there was the washroom. Of course, this was what all the low ranked enforcers used to prepare for the day. The washroom was larger than any of the rooms on this floor.

Also on this floor there was a grand study. It was just a place where the low rank enforcers could go and work. You see, if you wanted to advance in rank at all in this city, you must prove yourself in action and in how much you understand the law. For the more you study there were more chances to become something greater.

The last room on this floor was the bar. This room was nothing like the lounges I had seen before. The place was rougher. There were hardwood floors here, and the lighting here was dark. The place looked more like the bars I had seen outside the city.

There was a bar with stools around it, and scattered around the bar were wooden tables and chairs. The jukebox on the other side of the room had only rock and rap in it.

With the living quarters cleaned, our group gathered our cleaning stuff and all the clothes and bedding and headed back down to the basement. Once there, we headed into one of the rooms. Inside there were groups of both washers and dryers.

We then continued our work sorting through the clothes and sheets. Once sorted, they were thrown into the washers. Just as the washers were turned on, a bell rang from high above.

The fourth bell of the day told everyone that it was time for the afternoon meal. So our group headed back to the first floor. We then went into a pair of double doors. I soon found myself in a grand cafeteria.

Inside, you could see the division of class in this one room. On one side of the room at the high table were the justices. All nine were looking down on everyone with the Grand Justice in the middle of the nine. In front of them were the attorneys; there were several tables for them all. Behind them were the enforcers, who had the most tables set aside for them. And last and least was our table.

We all sat down, our backs to everyone else. We did this for two reasons. One, so no one at the other tables could say we made a funny look at them and get ourselves in trouble. As for the second reason, it was so we did not see what the other tables had to eat.

Even without looking, I could tell the other tables were eating far better than we were. I could smell things like roast pigs, grilled chickens, steamed vegetables of all types, and many kinds of steaks. The smell from the other tables made eating what was on our table harder. All we had to eat was some old mutton, stew, bread, cheese, and some wine.

Everyone ate in silence, keeping one's own thoughts to oneself. As I ate, I could not help but think about taking food from the other tables. Controlling my actions, I stayed quiet and ate my food with no complains.

After our meal, our group got up and headed back down to the laundry room. By the time we made it back to the laundry, the clothes were done washing. We threw the wet clothes into the dryers before heading back upstairs. As we left the laundry room, we could hear another bell ringing. The fifth bell was to tell people to get back to work.

I could tell you about my whole day working as a cleaner in the Grand Court-house, but I would not want to bore you. For the rest of the day, it was just cleaning the floors, washing windows, wiping down walls and ceilings, finishing the laundry, and a hundred and one other cleaning jobs. By time the sixth bell rang for the end of the workday, I could not wait to get back to the house.

Leaving the Grand Courthouse, I headed back to the home Enigma had set up for me. It was easy to find the right house. After all, the enforcers practically showed you where to go. All I had to do was find the right house number, and this was on my passport.

Once there, I found a new basket of food on the doorstep. Picking it up I went inside. Outside the bell rang for the seventh time. This meant that all white robes should be inside their homes.

At the table, I looked to see what I had to eat. There were some chopped up meat, some vegetables, some spices, a thing of cheese, half a loaf of bread, and a small thing of wine.

I put a pot of water on to boil and prepared the meat and vegetables for a stew. Waiting for the stew to cook, I helped myself to the bread and cheese. The meal was not the best in the world, but after the day I had it was enough. After everything had been eaten and drank, I cleaned up and placed the basket back on the step.

The light outside was fading fast. Lighting a candle, I headed back to my bed. Lying in bed, I looked up at the ceiling, my mind finally able to think clearly about my day.

My mind once more on my mission, the whole reason I was here was still fresh in my mind. When tomorrow comes, I would have to focus on finding the file room before I could find a way in.

Outside in the darkness, the bell rang for the eighth time calling for lights out. Blowing out the candle, I turned on my side and fell asleep.

Chapter 16

The Snail

After my first day in Lawmaker, I found it easier to adjust to life here. I could never stay here indefinitely, but for now I could act like I was a part of the city. So now I could focus on the real reason I came into this world of law and order.

In fact, I had already found the records room. It was on the third floor of the west side of the Grand Courthouse, but there was no way in. Not only was the door locked, but also there was always an enforcer nearby. In fact, the whole Grand Courthouse was heavily guarded.

But then again this was only during the day and evening; I did not know what the security was like at night. Indeed, nighttime would most likely be the time to enter the record room, but I would need to be careful.

So, I could get through the city to the Grand Courthouse with ease, but once there getting inside was another story. Only one thing was to my advantage, and this was anyone on duty at night would not be expecting anything to happen. Believing everyone in the city follows the law and the law was perfect, they would not think anyone would be stupid enough to sneak into the Grand Courthouse.

During the next few days, I began to make my plans to enter the records room. I took notice of everything around me. I memorized the number of enforcers during the day to estimate the number of enforcers that would be out at night. I even stayed up most of the night one night to learn their patterns and their numbers of the sentry, who patrols the city.

I also tried to familiarize myself with the layout of the Grand Courthouse as much as I could. I memorized what rooms were on what floors. How many windows each floor had, and which windows could be the easiest to enter. With all this information, I managed to come up with a plan and route which offered the best chance of prevailing.

My plan was to wait about two hours after the eighth bell before sneaking to the roof. Once on the roof, I could head towards the Grand Courthouse by jumping from rooftop to rooftop. Thankfully the roofs of the houses were close together, making it easy to move from rooftop to rooftop.

The only true problem was my white robes; it would give me away. But thanks to the city, I had an answer that problem. The sheets on my bed were as black as the night. I would use them to cover myself up and hide in the night air.

Once I had reached the last house closest to the Grand Courthouse, I would wait until the coast was clear before running to the windows on the east side of the courthouse. I would rig the window the day before to open from the outside.

Once inside, I would make my way to the third floor and to the records room using the servant stairs. I figured there would be around twenty to twenty-five guards on duty inside of the Grand Courthouse, but I should be able to avoid them.

After reaching the records room, I would need to unlock the door. It is a good thing I had long ago learned how to pick a lock. I could pick a lock in twelve seconds or less.

Once inside the records room, I would be able to relax. After all, no one goes in the records room, and only the Grand Justice had the key to the door. I would just need to stay away from the door and make as little noise as possible.

Once I found out what I needed to know, I would make my way back to the house. Hopefully, Enigma would be there to aid my escape from Lawmaker.

On my sixth day in Lawmaker, I began my preparations. I managed to rig one of the windows on the east side to open with ease, making sure no one would notice what I had done. I also managed to sneak out a thing of black thread and needle from the laundry. This I would be used to alter my bed sheets.

Before leaving that day, Stan had stamped my passport for tomorrow. For you see, everyone in Lawmaker was bound by law to take at least one day off from work each week. So, after working six days in a row, they want to get a mark on their passport from a superior granting them the time off. This law was, of course, made to stop the white robes from rioting from being over worked.

Tomorrow was my day, and I needed the time to make final preparation. I was going to put it to good use. Back home, I quickly prepare my food, cleaned up, and was in bed long before the eighth bell rang.

At first bell, I was up, dressed, and ate my breakfast. At second bell, I just sat at the table waiting. After the third rang through the city, a knock came from my door. I quickly went to the door, my papers in hand.

At the door was an enforcer, just as I knew there would be. Handing over my papers, the woman flipped through it. She took note of my name, made sure this was my assigned home, and I had permission for a day off.

Once she was satisfied everything was accurate, she handed me my paper, wished me good day, and left. On her way out, she placed a yellow card on my door. This card would tell other enforcers I had the right to be here, and to have food to be given at the afternoon meal.

Once she had left, I was once more left to my own devises. But there was still nothing for me to do but wait. I knew there would be more visitors to come. Not only would the enforcer check on me from time to time, a crew of white robes would come by with a guard at their sides to change the bed.

Until the cleaning crew came for the bedding, I could not start work on my nighttime clothing. So I went back to bed as most people in the city did on their days off.

I was awoken an hour before the fourth bell by another knock on the door. This time it was the cleaning crew with an escort. While the cleaning crew started their work, the enforcer checked my passport once more.

It only took the cleaning crew fifteen minutes to finish cleaning. The three-man crews were quick and efficient. But with over a hundred homes to clean, one would have to be. Once both the crew and their escort had left, I set myself to work. Pulling the fresh clean sheets off the well-made bed, I headed for the kitchen.

Throwing the sheets onto the table, I grabbed the needle and black tread I took from the laundry room yesterday and began my work. Using the kitchen knife, I began cutting the sheets into pieces being careful not to make any mistakes. By the fourth bell, I had made all my cuts. The pieces of cloth now covered the small table.

Taking a break, I retrieved the basket of food outside the door. Putting the black cloth pieces to one side, I made a quick lunch. After I ate, I cleaned up and returned to my work.

I took my time sewing the pieces of black cloth together. There was not a need for neatness, but I needed to know that the stitches would hold.

Only once more was I interrupted as I worked. An enforcer on his rounds knocked on my door just to see I was still there. I quickly hid my work before answering the door.

Afterwards, I had finished all the finishing touches on my new suit. By time the sixth bell rang, I was finally done. I stood in the room wearing my handiwork.

As I looked at myself in the mirror the city was too kind to provide, I was reminded of the ancient ninjas my father once talked about. I just hoped the spirit of the ninja could aid me tonight.

I sat in the dark waiting for the time to past. It was almost time for me to go. I was just waiting for the guard on patrol to pass the window. Once he had passed, I would have an hour before another patrol passed.

I watched as the lantern light passed my window before opening it. As quietly as possible, I stood on the window seal and reached for the gutters. With a firm grip on the gutters, I pulled myself up onto the roof, closing the window with my foot as I went.

Once on the roof, I crawled up and over the peak and down to the next roof. I moved in the same way all along the rooftops only stopping when a guard patrol came close to me.

Up on the roofs, the patrols were useless. None of the guards ever looked up on the rooftops. Even if they had looked up, the lanterns that they carried could not shine light that high to see me.

About an hour after I started, I had reached the last house. In front of me laid the Grand Courthouse and my goal. All I had to do was reach the courthouse, find the window I rigged, open it, and get inside before the guards saw me.

"Piece of cake," I said in a low whisper to myself.

I had already found the window I was looking for; from where I was, I was just waiting to see where the next guard was. As if on cue, one of the guards was coming around right below me. I watched as he took a left down one of the side streets before I made my move.

Landing silently, I ran to the courthouse aiming for the window. Taking a quick look inside, I opened the window. It opened with ease, and I was in without a sound.

Inside, I made my way the maintenance stairwell. I was thinking the stairs would be the easiest to reach the third floor without being seen. On the third floor, I looked out the door. I didn't see a guard nearby, but that did not mean they were not there.

The real problem was the room I was looking for was on the other side of the floor. Sneaking out, I slowly made my way to the records room.

Once outside the stairwell, I could hear there was at least one guard patrolling the floor. Thankfully he sounded like he was on the far end of the floor. Meaning I should have enough time to get to the records room and get inside before he made it around.

At the door, I pulled a small bit of wire and quickly worked on the old lock. Just then I heard a noise coming from the maintenance stairwell that was by me. It sounded like a guard was on his way down the stairs.

Not knowing if he was going to get off at this floor or not, I unlocked the door. Even if the guards keep going down the stairs, the records room's door was in the directed line of site of the stairwell door. If the guard looked out the window, he would see me.

With a click, the door opened. With the footsteps getting closer, I stepped in the room, closing and locking it at the same time. I then hid behind one of the cabinets in the room and waited. About five minutes passed before I moved out from the cabinet.

I looked in amazement at the sight around me. Their file cabinets were filled to bursting throughout this room. I would say it was around fifty cabinets within this one room. Now, I needed to see if it was worth my time coming here. I needed to find something that would help me find my father's killer or all this would be for nothing.

I began to go though the files on the far end of the room, using candles I brought with me. When I grew restless, I curled myself in a corner and slept with files all around me. Knowing this might take days, I manage to smuggled out some bread and cheese from the lunch table. I also had brought some water using the canteen that came with my evening meal.

By the first day, I had already gone through one-third of the files with no luck. It was far easier to move through the file then I first thought. Most of the files had pictures to look at. Those that didn't, I menially looked for the crime that was committed. By looking for the only the more violent crimes, I moved though the files fast.

By day two, I had gone through more than half of the files, and still I did not find anything. Every time I read something that sounded close to the stranger's pattern, I always found something which did not fit with him. And every time I would tell myself, 'The next one, and the next one.'

By the third day, I was nearing the end of the last file cabinet. It was not the only thing I was running out of. I was also running out of food and water, but more importantly I was running out of hope. I now believed this was completely pointless.

'The stranger did not have a record,' I thought to myself. 'He just picked up the jumpsuit off a corpse. He was never imprisoned, though he should have been.'

Just when I thought I might not find anything on the stranger, I opened a file that had a picture of him in it. With the last rays of sunlight fading, I sat down and read.

In the file, I learned the stranger's name was a Chad Michael, but he had another name too: The S.A. Killer. The FBI gave him this name for the way he killed his victims. For he would be invited into a person's home and in the dead of night sneak into everyone's room and stab them in the throat with a knife. Once everyone was dead, he would then set fire to the home and watch as it burned to the ground. And that is why he became known as the Stabbing Arsonist Killer, or S.A. Killer.

As I read, I found for the longest time most of his murders were thought to be accidental. If it were not for one home he had visited which did not burn down all the way, he might have gotten away.

In those charred ruins, investigators found evidence of arson. What's more, one of the bodies was not destroyed. On examination, they found that the girl had died before she was burned, and that she died from a stab wound to the throat.

The police started an investigation and search for how this could have been done. It wasn't long before the local police found the trail went cold and began asking around for other incidents like theirs. Within a week's time, they had over a dozen cases of unsolved fires, all having one common element. Each of the homes was either a bed and breakfast or had a room for rent.

Soon more bodies were found in the same way, leading investigators to believe they had a serial killer on the loose. The FBI was called in to create a profile of this man.

The FBI's report said the S.A. Killer seemed to have a blood mania. He loved the sight of a person's blood, but not just the sight, but also the feel of it, the smell, the taste of it, and even the sound it made. This was why he went for the throat, because it would gush out blood.

The FBI then believed that the S.A. Killer's first kills may have been an accident and he tried to hide the evidence by burning the body or bodies. In this act, he may have become even more excited by the act of burning the corpses. He may have even found the scent of burning flesh appealing. Like all other serial killers, he reveled in the idea of the chance to do it again and again.

With this profile, the FBI tried to map the killer's movements. But without knowing what arson-related deaths were truly caused by the S.A. Killer, all unsolved arson deaths were considered possible S.A. Killer murders.

The only true break came about a year after the first proven S.A. Killer murder, when the S.A. Killer was arrested.

As I read, I soon saw some similarities in the arrest report and my own encounter with the man. The report said that he was staying at a home of a small family. That night he began to murder the family. After killing the father, mother, and the young baby boy, he headed to the little girl's room. Inside the room, the girl woke to see the man in the room. Seeing the blood on his hands and holding a knife, she screamed.

The neighbors heard the scream and went to see what was going on. They saw a large amount of smoke coming out of the house and called 911. They then went to see if there was anything they could do before the fire department arrived.

On arriving, the people and the fire department found the place was engulfed in flames. As the fire department battled the fire, one man came though the flames. His hands were bloody and he smelled of both blood and gas. The police quickly apprehended the man, who didn't put up much of a fight.

Back at the station, the man confessed to the murders and the fire, and admitted to being the S.A. Killer. Hearing this, the FBI was informed, and they had the prisoner transferred into their custody.

The now confirmed S.A. Killer told the FBI about all the murders and fires he had committed. He had admitted to committing over a hundred different deaths over a four-year period.

At his trial, he didn't wish to be represented by an attorney nor did he wish for mercy from the court. Instead, he asked, and I quote, "I am not here to be acquitted for the things I did. I am not here to seek or be given help. I do not now or will ever feel bad for what I have done. In my mind, I see what I did was not wrong, but was right. In your world, I am guilty, but in mind I am not. Those I killed were too weak for the world that I live in, so they had to die. In my world, the strong survive and the weak die. So, I ask the court to show me that you are stronger than me and sentence me to death. If you don't, you will all prove to me that you are all weak and I will come and kill you all."

In the end, he was sentenced to death. The sentence was to be carried out one month after the court date. The execution was to be held at the Cornwell Corrections Facility that was located somewhere in the mountains.

This was the end of the files. There was no more information I could find on this man. The file did contain the basic pattern he used in his killings. I now knew the direction he may go.

But this was not what I had a problem with. My problem was how this man was still alive. If the court had him executed, how could he be here now?

I had to find out. So, I looked over the whole file once more. I read every word, every sentence, and every little note that was in the file. It was only when I read the court date and the date when the execution was to be performed.

It was the Great Disaster. This monster had been tried, convicted, sentenced one month before the Great Disaster happened. The prison itself could have saved the guards and the prisoners from it, but with the world going to hell, the guards could not have known what to do.

But something must have happened. Riots and massive escapes, something for the S.A. Killer get out and travel then kill my father and all those people. What's more, he was still out there killing people when by all rights he should be dead.

I now had more information than I ever thought I would ever find out. I now needed to get myself out of Lawmaker. Taking the picture of my enemy, I replaced the file and headed to the door.

By the bells, it was about an hour after the eighth bell. It was my time to move. Looking out the window, I checked to see if it was clear. Seeing no one outside in the hall, I crept out of the records room and locked the door.

Just as I had closed the door, I saw the light from one of the guard's lanterns coming near. I quickly headed towards the maintenance stairs. But I was forced to stop in my tracks because through the window I could see another light coming up the stairs. I turned to head to the stairs on the other side of the floor. I didn't get two steps before I was forced to stop again.

I had found myself cornered. The stairs near me had a guard coming up, and I had two guards on this floor. Soon the two guards were on top of me and I had no way out. There were no doors near to me to hide in. There was only the record room, which I locked, and I did not have the time to unlock it.

Before my mind could come up with a plan, the two guards had come around the corner and found me standing there. Before the two guards could get over their shock, I moved.

I charged the guard, who was in the direction of the far stairwell. I thought if I could get by him, I could make it to the stairs before the other guard could stop me.

I did manage to knock the guard down, but his senses were better than I thought. On his way to the ground, he had grabbed my leg and held on to it.

This gave the second guard time to tackle me. Now on the ground, I began to fight, like a madman. But nothing I did could get the two men off me.

Meanwhile, the sound alerted the guard on the stairs. Seeing what was going on, he quickly joined the battle.

Outnumbered, I was overpowered and found myself tied up. With my hands and feet tied, I lied on the ground as the three guards discussed what needed to be done now.

It was decided one would go and report to the Captain of the Enforcers and to the Grand Justice himself. Both needed to be informed of what had just happened now.

So, while the one guard went running with his duty, the other two carried me up to the fourth floor. On the fourth floor, the two guards guided me into one of the rooms.

There was not much in this room. There was only one small chair in the center of the room and a desk and chair right in front of it.

I was forced into the chair in the center and tied down to it. Just then the door opened and a man in a blue robe came in. On his robe was an insignia that showed his rank as a captain.

With a quick glance at me, he went over to one of the two guards who brought me into the room. He started to question the guard, making sure he understood everything. The guard handed the Captain the picture that I had taken from the record's room.

The Captain looked at the picture then at me before pocketing the picture then went and stood by the desk.

A few minutes later, the door opened once more; this time it was a man in a red and gold robe walked in, the Grand Justice himself. He stood tall as he walked in the robe gliding as if he was floating instead of walking.

His hood was up as always, and his mask covered his face. The mask itself had a human looking face but was also different. It looked as if it was trying to look more godlike.

Behind the Grand Justice, another man came in. This man was wearing a black robe, which made him an attorney. Bowing low, the man came over and stood next to me.

Reaching the desk, the Grand Justice stood as everyone, except me, bowed and cried, "Your Magnificent Grand Justice." At this, he sat down behind the desk, looking at me through the mask.

"To all those here, in law we speak, only truth do we seek," the Grand Justice said, his right hand raised in pledge.

Mimicking the Grand Justice's movements, those in the room in unison cried, "Amen!"

All eyes then turned to me, for I had remained silent during the Grand Justice's prey. Only after a sign from my attorney did I speak.

"I always speak the truth, and we will see just how lawful you are."

At my words the room became quiet as everyone looked to the Grand Justice. I found it hard to read, the Grand Justice's mood under that stupid mask of his. Only his eyes could be seen, jet black and unblinking.

Finally, the Grand Justice spoke; his voice was deep and rough, "Speak, criminal. Tell us who you are, why are you here, and what is it you want?"

"Why should I answer the questions of a madman and his mad dogs?" I shot back defiantly.

Surprisingly it was my attorney who said next, "As your legal adviser, I would tell you to answer all of the Grand Justice's questions."

"Why should I?" I said looking at my "attorney." "Will answering his questions aid in my release?"

A small chuckle from the Captain turned my attention to him. "Release?" he repeated. "There is no release; there is only guilty. You are a criminal in the eyes of the law, and you will be punished for the crimes against the city."

"And what crime did I commit?" I asked playing dumb.

"As if you didn't know!" the Captain said. "But if you would like a formal charge, fine! You are guilty of entering the Grand Courthouse without authorization and without identification. I also have reason to believe you not only entered the Sacred Record Room, but also stole from the records as well."

At this the Grand Justice turned to his Captain. "How do you know this, Captain?"

"Because, My Lord, we found this man near the door on the fourth floor," the Captain explained.

"Maybe he just happened to be near when he was captured, Captain."

"Then, My Lord, he would not have had this on him."

The Captain pulled the picture out from his pocket and handed it to the Grand Justice. He looked over the picture before placing it on the desk.

"This is indeed part of the Sacred Record," the Grand Justice proclaimed. "But the question is how he could have taken it."

At this, the Grand Justice removed a key on a string from beneath his robes.

"I am the only one who carries a key to the room. So, Captain, how could he enter a locked room?"

"It is my belief he has the lock picking art, My Lord," the Captain said bowing as he did.

"I see," the Grand Justice said nodding in understanding. "The gift of thieves and criminals, it is the true mark of the guilty. After all, no honest man needs know this skill."

Looking back in my direction, the Grand Justice continued to speak, "We have now answered the what, but we have not answered why. Why would you want this picture, criminal? For what purpose does it hold to you?"

"For what purpose, do you ask?" I said looking from the picture to his eyes. "The reason for taking this picture and my whole purpose for being here is to find my father's murderer."

"You have just answered the where!" the Grand Justice said. "If you are looking for a murderer, you must be an outsider. For you see, there has not been a murder in this city for three years now."

"I never said I was looking for the murderer in the city," I said to the room at large. "Indeed, all I wanted from this city was information on that man."

"Why would we have information on your father's murderer?" the Grand Justice asked almost confused.

"Because I had learned he may have been a prisoner of the old world!" I explained. "I was told this place had records from the old world, and I hoped I could see them and find info on this man."

"You believe this man killed your father?" the Grand Justice asked.

"I don't believe. I know."

"You are mistaken."

"What do you mean?"

"I mean this man could not kill your father!"

"Why is that?"

"Because this man you are looking for is dead!"

"What?"

My mind began to turn, thinking what could have happened. Did he find this city, break in, and begin to terrorize the people? Did they catch him, try him, and commit him to death? Or was he talking about what it says in the file that he was executed long ago?

Either way I needed to find out. I had to know what he knew about him.

"You are wrong!" I said watching the eyes in the mask. "This man lives, and he had killed my father and about ten different households."

"Impossible," the Grand Justice said.

"Why is that?

"If I may, My Lord," the Captain asked.

With a wave of the Grand Justice's hand, the Captain begins,

"It is a well-known fact the purpose for the Great Disaster was to wipe the slate clean. It was to kill off all the killers and criminals and leave just the pure and innocents. So, with this said, this man here and indeed all the others within those files you read were killed long ago by the Great Disaster, leaving this new world to the right and the noble people of our world."

"Bull!" was all I had to say this! "If you all believe this you all are crazier than I had first thought you were."

"How dare you speak in that insolent manner?" the Captain said raising his fist.

"Captain," the Grand Justice stopped him with a word.

Controlling his anger, he bowed to the Grand Justice and remained quiet.

"I know it is hard to learn the reason why the Great Disaster happened, but the truth can help you to understand why," the Grand Justice said comfortingly.

"I still think you all are full of shit!" I said, and as I did, one of the guards beside me punched me right in the face.

Stunned, I stared at the Grand Justice thinking he ordered it.

"I am afraid cursing in not permitted in my city," he said folding his hand.

"Another unneeded law," I said under my breath.

"What was that?"

"I said what about my mother then?"

"What do you mean?"

"Well, if you're right about the end of the old world. Why did my mother die?"

"If she died in the Great Disaster then she must have had been a villain of some kind."

"You do know what you're fucking saying!"

The second punch had hit with far more force than the first.

I shook my head and continued speaking. "If you know anything, you know the world outside these walls is just as violent if not more than the old one. If things happened the way you say then why are there murders, robberies, rapes, and all manners of violence out in that world."

"It is true crime is rampant outside these wells and many innocents suffer." At this, I saw the Grand Justice's eyes close before he went on. "But all those who commit these crimes are only those who have felt great sorrow in their life. As we all have, but we have a choice. We can either move past it, or we can act out to cover our sorrow. This is the truth behind crime. Men do terrible things to those around them to try to put out their sorrows.

I am sure it is the same with you, criminal."

"You do like to hear the sound of your own voice, don't ya?"

"I merely speak the truth."

"You speak bullshit."

The third punch had knocked me to the floor. Tied to the chair like I was, I could not pick myself up. With the guards' help I was once again in a sitting position.

I spat the blood from my mouth onto the floor and shot daggers from my eyes to all around me.

"Are you telling me your mother and father's deaths did not cause you great sorrow?" the Grand Justice said.

"Of course it did, you fool," I said. "But their deaths gave me strength, and my father's gave me a purpose. To find that man there and kill him."

"Oh! You poor fool," the Grand Justice said. "How can I prove to you that the man you seek has been dead for decades? That he, like the rest of the filth, died during the Great Disaster. This is scariest knowledge that all man knows."

"So, you think I am mad," I said. "I saw this man with my own eyes kill my father. I am not mistaking this man for another. He is alive, and you are all wrong."

"Perhaps what you say is right," the Grand Justice said with joy in his voice. "Maybe you are mad. Yes, I can see it now; I can see how you believe a dead man killed your father. This man here is merely a tool you are using to hide your own guilt."

"What!"

"Yes, you killed your father in a blinding rage of madness."

"How dare you call me a murder!"

"Why is that? After all, madness is another clear sign of a criminal."

"What of my father's murderer, the person I have been searching for?"

"Of course, your father's 'murderer' is merely a figment of your immigration."

"What!"

"It is clearly a fantasy, my child, a fantasy. Something you created to ease your pain."

"You're the only one who is living some kind of fantasy."

"I only wish to help you, my child."

"If you really want to help, you will let me go, you asshole."

Again, all my words did was to add to the bruises to my face. Lying on my side, I spat out the blood in my mouth before I was helped up.

"You sit there refusing to follow even the simplest law in my city," the Grand Justice said his anger rising. "You are making it hard for me to find mercy for you. All I see is a rodent who deserves to suffer for eternity. Is this what you want?"

"No, you son of a—I want the *leave*!" I said screaming at him now.

"No one leaves my city. No one enters my city. This is how things are, and how things will remain," the Grand Justice said. "You and all those like you are a disease that if left to remain will infect the whole city. Therefore, you must be removed from my city, to protect my citizens."

"So is this why you wear that mask, to protect yourself from my disease? All this time, I thought you wear it because you are butt ugly."

Whack!

With a grand punch, the Captain hit me breaking my nose. I lied on my back breathing in my own blood, with the Captain standing over me.

"I will not stand by and let you insult the Grand Justice in that manner," he said looking down on me. "He is the purity of the law, and as such his radiance is too much for our eyes."

"He is just a nut behind a mask, and this city is a bastard child of law," I said spitting blood on the Captain's face.

He was about to strike me once more, but before he could, the Grand Justice called him off. Wiping his face, the Captain ordered his men to pick me up. Sitting up I could feel the blood from my nose flowing down my face.

"You refer to my great city as a bastard child of law," the Grand Justice said speaking only to me. "But what would a lawless outsider know of law? I know the world outside my walls has no order, no laws to govern the people. So, what do you know of law?"

"I know more than you think, Your Grace," I said mockingly. "My father was a man of law in the old world, a lawyer. But when the Great Disaster happened and my mother died, he turned his attention to protecting me and teaching me. He told me everything he knew of the old law as well as everything he knew my mother, as a teacher, would want her son to know. You have mutated the law for your own purpose and for your own greed," I said, my voice growing with strength. "Samuel told me about your past and the history of this city, and I know from him you are a fraud."

"No one speaks that man's name in my presence!" the Grand Justice said rising from his chair.

"You mean the name of the True Grand Justice of Lawmaker, Samuel!" I screamed just as loud.

"Enough of this. Captain, remove him from my site."

"But, My Lord, we have not learned his name, or how he came into Lawmaker, sir."

"It matters not. What does a criminal need of a name? And as for how he entered, perhaps one of the guards allowed him to enter."

"Impossible, My Lord," the Captain protested, "the gate guards are the most loyal to the city and to you, My Lord."

"Yes, you're right," the Grand Justice said as he moved back and forth in thought.

Stopping in place he quickly turned to me. As if he were reading my mind, he came up with the answer that only he could.

"I know how you entered my fair city now," he said speaking as if we were the only ones in the room. "With help from my enemies on the other side of my wall, you made your plot. I have long believed that a copy of the plan for my city lay in the hands of the outsider. These rebels hope to use these plans to one day overthrow me, but it is impossible. My wall is inviolable; there is no way to enter my city without my notice."

"So how could he do it, Master," the Captain said.

"The wall, of course, he used the wall."

"The wall, My Lord?"

"Yes, the wall. He climbed the wall."

"But, My Lord, no man could climb the wall. The side is far too smooth for that."

"Yes, but the plan would tell a person how high it is and how much rope you would need to climb it."

"But, My Lord, I am sure one of my men would have seen him climbing down the wall."

"Captain, have you not noticed what he is wearing. His dark clothing is perfect for moving through the night. Add to the fact there has been a new moon for the past three nights. He could move through the city as if he were invisible."

"Of course, he must have used a rope covered in black coal so no one could see it.

And the lanterns our sentries carry did not help."

"Indeed, My Lord, the light they make is terrible."

"Yes, it is one of many things I have been meaning to improve."

"After climbing the wall, it would have been easy for him make his way through the slums to reach the Grand Courthouse."

"Yes, Captain, where he could have just opened the door and entered. Once in, he would have made his way up to the fourth floor and use his lock picking art to enter the record room."

"Where my men found him, My Lord?"

"Yes, but I believe only after he spent several days looking for his 'so-called killer.' I am sure if we look, we will find evidence of this in the Sacred Record Room."

"But, My Lord, neither my men nor I am worthy to enter the Sacred Record Room."

"Fear not, Captain, I will search the Sacred Record Room myself. You and your men focus on finding the rope he used to enter Lawmaker."

"I will do as you wish, My Lord, but what of his name?"

"It matters not; we know how and why he did what he did. With this and the evidence we will find, we have more than enough to put him on trial. His name will not aid him now."

"You two are too fucking much!" I said, reminding them I was still here.

A kick from one of my guards found me back on my side looking up at the masked man. He paid me no mind. He just turned and headed for the door. But I was not finished with him.

"Hey, freak, yeah you in the mask, I have something to say."

"And what is that?"

"I will give you one more chance. Tell your men to cut me loose and take me to the wall. If you let me walk through your gates out into the wild lands, I will never return. I won't even think of this hell of yours. But if you don't, I will return, and I will kill you all! Thus, says Matrix!"

Looking back, the Grand Justice just laughed. "Empty threat, Matrix, in a weeks' time you will either be dead or suffering for eternity. Captain, process the prisoner."

Chapter 17

The Jackal

My attorney followed the Grand Justice out, his notes in hand. As for me, I was released from my chair and helped onto my feet. With much pushing and pulling, the Captain led us out the door and down the stairs.

On the first floor, we headed to one of three doors. I was pushed into this room to a concert cubicle. There was a large drain in the center of it and ropes hanging from the ceiling. On the other wall in front of the opening was a large hose.

In the center of the cubicle, my hands were cut free and tied to the ropes hanging from the ceiling. My hands tied, my clothes were then ripped from my body. The guards then stepped out of the cubicle and turned on the hose.

When the water hit my body, it was like cold, icy needles pricking my skin. Unable to protect myself, I just hung there praying for it to stop.

Now cleaned, I found myself lying on the cold ground shivering. As I lied their cradled in a ball, one of the guards dropped a set of clothes in front of me. Wanting only to be warm again, I quickly put on the clothes.

They were like the robes I wore before; the only difference was the color. They were no longer white; there were instead an orange color. Seeing this, I once again thought about the stranger's clothes. He also was wearing orange clothing, the color of the criminal.

Once I was dressed, my hands were once more bound together and I was dragged out to the room next door. Inside this room were several desks. I was pulled over to one of the desks and forced to sit. On the desk were only some paper and a flat pan of ink with a roller.

At the desk, they turned my hand palms up and rolled ink on both. My hand covered in ink, they had me press my hands down on the two pieces of paper.

My handprints taken, I was dragged off to another desk where a man sat looking very tired. Here I was forced to sit as the man picked up a board with a piece of paper on it.

I sat there, looking straight at this man listening to the sound of his pencil scathing away on the paper. He would look up at me at times before returning to his work. There were even times when he would erase some mistake then he would be back sketching away.

When he was done, he showed his work to the Captain, who nodded, and placed his work on the desk. Looking down I found that he was drawing my picture. I had to say it looked very good, all most like a snapshot.

With my mugshot done, I was pulled away and dragged out the door. I was now being shoved into the third and final room on the first floor. I was not surprised to see where I had ended up at—the jail.

The cellblock was placed in the corner of the floor with cells on both side of the hall, a total of ten on each side. I soon found that I was not the only one here. Five of the cells were already occupied, two men about my age, two small children, a boy and girl, and an elderly woman. All of them were asleep when I came in.

Opening the cell in between the two men, my guards threw me onto the ground in the cell. My hands were unbound, and the cell door closed before I could even get to my feet.

I watched through the bars of my cell as the guard left, thinking only of putting my hands around their throats. Unable to do a thing to aid my situation, I lied down on my cot and fell asleep.

My sleep was disturbed by the sound of voices talking around. They were speaking in low whispers, but it was clear that their conversation was all about me.

Unable to go to sleep, I opened my eyes and sat up; as I did the voices went silent. Looking around, I found only the children were still asleep, but the older people were awake and were looking intently at me.

"Good morning," one of the two men said.

"What is good about it," I said irritated. "We are in jail, and in the hands of mad men. So, I ask you, what is good about this."

"Well… ah… mm," he said muttering.

"Don't mind him; he is always in a good mood," said the other man. "By the way, my name is Jason, he's Derrick, and the twins are Danny and Stephanie, and finally her name is Susan."

"I'm Matrix."

"Good to meet you, Matrix," said Derrick. "Forgive me for saying so, but you don't look like you are from around here."

"You're right. I am not from Lawmaker," I said.

"I knew it!" Derrick said. "I told you guys his was a fellow outsider."

"You mean you are an outsider, too?" I asked. "What in the world are you doing in this hellhole?"

"Well, before the wall, I used to trade here in Lawmaker," Derrick said sitting on his cot. "I even had helped out with the building of the wall. Back then we believed the wall was going to make Lawmaker a sanctuary in times of great need. We were wrong. Once the wall was up, we on the outside were forbidden to once more enter Lawmaker. It was then we knew the madness of the new Grand Justice.

"Shortly afterward, the towns near Lawmaker moved on to look for a place that would trade with them. But I did not go with them. I could not for I had left something in Lawmaker, and I wanted it back. So, I came up with a plan to enter Lawmaker to get it back."

"Why would you risk so much that you would willingly sneak into a place that wants nothing to do with you?" I asked.

"Me!" replied Jason.

"You?" I said looking at one then the other.

"You are too close in age to be father and son," I said, "and you do not look as if you are related by blood at all, so that would make you…"

"Lovers," Derrick said his head down.

"Ah! I see," I said understanding.

"Are you repelled by the idea of two men being together, as all others are, Matrix?" Jason asked.

"No, I could not care less about what you two do, and with who you want to be with," as I said this a look of confusion came over Jason's face. "You find this strange, Jason," I said. "I come from the outside world. I have seen weirder things out there than two men living together."

"Well, I managed to get myself into Lawmaker and find Jason but was found out before we could make it back out," Derrick said finishing his story.

"And for all your trouble, you were put in this jail," I said.

"Yes!" Jason said. "And even now we are kept apart."

"And what about the two little ones>" I asked. "What horrific things have they done to be put in jail?"

"I'm afraid the only thing these two are guilty of is being orphans," Susan said.

"What! How can being an orphan be against the law?" I asked.

"Well, it isn't really," Susan said, "but it is the law that all children under the age of eighteen must have a legal guardian, by blood or by law. If they do not, then the city takes custody of the children. But what that means is that the children come here to the Grand Courthouse to start their training to become enforcers."

"You mean they would make someone as young as them enforcers."

"Even younger."

"So, I guess they didn't go."

"No, it seems their mother told them to hide from the enforcers after her death," Susan said.

"What happened to their mother?" I asked.

"She became sick one day and died a week later," Susan said. "It is an unfortunate reality here in Lawmaker. Low class people do not get much medical attention by the higher-ups and because of that many die from common diseases."

"Is that what happened to their father, as well?"

"No, as far as they know their father is still alive."

"What do you mean?"

"Well, their father had wanted to leave the city and take his family with him," Susan said. "But you of all people would know how hard it is outside these walls. So, he was going to leave first and find a place for them to live then return for them."

"So, what happened?

"Well before he could get them out, their mother died, and they went on the run hiding from the enforcers."

As Susan spoke, one of the twins turned on their side still fast asleep.

"After their mother's death, they were still hopeful that their father would find a way to save them," Susan said with a heavy sigh. "Even now they believe their father will find away to get them out."

"In the minds of children, their parents can do anything, can save them from any harm or danger," I said watching the twins sleep. "It is best for them to keep this idea of their father, for I bet right now it is the only thing that gives them the strength to go on."

"This is my feeling as well," Susan said, and as she did the twins sat up on their bed rubbing the sleep from their eyes.

"Miss Susan, has breakfast come yet?" Stephanie asked in a tired voice.

"Not yet, sweetie," Susan said with a grandmotherly touch. "It should be here soon, but before it gets here, I want you two to meet Mister Matrix."

"Good morning, Mister Matrix!" the twins said together.

"Good morning," I replied.

I watched as Susan tried her best to entertain the twins. Even Derrick and Jason in the cells across from the twins told jokes or made faces at them just to make them laugh.

"You're quite the woman, Susan. I see now why Samuel loves you so much," I said.

"What was that?" she asked stunned.

"What is a founder of Lawmaker doing within its jail?" I said. "I only ask because Samuel never said you were imprisoned in all the time he talked about you. So why are you here, and why doesn't your husband know you're here?"

"I did not know you knew Samuel," Susan said.

"It was he who helped me get inside, but you have not answered my questions," I said hanging over the bars of my cell.

"To answer your second question, it is because I do not want my husband to know I am here," Susan said looking worried. "I know my husband; if Samuel found out I was I jail, he would do whatever it took to get me out. But by doing so he would lose his only chance to return Lawmaker back to the people."

"So are you here to insure he doesn't?" I asked.

"No, this was the reason Marcus would not let me leave with Samuel," Susan said. "Marcus fears Samuel's return, for he knows when he does, the people will fight for him to overthrow Marcus. With me still in Lawmaker, Marcus can threaten my life or use me to kill Samuel."

"So, he put you in this cell for safe keeping," I asked.

"No, I am afraid I put myself in this cell," she said looking down-hearted.

"So, what did you do?"

"If you were with Samuel then he would have told you about the punishment here, right?"

"You mean the hole, right? A twenty-foot deep and twenty-foot diameter abyss."

"That's it. A terrible place created by Marcus to scare people to follow his laws and to keep quiet about it."

With tears in her eyes, Susan sat herself down on her cot.

"Those poor people, I cannot imagine what it must be like to live in total darkness. To not even be able to tell what is around you or who. To eat whatever is by you, not knowing if what you are eating is even food, or one of you follow prisoner, or even something else."

"I could not stand the thought of those people living like this," said Susan shaking her head as if to erase the thought. "But there was not much I could do for them; there was no way to get them out of the Hole. The only thing I could do was make their lives easier. So about once a week I would sneak out to the Hole and drop some fresh bread, vegetables, and clean water for them all to have. I even managed to drop down some warmer clothes and blankets."

"How did you get all that stuff for those people?" I asked.

"Well I was not just anyone; I was an attorney," Susan said. "And as an attorney I could get people to give me whatever I wanted. All I had to say is it was for official business and no one questioned me. After all I was not just an attorney; I was also a founder. What right did anyone have to question me?"

"So how did you get found out?" I asked.

"By letting my small successes go to my head," Susan said. "I had made great progress in gathering supplies for those in the Hole, but I still wished to get them out. But I would have a hard time trying to get enough rope to reach the bottom of the Hole. That much rope would get even the dumbest man thinking why. So instead, I stole small pieces at a time. Some I took from the warehouses and storage areas; I also grabbed any pieces of rope I found lying on the ground, or in the dump."

"It took me the good part of two years, but I did it. I used the rope pieces and made a rope ladder that would make it to the bottom of the Hole. I could finally truly help those who had suffered the most from Marcus. I made my plan, and one night I left the courthouse and went to the Hole. With me I had my rope ladder, some food, and some water. My plan was simple: sneak up to the Hole, drop the ladder down, and hope the people down there would see it and climb up. If I needed, I would go down myself and carry those who couldn't get out of the Hole on their own.

"Once they were all out of the Hole, I would let them rest and eat as I told them the next part of my plan. Which was to go to the nearest part of the wall where I knew there was one of Samuel's secret openings in the wall and I would help them all out. After that, I was not sure what I would do. On one hand, I could leave with them and see Samuel again, or stay in Lawmaker and hope to help everyone else here. To stay or to go, it was the one thing I did not figure out. In the end, I decided that I would make the decision at the wall and not before."

"Your plan is very clever, Susan, but what was the factor did you not think of?" I asked.

"The full moon and a cloudless sky," she said. "My mind was on the plan and not on the condition outside. I should have waited for a moonless night, but I was too eager to start my plan and I went for it. I made it to the hill where the Hole is and made it to the top. It was there two young enforcers found me. All they saw was an old woman on top of the Hole with a rope ladder, bundles of food, and several canteens of water with the opening of the Hole wide open."

"If only I could have run away from them, they may have never known who it was. But I am not as young as I used to be; they caught me before I could make good my escape. To say they were surprised to see it was me would be and understatement. And if the enforcers were surprised, you can only imagine what went through Marcus's mind when he heard what had just happened. Indeed, when it came time to question me, he seemed to be enjoying the sight. But I also saw fear in his eyes, fear at what would happen if Samuel heard what had happened.

"Would he come and try to save me? If he didn't, what would happen after my trial? My crime would surely put me in the Hole. Would he come then to free me from that hell? And what if I was tried and convicted and Samuel never came? Marcus would lose his only leverage on Samuel! He would have no defense against Samuel. But he could not just let me go, without punishment? No! If he did that, he would show the law is bendable, and that would not do! So, what should he do with me?"

"So, he is just going to have you sit in this jail for the rest of your life," I said.

"It would seem to be his plan," Susan said. "This way, I can serve his means. When Samuel comes to take the city back for the people."

The jail became quiet after Susan's story. Everyone was left to think of one's own future. It was Susan who finally broke the depressing silence. "So, what is your story, Matrix?"

"Yeah, Matrix," Derrick said. "What crazy thing brought you in here?"

"I was looking for a murderer," I said.

"In Lawmaker?" Jason asked.

"There are no murderers in Lawmaker," Susan said. "There hasn't been one in the history of the city."

"I know! My murderer lives outside Lawmaker," I said.

"So why are you looking for him here in Lawmaker?" Derrick asked. "He didn't sneak into Lawmaker like I did?"

"No! If he had Lawmaker would have been burned to the ground and all the people would be dead," I said. "No, I know he is not here, but I had evidence that he was a killer in the old world."

So, I told them all about my father, the stranger, and all my adventures here in Lawmaker.

"You really went into the Sacred Record Room?" Jason said. "That is suicide."

"Indeed," Susan said. "I am sure Marcus is not going to wait long for your trial. A crime like this is a one-way ticket to the Hole for sure."

"Well, he did tell my attorney he had a week to prepare for my trail," I said.

"A whole week, I would have thought he would have it today or tomorrow," Susan said, "but there is something else troubling me.

"What is that, Susan?" Derrick asked.

"Matrix, are you sure the man you found in this file was the man who killed your father?" Susan asked looking deeply into my eyes.

"Without a doubt," I said.

"So, the S.A. Killer survived the Great Disaster," Susan said leaning up against the bars. "Of all the monsters of the Old World, why, oh why did that one not perish with it?"

"Is this S.A. Killer that bad Susan?" Jason asked.

"He is nothing like you two have ever seen," she said. "In many ways, Matrix is possibly the only person who has ever survived an encounter with him."

All further conversation stopped as a door was opened to the cellblock. Through the door came two enforcers; the man in front carried a basket of rolls while the other had a large bucket of water hanging from his shoulder.

Looking around I found a small jug on the windowsill. Grabbing it I placed it on the floor by the bars. We were all given one roll and water. When the enforcer reached my cell, there was a moment of hesitation in the man's eyes. He was thinking of not giving me a roll, but to do that would be illegal; after all the Grand Justice wanted me to be alive at my own trial.

The man, realizing this, threw the roll at me as hard as he could. With lighting speed, I caught the roll in mid-air. The enforcer seemed shocked at my speed, but quickly moved on with his duties. As for the man with the water, he merely kept his head down, filled my jug, and moved on.

The door slammed at the other end of the cellblock. Only then did I strike up a new conversation.

"Well, they truly dislike me now, don't they," I said.

"Well right now, I would say you are public enemy number one," Susan said, and as she did, I watched as Jason and Derrick ripped their rolls in two.

"It's for the little ones," Derrick said tossing half over to Stephanie.

"We adults always give them half what we have so they fill better," Jason said tossing his other half to Danny.

"We do what we can for them," Susan said getting ready to split her own into three pieces.

"Wait!" I said ripping my roll into two pieces.

"Give this to Stephanie," I said tossing half to Susan.

"You are too kind, Matrix." She handed the roll to Stephanie.

She then ripped her roll in two and handed one to Danny. The twins smiled as they ate their rolls in peace. As for my half, within two bites it was gone only to leave my stomach wanting more. But I had more important things to worry about besides my stomach.

Sometime after the fifth bell, my attorney walked into the cellblock. Behind him were two enforcers who were clearly here to ensure our meeting was a peaceful one. But I did not see a point to this whole ordeal. I already knew I was on my way to the Hole.

But still my attorney felt it was necessary to come down to my cell. Sitting in a chair one the enforcers brought, we began to talk.

I won't bore you with what we talked about. Let me just say it involved a lot of shouting, cursing, name-calling, and then whatever my attorney was saying. He only stayed for an hour, and as he was leaving, he said he would see me by the end of the week.

"What an ass!" I said after the three men had left.

"Well, this is what the attorneys are like in this city, mindless puppets," Susan said. "None of them have had a thought of their own for years now. Marcus has told them what to think and how to think, and there is nothing we can do about it."

Chapter 18

The Rat

The days in my cell went by far faster than a man would want. But this is what happens when you find yourself in good company. Even in this place, I found myself enjoying myself. We found ourselves enjoying what time we had with each other, talking, telling jokes, stories, even making funny faces for the joy of the twins. It seemed like time flew by, and in no time my date in court had arrived.

I remember the day clearly; I woke early that day. Looking around, I first saw I was not the only one who was up. Susan was sitting on her cot looking over into my cell. Even in the pale light, I could see she was crying.

When she saw I was awake, she quickly wiped her eyes and smiled at me. Standing up, I walked over to the bars and hung my arms over them.

"Can't sleep?" I asked knowing the answer.

"No," she replied standing as well. "The day of a person's court date always keeps me up."

"You feel pain for that person?"

"Yes! But I also think about those of us still here as well."

At this, her eyes looked first to Stephanie then to Danny both who were still a sleep.

"I think about the twins more than others," Susan said sitting back down. "I know when their date finally comes, they would be taken separately. It is Marcus's way; he would want to get as many court cases out of us. So even if two were charged with the same crime, their day in court would be different. I also know when this day comes, the one who would most likely go first will be Stephanie."

Susan then begins to sob once more. I am sure the image of little Stephanie being dragged away by the enforcers was all she saw. Stephanie's eyes filled with tears, her hands tied, her brother crying out for them to take him instead, his face turning red in an attempt to look brave while fighting back the tears. Jason and Derrick both crying out curses, while Susan is on her knees pleading with the men to spare the girl.

My eyes turned and looked at Stephanie still asleep in her cell. They are both too young to be in this place. At their age, they should be running outside playing and getting into mischief. But here in Lawmaker, a child is not allowed to be a child. In this regard, the twins and I are the same. Always on the road, I never had the time to be the child that I was. I was forced to grow up faster, but if I get the chance, I will save these kids from the fate made for them.

As the hours passed, the others woke, but other than small talk the cellblock was quiet.

It seemed like no time before the door opened and the enforcer came in to take me. I had thought the only chance I might have to escape was when they came for me. I could beat down the enforcer and make a run for it. Then return for the others, once I had my weapons.

But this plan was not going to work now. No less than ten enforcers came into the cellblock to escort me. Out numbered, I found my hands and legs tied, being dragged out of my cell. The only sound that could be heard was the sound of Stephanie's tears, while her brother looked as if he were fighting back his own tears.

As for the others, they were quiet as they watched as my guards and I left the cell.

Up to the fourth floor we went, my guard half-carrying me up the stairs as we went.

On the fourth floor, there were four courtrooms, the First Level Court Room, the Second Level Court Room, the Third Level Court Room, and the Supreme Court Room. These courtrooms are named for the level of your offense. If you commit a small crime, like littering, you will find yourself arrested and brought to the Grand Courthouse up to the fourth floor. Now, if it were your first offense you would be trialed in the First Level Court Room where you would be seen by one of the justices.

This justice would question you then mark in your passport that you were here in the First Level Court Room. This is your first strike, and you do not want more. But if you are unlucky and are seen committing another small crime you would then go to the Second Level Court Room where the same thing would happen as in the First Level Court Room.

But things change if you find yourself in the Third Level Court Room. Here instead of being seen by one of the low rank justices, you would be seen by the Grand Justice himself. Further more you will no longer have any more chances; you will be named a criminal and find yourself processed and put in jail, downstairs.

Now, the Supreme Court Room is the place where all criminals go for them to receive their sentence, and this was the place my guards and I were heading to. Being that my crime was not a small crime but a big crime, I skipped the three small courtrooms and went right to the Supreme Court Room.

The courtroom was very large. As I entered, I saw there was a long bench on my right; this is where the nine justices would sit during my trail. To my left there were two small tables were my attorney and the district attorney would sit. Behind them there were two rows of benches where people could watch the trail. They were mostly attorneys and enforcers, but I also saw a few white robes in the crowd. Among the white robes, I saw Enigma; his dark skin was easily seen in the sea of black and blue.

Sitting by my attorney, I waited for the start of the trail. We didn't have to wait long for the bailiff to ask all to rise for the Grand Justice and the associate justices. With my guards' aide, I stood and watched as Marcus and the other eight justices entered from the left.

Dressed in their normal red and gold robes, the nine members found their seats behind the bench. Mask and hooded, I could see each member's mask had the same godlike look, each with different characteristics; one even had a female look. Of course, this belongs to the only woman justice; not even her robe could hide that from the world.

Once all were sitting, the Grand Justice raised his hands for silence before saying the prayer. "To all those here, in law we speak, only truth do we seek," he said

And with a great "Amen" everyone sat leaving only the Grand Justice still on his feet. Speaking to the whole court, he told the crimes I had committed against the city. Those in the crowd stayed quiet, but I could feel the anger and the hatred toward me.

My crimes laid bare, the Grand Justice then asked for the district attorney to state his case. Standing, he first bowed to the nine justices then to my attorney then finally to the crowd. He then stood tall and began to speak to the court as if he were a preacher in a church.

I won't bore you with all he said, but for the most part he told all how I was a monster and a criminal. He spoke about my entrance into Lawmaker, and he even held up a blackened rope and hook that someone obviously created just for the purpose of the trial. He told how I made it into the record room and stole a picture from the records. He described my capture and all that was said in my interrogation, focusing on the photo of my father's killer saying it was madness that I could think he is alive and killing. He even went so far as to say I killed my father.

He ended his sermon by saying my crimes to the city did not deserve mercy. Saying I was a born criminal and I deserved to be thrown into the Hole so I could rot for all time. Taking his seat, the Grand Justice asked if my attorney wished to speak.

Nodding, my attorney stood and preformed the same bows as the district attorney did before starting his sermon. In the end, my own attorney said nothing new. Indeed, his sermon sounded much like the district attorney's sermon. The only true difference was that his sermon was more compassionate then the district attorney's.

In the end, my attorney focused on my father's death, saying that it drove me to madness. And without my father, I had lost my way and I had found myself in the shadows, but then my mind created a figure to focus on. This figure became the light in the darkness and was the only thing which now guided me.

But the figure had no form, no body, and so I searched for someone to become my villain. He said when I saw this man in the photo in the record room, my mind made him the villain.

He went on for another ten minutes before finally saying to the court I had suffered enough, and I should be put out of my misery. Sitting down by me, he smiled as if he had done wonderful job and wanted me to thank him for all he'd done. I just looked away and focused on the justices in front of me.

"Mister Matrix," the Grand Justice said turning to me. "Is there anything you would like to add before we pass judgment?"

"Yes, there is, Your Honor," I said standing up.

"Who do you think you are?" I started. "Everyone here thinks what is gone on in this room is justice. You believe order is made by holding trials and sentencing men like me to death or the Hole is the act of justice, but it's not. This place is a bastard child in the eyes of pure justice, and you all up there are the whores.

"In many ways, you are no different to those men outside this wall who prey on the weak and the helpless. They use the fear of men to take control over them, and so do you. The only true difference is you think what you are doing is the right thing. The men out there know what they are doing is wrong, but they just don't care.

This place makes me sick. But I will give you all one more chance. Let me go! Take me to one of your doors and let me walk through and I will never return. But if you go through with this insult of justice, I swear to you I will find a way to tear down your wall and turn your world into chaos."

Sitting down, I watched as the Grand Justice stood once more and spoke to me.

"Your words held great power, Matrix, but they were not stronger than the power of our law," the Grand Justice said looking down to me. "You say we are a bastards of the law, but I say we are the law's true children. We live, breathe, eat, and sleep the law. To us there is nothing more important then the law. We would sacrifice anything in order to protect it. Even turning in one of his own family. All who turned their backs to the law must be punished. As for our wall, I assure you it is far stronger than you give it credit. For it is powered by the strength and the faith of the people in the law. Nothing in the world could ever make our wall fall. You will be judged here and now by us, and you will face you fate."

Sitting down he and the other justices began to speak in low whispers. In no time, the nine members were silent, and the Grand Justice once more was on his feet. He was not the only one. As he stood my attorney and I too rose.

"In the case against the criminal Matrix," the Grand Justice began, "the justices and I have deicided that Matrix has no remorse for the crimes his has committed. It is our decision that Matrix is to be thrown into the Hole where he will remain to the end of his days. May Justice watch over him! Enforcers, do your duty."

The trial over, I found myself being led out of the courtroom. Down to the first floor, we made our way to a small door on the north side of the building. Though the door, we found ourselves in a small room with another door right in front of us.

I could not see the reason for this room. The room was just big enough for the three of us. The room had nothing in it and seemed to have no purpose.

I was going to ask my guards what this room was for when I felt a punch in my gut. Gasping for air, I could not prepare myself for the kick to the head. The kick knocked me down to the ground, where the two enforcers began to beat the shit out of me.

It was then I knew what this room was for. It was here where the enforcers could beat up the condemned, where no one could see or stop it.

Here and now, I had become a ghost in this city. I no longer existed; I had no rights, dead to the world, and the laws could not save me. This meant that everything they did to me in that room did not count. These men could commit murder and they would never be charged.

And this seemed to be their plan, or at least to knock me out. Seeing that was what they wanted, I stopped fighting and let them hit me anywhere without trying to block. After taking two more kicks to the face, the enforcers stopped. Bending down, one of them checked to see if I was alive.

"Is he dead?" I heard the other guard ask.

"No!" his friend said. "But he is not far off."

"Good!" the first guard said. "Let's dump this trash then go eat."

Picking me up, the two men dragged me outside and headed in the direction of the Hole. The entrance to the Hole was on the top of a huge hill. I could hear the two men struggling as they dragged my limp body up the hill. At the top, I was laid on the ground, my feet facing the entrance.

The entrance itself was covered by wood boards with a small wooden door covering the opening. The opening itself was only big enough for a single man to fit.

As I lay there, I could hear one of the enforcers working at unlatching the door. With a slam, I knew the door was open. Opening my eyes, I could see one reaching for my feet while the other was over top of my head. Thinking quickly, I kicked out, knocking the man by my feet towards the opening.

I then reached up and put my hands around the throat of the man above me. He tried to remove my hands from his throat, but with my hands tied like they were he was finding it hard. So, he instead tried for my face, trying to put his fingers into my eyes, but before he could I gave his neck a great jerk. With a snap of his neck the man went down and did not move.

A yell made me look back at the opening of the Hole. There I saw the other enforcer picking himself out of the Hole. He then ran at me. Using his momentum, I was able to roll him onto his back and pin his arms down with my legs. Clamping my hands around his neck, I held him there until he stopped thrashing.

Sitting back, I sat down trying to catch my breath. But I could not stay there long; there was no telling when someone would come by. So, I began to search the bodies for anything that could help me. One for the enforcers had a knife that I used to cut my bindings.

But I couldn't go around in the clothes I had on. I was sill wearing the clothes of a criminal. But my answer to this was right in front of me. I found one of the enforcer's clothes fit me almost as if they were made for me.

Now with the enforcer's clothes and paperwork it was time to hide the bodies. But there was only one place I could hide them, in the Hole. So I dragged the bodies one by one over to the opening and let them drop. I could hear the bodies go crunch as they hit the floor below. With the bodies out of the way, I then threw down the robes and my old clothes, since I had no need for either one. I closed the Hole and walked south back to the houses.

Back in the residential area, I found myself drawn to the smell of food. Not having a decent meal for several weeks now, I could not resist the lure of the food. The smells led me to a small area that was set a side for the enforcers to eat while on duty.

The food was on warming trays over a large fire under a large wooden canopy. There were also two wooden tables and benches under the canopy. There were several enforcers sitting at these tables eating when I walked up.

Grabbing a tray, I headed right for the food where I began to load up my tray. Grabbing as much food that I could, I headed over to the tables and sat apart from the other enforcers. But I knew that I could not stay away from the others, for I soon found myself sitting around other enforcers who also just came in to eat.

My fears of being found out soon died out. No one there seemed to know my face, or at least believed I was indeed a newbie enforcer. So I ran with it; coming up with a fake name I quietly become one of the boys. After all, I did have a newbie look, the look as if you do not no what you are doing.

I had a scare when one of the enforcers asked about my broken nose, but I just told them I just got back from taking the criminal up to the Hole. I said before he went into the Hole, he smacked me once in the nose with his head.

The others just laughed after I told my story. Then they started to poke fun at my nose and cursing the criminal who broke my nose. Not knowing I was supposed to be that criminal rotting in the Hole.

I forced myself to laugh along with the others as they laughed and talked about the white robes. In many ways, the enforcers had a low opinion about the white robes, thinking of them as low-class filth, and as useless pieces of scum.

"I don't see how they can live like they do," one of the enforcers said speaking to the group. "I mean if they would only pick themselves off the floor and commit to the law, they could be just like us and then we would not need to worry about crime, right boys."

"You said it," another enforcer said.

"Yea," I said raising my cup for a toast. "Speaking of the low-class filth, I need to go on patrol."

With this I got up, returned my tray, and left. My departure was accompanied with farewells and more dirty jokes. In many ways, I could not have stood to sit there much longer. For the white robes were not the only ones being bad-mouthed; so were outsiders. Several times I had the thought of punching or kicking every one of those men, but it would not look good for me if I did.

Away from the table, I now had to think of what I had to do now. Getting out of the city was what I had to do, but just walking out the door for some reason did not seem to work for me. It was by far the easiest way for me to leave. All I had to do was walk up to the guard on duty and tell him I was to relieve him and once he was gone open the door and leave.

But I didn't just want to leave Lawmaker. I wanted to leave a massage. I wanted to show Marcus that his walls were nothing to an outsider. Everything can fall and be destroyed, but to do that I would need help.

Heading into the city, I came onto a familiar road. Taking a right into an alley, I came onto another road, turned right, and went down four houses before stopping in front of one of the houses. I knew no one was home so I looked left then right before entering the door.

Inside, I saw that the house looked just like the house I had used in my time in Lawmaker. Making my way to the back of the house, I lied myself down on the bed, and I fell the sleep.

It was the sixth bell that woke me. Getting up I made my way back to the front room to wait. While I waited, I grabbed a pencil and paper and started to write.

By time the door to the house opened, I had finished what I was writing. Sitting there, I watched as the look of surprise came over the man who walked into the door.

"It's good to see you again, Enigma," I said.

Enigma's shock wore off. He quickly closed the door, scared someone might see me. His back on the door, the basket of food in his hand, Enigma tried to find his voice.

"Wha—how, whe—," Taking a deep breath, he tried talking again, "I thought you were in the Hole. How did you escape, and how did you know this was my place?"

"Well, how I know where you live is simple," I said. "One day while I was on my way home, I saw you walk by; without the enforcers knowing, I followed you here before heading back to my place.

As for my escape from the Hole, it was easy. I never went into the Hole." Standing up, I showed off the enforcers robes I was still wearing. "Do you like my new clothes? It was unfortunate the enforcer who was wearing them before me had to take my place in the Hole. But what was I to do? After all, I was not just going to go to the Hole quietly. I would rather fight than go into that hell."

"But what are you doing here?" Enigma asked. "With those clothes, you could have headed to one of the gates and walked out. You could have been free of this place. I do not get why you are still here, and why you are in my house?"

"Because," I said, "I need your help to teach a lesson to Marcus and to this city. Sort of outsider justice as it was."

"And what does that mean?" Enigma asked.

"I mean I am planning to blow a hole into the Grand Justice's Great Wall and show him how fake his power is," I said watching his eyes widen.

"You can't," Enigma said as if saying this could stop me.

"You're right. I can't," I said, "at least not without your help."

"My help, what do you need my help for?"

"Samuel is holding some things for me. I need them brought inside."

"You want me to smuggle item into Lawmaker? No way!"

"Yes, you will!"

"And why would I do that?"

"Because I can still turn you in to the enforcers if you don't."

"You wouldn't?"

"I would!"

"But then how would you get the things you need into Lawmaker?"

"You forget I could still walk out of Lawmaker at any time I want?" I said standing up and walking over to Enigma.

"And what? Forget about you plans?" Enigma said trying to keep his distance from me.

"Oh, no my plan will go forward whether I am inside Lawmaker or outside Lawmaker," I said standing within a few steps from him. "But my plan would work so much better inside than outside. And more innocents' lives could also be saved if my plan were to happen inside, but again I need your help, Enigma."

"If I were to help," Enigma said stuttering, "what would I have to do?"

"Just get this note to Samuel," I said handing him the note. "It has all the items I need and instructions I would need him to follow. Once those items make it into Lawmaker, your job will be done. After that, it will all be up to me."

"Ok, but only so I can get rid of you," Enigma said walking over to the rug on the floor. "It will take time for me to do everything you want me to do, but until then you are going to stick out like a sore thumb. Even in that outfit you won't fool them for long. So, until everything is ready, you are going to have to use my guestroom."

The "guestroom" turned out to be a small place beneath the floorboards.

"May be a little uncomfortable, but it is the only place you can hide out of site," Enigma said.

"Don't worry, I am an outsider; uncomfortable is all I know."

With this said, I slid myself under the floor. Once I was settled in the floor, Enigma handed me a large loaf of bread and a big water skin.

"I may not be able to let you out every day so you may need to stay down there for several days," Enigma said picking up the first board. "So I would make what you have there last as long as possible, and you will need to stay quiet."

"I understand!" I said as the boards were placed over top of me.

Lying there under the floor, those long hours in the dark, you find yourself doing anything to try in make the time fly by. But without being able to speak or make any noise at all, you find there is not a lot you can do.

So, I spent my time going over my grand plan to leave Lawmaker. But there are only so many times you can go over something. After a while, you get tired of even your own thoughts. But with nothing else to do, you find yourself becoming bored, and with boredom comes sleep, and when you are not asleep you find yourself eating. And this is mainly what I did while I laid there—eat, sleep, and think.

Only twice was I able to get out from beneath the floor. The first time, Enigma told me my note had made it to the outside and he was now just waiting for a response. He also told me the two enforcers who I killed and threw into the Hole were finally missed. Everyone was to keep both their eyes and ears open for any sign or news of them.

"They are even saying if anyone ever learns what became of them will get a reward of extra food," Enigma told me as I saw to pressing matters.

When I emerged from the floor the second time, Enigma told me he had word from Samuel. The message said he was for the plan and he would do what he could to get the item into Lawmaker. He also said when the time came, he would see the second part of the plan would be ready.

"Good, everything is so far going like clockwork," I said throwing the note into the fire.

It had been five days after my escape from the Hole. All I had to do was wait a few more days and then I could leave this city with a bang.

It was three days later when Enigma removed the board for the last time. For on the table was everything I had asked for. Not only were my clothes, guns, and sword there but so were the explosives I had asked for. It was a good thing I just so happened to have been carrying all those things in the back of my vehicle.

With the item was a note from Samuel, as well. It said:

Dear Matrix,

Everything is ready on our side. A person will be waiting on the northwest side of Law-maker in the vehicle you told us about. This person will be there from midnight to dawn the perfect time for your plan.

I am hoping everything goes well and am hoping to see you again, as well as my wife. Please take care.

Samuel

"You told him about Susan?" Enigma asked reading over my shoulder.

"Yes, I did," I said throwing the note in the fire.

"But why? There is nothing he can do for her," he said sitting down. "Why did it sound like he will see her again?"

"You haven't figured it out," I said getting ready to go. "I am going to free her and all the others from their prisons."

"You can't," Enigma said standing up quickly.

"Watch me," I said looking over my guns.

"But you do not know what this will do to the people here."

"It should show Marcus's power is not all powerful. It will show that he is human," I said now wiping down my sword.

"I don't know," Enigma said falling back onto his chair. "It is too rash; too many things could go wrong. I can't believe Samuel would let this happen."

"This is because you forgot how much he loves Susan," I said placing the last explosive on my person. "It was because Susan knew how much Samuel loves her that she told people like you to never tell him that she was in jail. But I never made that promise, and I am not with Samuel, so I can say and do what I want."

"I could have left them all to suffer, but I owe a debt to Samuel. If it wasn't for his and your help, I would not be so close to meeting my goals."

Throwing my jacket on, I opened the door and walked out into the cold night.

Chapter 19

The Robin

I could smell the rain in the night air. Hopefully, the rain would hold off until we had made our escape.

I found my way though the houses as easily as my last midnight stroll. There were no signs of increased patrols. The Enforcers still did not think anyone would ever do what I was going to do. It was this that allowed me to make it through the houses without being seen.

With a quick dash, I cleared the area between the homes and the Grand Courthouse; once at the courthouse, I made my way around the east side, staying low as I moved.

Making my way to the east side of the courthouse, I lined myself up with the windows to the jails. Turning from the windows, I sprinted in the eastern side of the wall.

I picked a spot that was in between the east gate and the northeast corner. There I placed my first set of explosives. With the detonator and remote ready to go, I headed back to the courthouse.

Setting myself under the windows to the cells, I jumped up grabbing the bar and pulled myself up. Looking into the cell, I found the cell was empty, but the cells to either side each had a man in them.

Dropping to the ground, I walked over to the cell to my right. Jumping, I lifted myself up to the window. Inside I saw Jason sleeping.

"Jason," I whispered, "Jason, wake!"

Jason sat up in bed rubbing his eyes; he tried to see what had awakened him. Looking up at the window, he saw my face looking through the window just before I had lost my grip and fell to the ground.

"Matrix," I heard him say as I hit the ground.

My hand hurting, I began to rub them so to get the feeling in them before Jason fell back to sleep. But there was no need, for I could hear something being pulled closer to the window. In no time, I saw Jason's shocked face looking out the window.

"Matrix, it is you," he said in a whisper. "You're not a ghost, are you?"

"No, I am alive and well," I said trying to put him at ease. "But there is no time to tell you how I escaped. I need you to do something for me."

"What is it you need?"

"I am planning to break you all out tonight."

"How?"

"By blowing a hole in this wall and then another hole in the great wall."

"What!" Jason said in surprise.

"There is no time; take these," I said throwing what looked like black wires. "Those things in your hand will destroy the locks to your cells," I explained to him. "You need to hand those things out. Give one to Susan and two to Derrick. Then you all will have to put the tubes into the keyhole with the big cap sticking out. When you are all ready, all you need to do is pull on the big cap. You should not stand behind the door when it blows. Once it blows you and Derrick should then run over to the twin's cell and do the same.

"While you two are freeing the twins, I will blow a hole in this wall so you can all escape. Once you are all out, you will need to head for the wall, not to the door. I have placed more charges on the inner wall. Once we are all at the wall, I will blow those charges and we can leave Lawmaker forever."

"I don't know, Matrix," Jason said looking at the wires in his hand. "Do you really think we could do it?"

"We won't know until we try," I said. "If you have doubts, you do not have to go. But you should see what everyone else wants to do. You should know no matter what you all say I am leaving Lawmaker now."

Nodding, Jason turned away from the window. I could just hear him trying quietly to wake the others. Not wanting to waste time, I set the charges that I would need to blow the wall. Ready, I looked to find Jason once more looking out the window.

"I told everyone about your plan, Matrix," he said, "and we all are willing to try."

"Good," I said. "Then get ready to blow your locks. Once they go off, the guards will hear, so move quickly and get the twins out. Once I hear the explosion, I will wait three seconds before I blow the wall. So, you better be out of your cells by then."

"Okay, let's do it!"

Getting down from the window, I could hear the cot being moved so it was not in the way once the hole was made. After, I just waited. All was ready on my side; I just needed to wait for the sound of several explosions.

With a bang, I heard the explosions. Counting to three, I detonated the wall charges. The hole it made was about the size of the cell. Looking inside, I saw Jason and Derrick running out with one of the twins in their arms.

Running by me, I directed them into the direction of where I had set the explosives. With Susan running just in front of me, I began chasing after the others. I knew the explosions would soon gather a crowd to see what had happened, but once they learned the prisoners had escaped them they would be on the chase. So, all I had to worry about was to ensure the way was open before the chases began. But a gunshot changed my plans.

Turning around, I found myself looking at the four Enforcers, each one with a rifle in hand. Overcoming the shock, I quickly went for my gun and opened fire. Concentrating more on scaring the gunner, I made my target the wall around the hole instead of the men. All I wanted was to keep them from firing at us.

My guns empty, I turned and quickly regained the ground I had lost, reloading as I did. I was about to turn around and continue my assault when I felt one of the men's bullets fly passing my right ear. The near miss flew past me and found its mark in Susan. I watched, almost in slow motion, as the bullet entered Susan's left side and saw her fall to the ground.

Running to her, I quickly called to Jason and Derrick who had made it to the wall to return and help Susan. As they did, I fell to one knee and covered them. No longer was I aiming to scare; now I was now aiming to kill.

In no time at all, Jason and Derrick had Susan on their shoulders carrying her towards the wall. Knowing there was no time left to lose, I pulled out the detonator and detonated the charges knowing the twins were at a safe distance from the charges.

Reloading, I turned and ran watching as the twins ran through the hole in the wall heading for the vehicle, which I could see now. To buy more time for Derrick and Jason to get Susan out of the city, I found myself running backwards shooting as did. Once my clips were again empty; I turned and ran the rest of the way at full speed.

By that time, the twins made it to the vehicle. The driver had gotten out and picked up the kids in both arms and put them in the front set. Seeing Susan hurt and Derrick and Jason carrying her, he then opened the back and helped her in. Lying on Derrick's lap, I could just hear Jason telling Derrick to put pressure on the wound. Closing the door, Jason jumped in the bed of the vehicle and lied down.

Reaching the vehicle myself, I jumped into the bed as well. Falling to my knees, I told the driver to go. As the vehicle began to move, the riflemen had reached the hole, but before they could get a shot off, I sent a hail of bullets towards them. Soon, we were out of range of the rifles, and I put my head through the open back window to check on Susan. The rag in Derrick's hand was soaked in Susan's blood.

"It won't stop," Derrick said all most in tears.

"That is not our only problem," I said looking at Susan. "The bullet is still in there; I see no exit wound.

We need to get to the village now!" I said to the driver.

"Right," he said speeding up.

Sitting down, my back to the cab, I said to the air, "Hold on, Susan, hold on!"

We made it back to the village in good time, but whether it was good enough to save Susan, I did not know. As soon as we came to a stop, all hell broke loose. Both Jason and I were yelling out for help. The people who were running up in joy soon started running in concern.

In the lead, his face red, ran Samuel. Seeing the blood and the wound in Susan's back, he quickly took charge. Gently Susan was removed from the back seat and was now being carried by several of the townsfolk.

"To the doctor's place," I heard Samuel said.

As the group moved toward the nearest house, a man in white clothes came rushing out. Reaching the group, he quickly began to examine Susan. He saw that there wasn't an exit wound, and he insisted to those who carried Susan to hurry.

Susan's body was laid on a table just inside the Doc's house. Their job done, he told everyone except for Samuel to leave.

With the door closed in our faces, the people in the town came to us to see what had happened. Letting the others tell the story, I found myself heading back to my vehicle. Sitting on the ground by the back tire, I stared at the door where Susan was now fighting for her life.

As we waited, the storm finally hit; with a flash of lighting and a roar of thunder, the rain starting to fall. The townsfolk found shelter sitting down under overhangs, while others went into their homes. As for me, I stayed where I was, pulling up the hood I wore around my neck. As the storm raged, the people become more somber. It was as if the emotions of the people were being stolen by the storm.

But soon the storm seems to be letting up, and as the storm clouds passed the mood of the people seem to grow as bright as the light which come through the clouds. Finally, when the last of the clouds disappeared, the door to the Doc's place opened.

Getting up, I quickly made my way to the crowd around the doctor. Reaching the crowd, I could hear them all asking him the same question: "How is Susan?" Wiping his blood-soaked hand, he spoke to the crowd. "I was able to remove the bullet," he said speaking over the crowd. "The bullet passed close to Susan's heart, I am afraid, where it got stuck in one of her ribs. The damage caused by the bullet was too great. Internal bleeding is most likely, but I do not have the tools or the medicine to stop it. Not even the supplies Matrix has can help right now. I am afraid it is only a matter of time.

"If anyone wished to see Susan, you may," he continued, "but if you do don't over excite her. If she has any chances to survive, she has to rest." With this said, the doctor moved through the crowd heading to the well to clean the blood from his hands.

The news of Susan's condition was hard on everyone. Many fell in tears, while others tried to hide their tears. As for the rest, they didn't know what to do or how to feel. People just crowded the street in front of the Doc's place looking depressed.

It was my five companions and me that headed for the door to the Doc's house. It turned out the driver who helped us escape was the twins' father. He had been living here ever since he escaped Lawmaker, planning one day to save his family.

Inside the Doc's house, a woman, who looked as if she could have been the Doc's daughter, was busy cleaning up after the operation. With bloody rags in hand, she pointed us in the direction of Susan's bed.

The Doc's house was made up of two floors. The first floor was for his patients to use, and the second floor was where he and his daughter lived.

Passing the table where the Doc worked on Susan, our group walked into the next room. This room was filled with beds on both sides about five on each side. All the beds were empty except for one.

The curtains around Susan's bed were not all the way closed. Through the curtains, we could just see Samuel on the side for the bed, his hand holding Susan's.

Breaking from their father, the twins ran to the other side of Susan's bed. Stephanie wrapped her arms around Susan's neck and hugged her. With her spare arm,

Susan held on to little Stephanie's body as if she wished to ensure the little girl was real and safe.

Danny stood by his sister trying and failing to hold back his tears. Once in Susan's arms, the young man was unable to hold it in. For the first time in a long time, the young man was the little boy again. Looking up, Susan smiled at the man who now was holding Stephanie in his arms.

"So you are their Father?" she asked as Danny let go Susan turned to his Father.

"Yes, madam," the twins' father said. "I just want to thank you for all you did for my children. I also want you to know if I knew this was going to happen, I would never have left them. To lose my wife is bad enough. All I did I did for my children and my wife."

"You do not need to define your actions," Susan said taking the man's hand. "Your children told me everything. They know why you did what you did. What is more, they always believed that one day you would come to rescue them. You are a good man and very brave. Never be ashamed of what you have done and for whom you were doing it for."

The twins' father bowed his head to Susan, and with twins in hand he stepped back from the bed.

The next up was Derrick and Jason. Both men walked up to the bed and kissed her on the forehead before sitting. Both then held on to Susan's outstretched hand. The three speaking in soft tones, the two men trying their best to brighten the old woman's mood, trying their best to convince her and themselves that she would be fine in no time.

My mind was no longer here at this place. As I watched everyone sitting with Susan, seeing their sad faces, the only thing I could think of was this had all happened because of me. I was the reason Susan was dying. I was the cause of Samuel's wife's death. The more I thought about it, I knew I did not deserve to be here.

So, without a word, I turned and headed for the door.

"Matrix," Susan's voice seemed to stop me in my tracks. "Where are you going? Were you going to leave without saying a word?"

With my back to the bed and all those people who cared for her, I remained silent.

"You were?" Susan's said sitting up in bed.

"Susan!" Samuel said. I could hear him trying to get her to lie back down. "You need to get your rest."

"Not until Matrix turns around," Susan said looking at him coldly. "Why are you trying to leave, Matrix?"

"I do not belong here," I said my back still turned.

"What do you mean?" Derrick said standing up.

"Everything that has happened was because of me," I said. "Susan is dying because of me. It was my plan, but I didn't think there were guns in Lawmaker. I should have known or at least suspected there may have been guns in Lawmaker."

"And what would that have changed?" Samuel said.

"I would have had more guns brought in, bigger guns," I said hitting the wall. "I should have been ready to go to war in Lawmaker, but I underestimated my enemy."

"You could not have known Marcus had armed his men, Matrix!" Susan said; the strain of sitting up could be heard in her voice.

"She is right, Matrix," Samuel standing. "In our time, there were no guns in Lawmaker. We who sit in the seat of power did not think it would be wise to have such thing. But Marcus must have gathered some before the wall was complete."

"This is not your fault, Matrix," Susan said. "If we the ones who founded and now fight to protect and save the city didn't know of the guns in Lawmaker how would you a stranger to our land know?"

"But I should have been the one to be shot," I said turning around facing the bed.

"Why do you say that?" Susan said with a sigh as she laid herself back down on the bed.

"The bullet missed, just missed hitting me," I said hanging my head. "I should have been the one that got shot."

"Why do you say that?" Susan asked a look of concern flooding her face.

"Because I felt the bullet pass by my ear. I heard it fly by," I said not looking at Susan. "If it was a few inches to the left I would have been hit, should have been hit."

"I see!" Susan said. "But are you sorry that that bullet didn't hit you, or are you scared that the bullet was so close that it almost did."

"I didn't," I said not really knowing what to say.

"So, what would have happened if the bullet hit you and not me? What then?" Susan asked.

"What?"

"If the bullet hit you and not me, what would have happened then?"

"I don't know!"

"Would you have died?

If the bullet was as close as you say it was, wouldn't it kill you?"

"Most likely," Matrix said.

"Then what? Could we have made it out without your help?"

"You would have survived!"

"Maybe, but would we have been able to get out of the city, for you had the detonator."

At this I remained silent. I did not know how to answer her. In truth, I didn't know what to say.

"The rest of us do not know anything about your explosive," she said. We would have not been about to get out of Lawmaker if it was not for you," Susan said then paused before continuing. "You are the very reason we have all made it out of Lawmaker. Thanks to you, Stephanie and Danny are now with their own father. Would Derrick and Jason have the chance to be together, to have the chance to make their own lives away from Lawmaker? Even I have the chance to be with my husband even if these will be my last days.

All this will mean nothing if you blame yourself for my death," Susan said. "I do not want you to feel my death is your fault. This old woman will not rest in peace knowing you do feel this way."

"I promise I won't," I said. "The only one I will blame is Marcus. He is the cause of all of this, and I will have my revenge."

"Yes, but not today," Samuel said. "We have other things to attend to."

At this everyone looked down at Susan.

"Besides, now we know there were guns in Lawmaker; we now need to know what kind and how many they have," Samuel said. "As for you Matrix, isn't there something else you need to do? Another promise you made to someone else?"

"You're right, my father's killer," I said thinking about all the information I gathered in the Lawmaker records room. "I will find my father's killer, but when you are ready to attack Lawmaker and take down Marcus, I will be ready to fight with you. After all, I already told Marcus I would return. I don't want to look like a liar,"

"When the time is right, we will wait for you, Matrix," Samuel said. "Lord knows we could use all the help we can find. But know if we can't wait, or those sent to find you cannot bring you back in time."

"It will be fine," I said, "as long as Mucus is taken down it will be fine."

The time after the visit seemed to fly by. The twins' father Michael put us up for the night. Even with the twins now living in his home, he still had two extra rooms available. I laid in bed, my eyes on the ceiling, my mind on Susan's condition.

I wasn't the only one getting a sleepless night tonight. Everyone in town I was sure was having the same problem. As for Samuel, he was last seen in the same chair, his head on the bed sleeping with his wife.

Tiredness must have over taken me, for the next thing I remember was waking up to a loud cry of pain.

It was still early when I stepped outside, an orange light coming from the east. I was not the only one up; the whole town seemed to have heard what I heard and had come out to see what had happened. Turning to the doctor's house, the mob of people moved as one to check on Susan.

On reaching the house, we found Samuel outside his head in his hand sitting on the ground. Once there, the people just started to probe the grief-stricken man with questions. But in many ways, everyone knew what had happened. Susan was dead.

I had never been to a real funeral before, never having been in a place long enough and knowing any one for long. Even in the small village my father and I lived in, we didn't have a funeral take place. I did bury the members of the Shadow Matrix, yes, but a burial and a funeral were two different things. Anyone can bury a person, but only family and friends would ever celebrate the person's life and death.

In many ways, Susan's funeral was the only thing keeping me in the town. Normally, I would have left as soon as possible, but this time, I felt I like I needed to stay a little longer.

Not knowing what was needed for a funeral, I stayed out of the way for the most part. Though when I was asked, I lent a hand when needed. One of the things I was asked to help with was the digging of the grave.

Next to the town not too far away there was a place where the townsfolk buried their dead. The graveyard was not that big and had very few graves. The site for Susan's grave was close to the middle of the graveyard.

Grabbing a shove, I began to dig along with the three other men who were given the job. By time the sun was high in the sky, the grave was finished, and we headed back to the town. When we got back to town, there was just enough time for us to wash up before the funeral.

Once cleaned, I made my way to where the funeral was to be held. Due to the fact that the entire town was going to be at this funeral, it was to be held outside.

Right on the main road, chairs and stools had been set up in two groups of eight rows leaving a path between the two groups. In front of the rows of seats was a long bench. On top of the bench was a large wooden box; inside was Susan.

After I paid my respects to her, I found myself a seat and sat down. Once everyone was seated, there were several men and women who stood up before the group saying a few words about Susan and her life. Among those who spoke were Samuel and the holy leader of this town. After everyone who wished to speak said their peace, I stood up and with Samuel and two others picked up the box with Susan's body and carried it to the grave.

Gently we lowered Susan into the freshly dug earth and stood to one side. Once more the holy leader said a few words over the grave. Then one by one the people of the town said their final goodbyes to Susan before heading back to the town.

Once Samuel departed, the holy leader beside him, it was time for us who dug the grave to fill it with dirt.

I did not spend too much after the funeral. I had planned to leave early the next morning. So, it was two hours later, and I excused myself and headed back to the twins' father's home. Back in my room, I quickly undressed and went right to sleep.

I woke up shortly after sun rose; I dressed and headed outside. On my way out, I grabbed some of the food from last night and began to eat as I stepped outside.

My vehicle was parked on the side of the house, my bags already inside. Turning the corner, I found there were several people standing near by. It was Derrick, Jason, the twins, and their father, and Samuel.

"Well, I didn't expect to see you all here," I said walking up to them.

"You mean to say you were trying to leave without saying goodbye," Derrick said grinning.

"Trying but failed," I said shaking his hand. "So, are you two going to be staying here?"

"No!" Jason said with his hand out. "Derrick and I are planning to leave sometime after you."

"Going out to see the world?" I said with a smile.

"Something like that," Jason said.

"Well, good luck to the both of you," I said.

"You too, Matrix," Derrick replied.

As Derrick and Jason stepped back, the two twins came running towards me. Bending down, I let the two wrap their arms around me. Both seemed to be on the verge of tears.

"Mr. Matrix, do you really have to go?" Stephanie asked with tears in her eyes.

"Yes, I do little one. I do," I said.

"But why?" she asked.

"Because there is thing I need to take care of," I said. "Things that are important to me, and I can't do them here."

"What things?" she asked, and here I chose my words carefully.

"I made a promise to someone, and I need to go and do it for them," I said. "Because they were important to me like your father and brother are to you. You understand?"

"I think so," she said wiping her eyes.

"Good!" I said before turning to her brother. "You will take good care of your sister right."

"I will!" Danny said drying his eyes and trying to act tough.

"That is what big brothers are for, to watch out for their sisters, right?" I said.

"Right!" he said standing tall.

"Good, then I will not have to worry about you two, not while you are together, right?"

"Right," they said as one.

Nodding the two headed to their father who held out a hand to me.

"I don't think I will ever thank you enough for what you have done for my family," he said.

"I am glad I was able to help," I said standing and taking his hand. "You have two great kids. Take care of them."

"I will, and thanks again."

Walking over to my vehicle, I found Samuel there holding the door open for me. When I came close, we shook hands before speaking.

Good luck to you," he said trying to hide the sorrow for the loss of his wife.

"And to you," I said.

Stepping inside, Samuel closed the door behind me, before peering through the open window. At first, it looked as if he wanted to say something more, but then he seemed to decide not to. Instead, he banged on the window doorframe and stepped back.

Kicking the engine into life, I waved to my friends before slowly driving off. In the mirrors, I could see them waving back, the twins running after me. In no time at all, I passed the last of the homes heading back into the wild world.

Chapter 20

The Coyote

"I never knew your life was filled with so much misery," the bartender said.

"We have all felt great misery since the Great Disaster," Matrix said. "There are just those who have seen more than their fair share of it."

"So, where did you go after that?" the bartender asked.

"Many places," Matrix said, "but what is important is what I found."

"What?" the bartender asked.

"Why not cook me something good to eat and I will tell you," Matrix said.

The bartender went right to work preparing a dish worthy of a king. With the smell of food cooking in the air, Matrix continued to speak.

Once I was on the road again, I had turned my thoughts back to what I had learned back in Lawmaker. I had made sure the knowledge had been engraved into my mind. Even in my cell, I had spent many hours recounting what I had learned and did the time under Enigma's floor.

Now I was away from it all, I could recall everything I read in that file. I just hoped the knowledge would serve me well.

The hardest part was making the journey back to my father's village. I still hated to think about what happened there, but it was the only starting point I had for the stranger.

The file spoke of a pattern the stranger used when he was the S.A. Killer. I knew which direction he came from so if he followed the same pattern as before, I should be able to go in the same direction he would have gone afterward. That is if he hadn't changed his ways since then.

I soon found out he hadn't. For two days later, I found the charred remains of a town. From what I could see, the town had been built from the bones of the old world. The place was badly burned, but what was left was enough for me to believe the Stranger was here.

So, I followed the path the Stranger left. Following a new direction every time I found a new town or village destroyed. My eyes fell upon dozens of towns and villages which were destroyed by the Stranger, and I soon found myself feeling nothing for those who lost their live. I only felt excitement at the new discovery.

But I did not just find direction on my journey; I also found life. For there were several towns and villages that did not fall victim to the Stranger; there were some that the Stranger left alone. At these rare moments, I would speak to those in the town or village and ask them about the Stranger.

They were surprised about what I had to say about the man, for they would always speak of him in high favor, calling him a kind and gentle man. When these people asked why I was looking for him, I would simply say he was just an old friend I was looking for. The people would then point me in the direction he went, and I would keep moving.

On my travels, I came to another destroyed village. Driving through I quickly estimated the destruction couldn't be more than a week or two old; this meant I was not too far away from my goal.

As I drove through the destroyed homes, I saw an old man lying in the road. Slamming on my brakes, I stopped just short of the man. It was like the old man was unaware of me or how close I came to killing him.

Lying there swinging his right foot on his left knee, the old man seemed to be humming a tune, his eyes on the sky. Stepping out of my vehicle, I walked around to the old man.

"Hey, old man," I said walking up to him. "Can you move, sir?"

The old man did not move at all, or even respond to my question. He just lied there humming his tune. Getting mad, I walked around the old man to get in front of him.

"I asked," I said, "are you going to move, or do I have to move you?"

Now in front of the old man, I could see his eyes were closed and his humming had grown louder. My anger raging, I grabbed the old man and pulled him to his feet.

"Are you deaf, old man, or just dumb?" I said shaking him.

"No!" he said caching me by surprise. "I was just waiting for you to try to make me move."

With speed I would not expect from a man of his age, he struck me in the stomach with his palm. The sudden move made me release my grip on the old man and stumble backwards. Holding my stomach, I looked up just in time to see him jump in the air and kick me on the side of my head.

Falling to ground, I soon found myself at the point of a sword. Looking down I recognized the blade as my own. Feeling for my sword case, I found that indeed it was empty. The old man's speed was incredible; not only did he hit me in the stomach he also stole my sword from the case.

Lying there beaten and humiliated, I waited for the old man to finish me off. But he did not make a move to finish me; he just stood there over me, the sword in his hand, the tip under my chin.

"What are you waiting for?" I demanded. "Are you going to kill me or not? If you are, then do it already!"

"And what would a boy like you learn from me killing you?" the old man said.

The question was an odd one, and I did not know how to answer it. I was just lying there looking at the old man as if he were speaking in another language.

"I see you are more hopeless than I could image," the old man said. "To think you have such a wonderful weapon in your possession, but you do not know how to use it."

"Give me my sword back, and I will show you how I use it," I said to defend myself.

The old man then cracked a smile and took a few steps backwards. Confused, I slowly got to my feet never taking my eyes off the old man. Once on my feet, the old man grabbed the sword by its blade and pointed the handle to me. I saw he held the blade so I could neither slash his hand nor stab him in the stomach with the sword.

As I grabbed the sword, the old man released the blade and stood in front of me waiting. Up to this point, I truly had very rarely used the sword for anything. I relied more on my guns than I did with the sword. The only times I did use the sword were when I was in a fight those who came at me with knives or daggers, and for those times I used it just for intimidation reasons.

But now I was fighting someone who obviously knew more about fighting with swords than I did. But I was not going to be stopped by an old man; I was going to find the way to beat him just so I could keep moving forward.

Grabbing the handle tightly in my hand, I charged the old man swinging the sword as I did. In spite of my best attempt to hit the old man, he managed to dodge my swings. As I swung the sword, my anger grew as I continued to miss my target. My anger growing to its peak, I grabbed the sword in both hand and swung it down trying to split the old man in two.

With great skill, the old man caught the blade between his hand just inches from his head. He then managed to bring the blade down and to the side and held it there. I then felt my hand releasing the handle as the old man's foot made contact with my stomach.

Quickly catching my breath, I went for my gun not ready to give in to this old man. But the old man was ready for me. Flipping the sword around, he caught it and swung it at me. Before I knew what happened, the old man had knocked my guns out of my hand and in the same move kicked me to the ground.

For the second time, I was on the ground, my own sword under my throat. Turning my eyes away from the old man, I just waited for death. But again, death did not come quickly; it seemed as if the old man just didn't have it in him to kill me. Now for the first time, I truly wondered why.

"Why?" I asked. "Why won't you kill me?"

"Are you in a hurry to die?" the old man asked.

"No, but in this world, it is kill or be killed."

"Is that truly how you see the world, young man?"

"It does not matter how I see the world; it is just how it is."

"So, you mean to say that if I do not kill you, you will kill me instead."

"Yes, no, what?"

"You said you wanted to kill me; isn't that true?"

"No, I didn't. I just wanted you to move, that's all."

"Well, then you must have expected I planned to kill you then?"

"Yes, no, I mean I don't—"

"Well then, if you weren't going to kill me and I am not going to kill you then is this really a kill or be killed world?" At this the old man took a step back allowing me to sit up.

"I don't know," I admitted more to myself than to the old man.

"Of course you don't," he said handing me my sword. "After all, you are still so young and know only the violence of this world. You never had the chance to experience the peace of the old world and it is a true lost.

Walking over, the old man picked up my guns, which he had knocked out of my hand. He examined them for a while before he returned them to me. He then sat down in front of me.

I was not there for this. I mean I remember everything that happened, but I didn't react to what was going on. My mind was just listening to what was being said.

"Tell me," the old man said breaking the long silent, "do you even remember how this fight started?"

I had to think for a moment before I could answer him. As I did, I found it was hard to think how things got started. I had only known this old man for thirty minutes, but I felt like it has been hours if not days. It probably made it hard for me to remember quickly. When I finally remembered, I hung my head.

"I started this," I said. "I was the one who tried to hurt you first. All you did was defend yourself. This is my fault."

"Yes!" the old man said. "Your anger bested you this day, and you were ready to harm an old man. If you had calmed yourself down, you would have seen another way and avoided this conflict."

"I, I don't know what to say," I said.

"The curse of youth," the old man said. "Always quick to action, but slow when it comes to thinking things through. If you did you would know you could have just gone around me instead of through me. In many ways, it would have been the faster route to take."

"But now why don't you speak of the reason for your haste," the old man said. "Come, my tent is not far. We can speak in private and share a meal while you speak."

Getting up, I followed behind the old man as he led me to a small tent that was pitched next to one of the burned-out buildings. With my large bag of food in hand, I walked into the small tent.

Sitting down in the center of the tent, the old man offered a canteen of water. Taking the canteen, I drank deeply before handing it back to him. Putting the canteen down, the old man then tossed a can of food at me.

Catching it, I thanked the old man before opening it. As I did, I felt a sense of familiarity as if the can was familiar to me. On a whim, I looked down at the bag to my side. Looking closely, I found the bag had been opened.

Looking at the old man, I saw a small grin cross his face. The fact was the old man had taken several cans from my bag in that small time I spent drinking from the canteen he handed me.

"You are good, old man," I said knowing there was nothing I could do about what just happened.

"What do you mean?" he said playing innocent.

"I mean the way you took the cans from my bag without my noticing you," I said. "You are good."

"Or you are just not that observant of what is going on around you," he said. "Remember you did not even notice when I took your sword in our fight as will. You need to become more aware of your surroundings. You never know what your enemies may use against you.

But enough of this," the old man said. "Tell me now where you are heading, and why you were willing to fight an old man to get there."

So, I told him everything that had happened. I told him about my father and the village we lived in. I described to him about the night my father died, and everything I could remember about the Stranger, including what I learned in Lawmaker. I talked for several hours without stopping.

As I talked, he sat quietly eating as if he had never eaten before in his life. Finishing off his tenth can of food, silence fell as my story came to an end. I had eaten with him, but only to help to keep my throat from going dry. Unlike the old man, I was only able to eat three cans to his ten.

Finally, the old man placed the can on the ground leaning back and placing a hand on his stomach. Closing his eyes, it looked as if he was locked in deep thought. For close to twenty minutes, he sat there thinking before sitting up straight.

"You intend to find this man and kill him, do you not?" the old man finally said.

"I do!" I said without hesitation.

"But how do you plan to kill him?" the old man asked.

"With these," I said pointing to my guns.

"Your guns?" the old man started. "Your guns, I think, will not help you. By your own words, you caught the Stranger by surprise when you wounded him. Then when your father faced him and died, he avoided your father's shots. It's true your father wounded the man first, but you told me that your father was a peaceful man who could not kill a man. I am sure the Stranger saw what was in your father and let the first shot be fired, but when they faced each other again your father could then kill if only to save you.

"No, I do not think you will be able to get a shot off unless you are extremely lucky to catch him off guard, but after your last encounter, he would most likely start protecting himself better than when you first met. But maybe I am just thinking too much. It is a problem; I have some time. Just unable to shut up my own mind.

"My point I am trying to make is your skills as a marksman and hunter may be fantastic, but you have no skills as a swordsman or fighter. If you were to add these skills to the skills you already have, you could become something greater. You could become a warrior. This man you seek seems to be a great warrior himself. His skills seem to allow him to predict what his enemy will do before they do it. But it is clear this man focuses more on power than on speed. I know this just in the way you say he kills, a powerful strike to the throat with a dull knife.

"If you truly want a chance to beat this man, you need to become faster than your enemy, for only incredible speed can match incredible strength. Speed you can gain, but only if you train with me. If you want to learn what I have to teach, you must listen to everything I say and do everything without question. I will even show you how to use the sword by your side like a true master."

"So, what do you say?"

I do not know why I did at the time, but I agreed to be his student that day. Something inside me told me the things the old man said, or from this point on my Master, was right. The skills I had at that point were not enough if I were going to fight the Stranger, again. I needed to become stronger and my new Master had the skills I needed to get stronger.

The time with my Master seemed to move fast. It seemed that in no time it had been almost two weeks, and within those two weeks, I had already mastered the basics of fighting. Though, how I could not tell you, my Master's ways of training were hard to get used to.

From morning to night, I was told to wear weights on my legs, hands, and body. At first, it was difficult to move with all the extra weight, but as time went on, the weight became easier for me to move. Though, when it became too easy, my Master would just add more weight to my body.

For two weeks, I trained in this fashion, my strength and speed growing along with my new skills. Like when I was taught by my father, I learned fast. I quickly had the basics down pat, but my Master did not seem to think I was ready to move on.

"Master, may I ask a question?" I had asked after a long day of training.

"Indeed, you can, and I can answer your question if I have the answer to your question," he said speaking in riddles as always.

"Well, it's just, when do you think we can move on with my lessons?" I asked. "I mean, we have been doing the same thing for two weeks now. I thought we would have moved to something more advanced by now."

"So, you feel you are ready to continue your training with me?"

"Yes, Master!"

"You may say you are ready, but I do not know," he said. "The advanced training is not as easy as what you have done so far. Moreover, I am not sure if you can even perform the training at all. Many things must happen if you are to succeed. You may not have what it takes to succeed."

"Whatever it is, Master, I know I can do it! I have no doubt or fear I will not succeed! All I ask is the chance to try."

"If that is what you truly believe then I will consider the matter, but for now get some rest. You have a long day and you need your sleep."

Knowing there was nothing more I could say or do to convince my Master's mind, I bowed my head to him. I then rolled out my bedding, removed the weights from my body, and went to sleep.

I had slept quite peacefully ever since I started my training. Every night, I found my body worn out. The carrying of those weights while performing everyday tasks as well as my exercises drained me of all my strength. There were times I woke up seeming more tired than when I went to sleep.

When morning came, I was up and dressed in no time. By time I started to put on my weights for the day, I noticed my Master was not in the tent. Normally, he would still be asleep and would not wake up until I had the morning meal done. But today for whatever reason, he was up before I was.

Sure, my Master would be back, and when he returned, he would want his meal. I began my routine. Stepping out of the tent I went to gather the water, the firewood, and the other morning tasks my Master made me complete since starting my training.

By the time my Master returned, I had the fire started and the food was almost finished cooking. Sitting down, I handed him a plate of food and we began eating. No one spoke during our meal; we just sat in silence eating. I knew if I wanted to know where my Master was, I would need to wait for him to tell me.

"I know you want to know where I was this morning," my Master said as he finished his food.

"I do want to know, Master."

"Well, the truth is I was thinking about what we were talking about last night." My Master paused putting his plate down. "I had decided that you may be right in that you are ready to continue your training."

"Really, Master, you think so?" I said unable to control my excitement.

"Yes! But I am still not sure if you will indeed succeed in you training," my Master said.

"I understand, Master," I said.

"Fine, then we will start now," my Master said standing up and walking over the opening. "To the east of here there is a river; I want you to find it and flow in it. Moving with the water you will come to a waterfall that falls into a pond. It then flows into a stream that moves through the forest. Behind the waterfall there is a cave; find the cave and stay there for one month."

"While you are there, you are to hunt for your food and survive. But there is a catch: You cannot take your guns, nor are you allowed to make any bow or spear to help you hunt. You can only use your bare hands, your sword, or your knife. Do you understand me?"

"I understand what you said, Master," I said. "But I do not know what this training will do. I mean, Master I have survived in the wilderness all my life."

"Maybe, but you have done so with a gun or a bow; you never had to get close up on to your prey," he said. "This part of your training will make you fight close up just so you can survive. And see how your prey will be faster than you; you will find your speed must increase if you want to live."

"But if I am wearing these weights how do I catch anything?" I asked standing up slowly.

"There is no need to fear, for once you get to the cave you can remove the weights so you may move freely," my Master explained. "But you will still be required to use the weights when you do your exercises either before bed or in the morning. After your exercises, you can go without for rest of the day or night. I leave it up to you."

"Very well, Master, I may still not understand the reason for all this, but I will do as you say," I said bowing to him.

Chapter 21

The Wolf

I spent the next few minutes preparing to leave. In no time, I was on my way. Traveling east, I made it to the river by high noon. Following the flow of the river, I moved with haste. I needed to find the cave my Master spoke of before nightfall.

As I followed the river, I watched as the current grew faster and faster which meant I was getting closer to the falls. Before I could see the falls, I heard the noise of the falls and found myself running faster.

In no time, I found myself on top of the falls looking down. It was just like what my Master said. The falls fell into a great pond which then passed through the forest in a small stream. Looking around I found a small path that would lead me down to the ground.

Turning from the site in front of me, I made my way down the path. The path was not big, so one needed to move slowly or risked falling. Beneath the falls, there was a small ledge that moved into the cave.

Walking on to the ledge, I made my way into the cave. It was very large inside the cave, and on the back wall was a small rock shelf. Moving to the shelf I removed the weights and laid them on the shelf.

Turning towards the opening, I made my way out and down the path to the pond. Once there, I undressed and jumped into the pond. Washing up, I redressed and moved towards the forest.

I needed to find some food before nightfall. I did not have the time to hunt properly, so I would just have to find some fruits and vegetables for the night. Thankfully, I knew what things were eatable and which were not.

Moving with the stream, I made my way into the forest. I soon found many fruit trees and eatable plants. Using my jacket, I gathered these plants and fruits as I moved deeper into the forest, and I soon found myself in a tree picking apples.

Sitting in the tree, I sat back, my jacket of food hanging from a branch. Grabbing an apple, I ate it hungrily. As I did, I sat there listening to the forest. I found peace in the place, a calm, that I had not felt for a long time.

Suddenly, the sound of wolves could be heard coming closer. Looking down I could see a hunting pack chasing after a doe.

Not moving, I watched as the pack hunt down the doe right below me. Killing the doe, I watched as the pack divided up the doe. Sitting in the tree, I found myself thankful that I had bathed before looking for food. But as I was waiting for the pack to move on, I found myself craving for meat.

I drew my sword and was prepared to strike. Perched on the branch, I readied to jump down; steeling myself I leaped off, my sword blade pointing down.

Landing on top of one of the wolf's back, my sword ran through it's neck. The wolf was dead almost instantly. Looking up from my kill, I saw the other wolves standing around me crouched and ready to strike.

Standing over my kill, I stood ready to fight, but as I looked into the eyes of the wolves around me, a strange feeling come over me. I was calm and relaxed not afraid of the wolves around me. At an impulse, I raised my head and howled.

Facing the wolves again, I found myself changing my grip on my sword. The blade parallel to the ground, I stood crouched ready to strike just like the pack. My left hand was just hanging in the air over my right hand, which was holding the sword. My face was taking on a fierceness to it in many ways like the snarling wolf pack before me.

I was ready to fight for my kill, and I was not going to let this pack get in my way. But the pack no longer seemed to want to fight; in fact it looked as if the pack was almost afraid of me. Several seconds went by and still the pack did not make a move. Finally, the pack grabbed what they could from the doe before turning and running back into the forest.

With the wolf pack gone, I finally began to relax. Putting my sword away to retrieve my jacket, which contained the fruits and other plants I had found earlier, I carried both it and the slain wolf back to the cave.

Once back at the cave, I put what was in my jacket on the stone bench in the back of the cave. Then taking my knife, some rope I had, and the wolf, I went back down to the edge of the forest. There I hung the wolf's body and began to skin it.

Once it was skinned, I used the water from the pond to clean both the hide and the wolf body. The hide I had planned on using like a bedroll for the hard-stone bench.

Once the hide was cleaned, I began to cut up the wolf into small pieces; any leftovers I had I buried a little way from my camp. On my return, I picked up wood I would use to cook the meat and keep me warm through the night.

Back in the cave, I started to work on the fire pit, using stones I had picked up earlier. In no time at all, I had a blazing fire going and had several pieces of meat cooking on two well-polished flat stones. Using some of the plants I gathered I was even able to season the meat.

By time I had finished eating, the sun had completely set. Picking up the wolf's hide, I went over to the stone bench and laid it down. Using by jacket like a pillow, I lied down on the hide.

In the morning, I found I was well rested, and I could sleep more freely. I was truly able to sleep through the whole night without the fear I would be attacked in the night. I ate a small meal from last night before getting dressed.

With my sword on my hip, I made my way to the opening of the cave. Walking outside, I found myself looking down at a large pack of wolves. Fearing for my life, I quickly hid myself back in the cave.

Poking my head outside the cave, I could see the wolf pack looked relaxed. They were just sitting and lying around the pond area. I could not tell if the pack was from the same pack I meet yesterday or if it was another pack. If it was the same pack, then were they here just here for a rest or did they track me here for some sort of revenge?

Either way, I was not about to go outside while a pack of wolves was outside. I was just going to have to wait and see what would happen.

Watching the wolves from the cave, I could see they made no moves towards the cave I was in. I did, however, see them go in and out of some of the lower caves I had noticed yesterday. To me this told me the wolves were not going anywhere soon.

By midday, I was becoming very hungry, but I had already eaten all the food I had from last night. Looking out, I could see there would be no way to get around the pack without being seen. Even if I went up the path in the direction I came from, there was not much food up there to last me at all.

Before I could make up my mind, I saw one of the wolves moving up the path towards my cave. Backing into the cave, I grabbed my sword and drew it. Turning to face entrance, I found myself facing down the wolf.

It moved slowing into the cave. In its mouth it looked to be carrying a leg of a deer. Seeing me, the wolf stopped just inside the cave's mouth. Not moving, the wolf lowered its head and dropped the leg. Backing away from the leg, the wolf turned and walked out of the cave.

With caution, I moved towards the leg and the opening. Looking out, I could see the wolf who had come into the cave was already back down by the pond. It seemed as if all it wanted was to bring me some food. I just did not know why.

Picking up the leg, I quickly made a fire and roasted the deer leg. After the scare at seeing the wolf pack and the wolf coming into the cave, the meat on the leg seemed to be the best thing I had ever had.

Done eating, I stood up and went to the falls to clean myself up, as well as get a drink and to get some relief. As I did, I was watching the wolves, both to make sure they were not going to attack me and out of general curiosity.

Looking down at the pack, I watched as the mothers bathed and watched over their cubs. Watching those same cubs playing and getting into trouble, all the while the males were looking and watching out for trouble, protecting the pack. It is the same with the humans, all just struggling to survive.

Heading back into the cave, I decided I wait for now before trying to leave the cave. I still did not have any idea what would happen if I were to leave to cave, and I did not want the upset the wolves right now.

Back in the cave, I put on my weights and started my exercises. When I finished, I went back out to the falls to clean up.

Sitting at the opening of the cave, I looked and watched the wolf pack the whole day. As the sun moved to the horizon, my friendly wolf from this afternoon returned with more meat in his jaws. He moved with caution towards me, dropping the meat just in front of me.

As he did, I slowly reached out with my hand to touch him on his head. He didn't snap at me nor did he move away. In fact, he seemed to move closer to me. Petting him between the ears, he sat down and kept me company for a time.

It was then I no longer felt afraid of the wolves. By the second day, I found myself out of the cave and down with the pack. It was strange at first to be in the middle of all these wild animals, but the same time normal. It was like I was more at home with the wolves than with humans.

As time passed, I became closer to the wolves. It wasn't long before I began going out with the hunting pack. At first, I was not able to keep up with the wolves. But within a week, I found I was becoming faster.

I was soon able to hunt with the wolves as an equal. At first I was using my sword to hunt, then with knife, and before the month ended, I could hunt with my bare hands.

It seemed like in no time, my time there was over. The night before I was to go, I spent the time with the pack. In the morning, I headed back up to my cave to gather my things. Once I was ready to go, I headed up the path to the top of the falls. Not surprised, I found many of the wolves there waiting for me.

During my time with the wolves, I had learned a way to communicate with them. I learned to understand them to a degree and them with me. It was with this method: I was able to tell the wolves what I was going to be doing today and that was why they were here now.

Walking up, the Sliver, the wolf who first came to my cave, scratching between his ears, I tried to tell him I would come back if I could. Through his eyes I could see he understood my meaning, but there was something more in there. It was like he was telling me if I were ever in need of the pack's help, they would come to my aid. Thanking them once more, I begin my journey back to my Master's

Thanks to my training, I found I could move faster than when I first started. By midday, I had return to the ruined city. It was now the matter of finding my Master.

Before I could even start my search for him, a masked man attacked me. Without words, the man attacked striking with fearsome moves. Blocking his first few attacks, I managed to fight back. But it seemed as if we were too evenly matcedh to get an edge over the other.

As our fight went on, I found my thoughts returning to my time with the wolves and the things I learned with them. It wasn't long before I began to use what I learned in this fight. So, my moves took on more of a wolfish style. Breaking apart, we stood facing off against one another.

"That is quite a welcoming, Master!"

"So you know it was me, did you," my Master said removing his mask.

"It was not hard to figure it out," I said scratching my muscles.

"I can see you have become a more skilled fighter," he said walking over to the tent.

Walking to the tent, we took a seat by the fire. Looking around the tent, I saw that not much had changed. The only different was my bag of food was half empty.

"I can see you have learned a lot in your time away, young student." He grabbed a couple of cans from my bag and tossed one to me.

"So why not tell me about your time in the wild."

The rest of my day was spent telling my Master all about my time with the wolves. With his head on his hand, my Master looked calm.

"To be honest, I do not think you are able do the training, but it would seem he was right after all."

"What do you mean and who are you talking about?"

"It is a long story," my Master said. "It all starts back before the Great Disaster, back when I was around your age. In those days, I was a martial artist fighting in mixed martial arts competitions and tournaments around the world. I would even fly to them in my own plane.

"One day I was flying to a competition when my plane crashed. I found myself lost in the middle of nowhere. My first few days were spent just trying to survive. With the wing of my plane, I was able to make it into a tent using things from my bag; I was even able to close it off for protection from the wind.

"I was even able to find water in the ground just inside my shelter, but still there was the problem about food. There was some food in the plane and I also had some snack bars in my bags, but they were not going to last long. So, I was forced to conserve my food and hope someone would come looking for me.

"So, I sat and waited for help to arrive, but no one came. But there was nothing more I could do. The nearest town was days away; there would be no way I could make it with the small supplies I had.

"One day a huge storm came rolling in. The wind and rain battered my shelter hard, but somehow it did not fall. As I sat there trying to sleep through this storm, a small group of coyotes walked into my shelter.

"At first, I was frightened at the sight, but that passed. The coyotes just sat across from me and did not move much. The only time anyone moved was only to drink from the watering hole in between us both.

"By the next morning, the storm had passed and the coyotes had seemed to have moved on. But I didn't have time to think about them for I was now out of food. I had to find something to eat or I was not going to make it much longer.

"I didn't know what I was going to do about food, but I soon found it would soon be resolved. For as I was about to head out in search of food, I was surprised to see the family of coyotes outside. What was more, in one of their mouths was a large piece of meat. Dropping it at my feet, the coyote stepped away from it and went back to his family.

"For the next month or so the coyote family and I lived together helping one another. I began to learn how to help myself in that place. It wasn't long before I was killing my own food and sharing it with my coyote friends. But I could not stay with them forever; I would have to leave them in time.

"One day while sitting on the cliffs by my plane, the coyotes and I noticed something was coming. Looking around we saw it was a jeep driving thought the desert and coming towards us.

"Seeing this, the coyotes jumped down from the cliff and began to run away. When I tried to follow them, the male of the group turned and growled at me. I tried to move closer to him, but when I did, he only snapped at me and growled some more. I could not understand what was going on, but then the coyote pointed his snout at me then to the oncoming jeep, and I knew what he was saying. He was telling me it was time to go home to my people.

"After saying my goodbyes, I watched as the coyotes faded into the cliff side. Turning back, I sat down by my plane and waited for the jeep to arrive.

"When the jeep finally arrived, the people inside looked as if they had been looking for me. The driver, a young Native American woman of eighteen, looked at me as if she could not believe I was here. She was very beautiful with long black hair and deep green eyes. Her passenger was an older man who looked as if he could have been her father. He too had long hair like her, but his eyes were white. He was blind.

"Greeting the two, I soon learned their names. He was Soaring Eagle, and his daughter was Dancing Doe. I then told them of how I ended up out here, but I kept my time with the coyotes quieted.

"On the way to their home, Eagle told me a little about himself in a cryptic kind of way. Born blind, Eagle said he never had a problem seeing. Seeing in a way different than you or me. He sees in what his people called spirit vision.

"His daughter explained everyone has a spirit animal; an animal defines and guides a person. Her father has the power to see these spirit animals in all humans. She also told me her father would also get visions of things, places, and of people. Sometimes, he would even disappear for days after having one of theses visions.

"I didn't really believe at first, but in the short time I spent with them, I soon became a believer. All the time I spent with Eagle and his daughter he would call me by the name Wise Coyote. When I asked about why he called me this, he said it was partly because of my sprit; the second reason was because of my time with the coyotes.

"Somehow Eagle knew about what happened with me with the coyotes. Doe would say her father always knew things about people he had never met. Things people never told anyone her father could see and know their deepest secret. She said it was always hard even hard her to hide anything from her father.

"When it was finally time for me to go, Doe handed me this pendent." As he spoke these words, Coyote pulled a pendent from his shirt. It looked like it was made of stone and it had been shaped in the way of a coyote's head. Coyote stared at it for some time before returning it.

"From that day on, everything changed," he said. "I returned to competitions, and as I fought, I found my fighting style had changed. I began to fight more like a coyote than a man. My moves were more powerful. It wasn't long before I was given the nickname The Coyote."

"What did this have to do with me?" I asked feeling like it would take all day to find out.

"When the Great Disaster hit, I found myself once more alone in the wilderness, but this time I was not afraid. As I wandered through the world, I ran into an old friend.

"It was Eagle! I don't know how he found me, or even how he had traveled all that way, but he did.

"He said to me, 'The Young Wolf is on the move. He has gained the strength from the Mighty Dragon but is still in need of wisdom from you, Wise Coyote. Show him the path you walked and let him find his way.'"

"How did you know he was talking about me?"

"Because," my Master said, "of your sword."

"My sword," I asked in wonder. "What does my sword have to do with an Eagle's words?"

"It's not really the sword but the man who made the sword," my Master said. "He is the one Eagle refers to as the Mighty Dragon. To know this, you must know the person well enough to know who Eagle is speaking about."

"How is it you know him? And how did you know this was one of his swords?"

"Simply because I had met him before, and I remembered the symbol that is on your sword was the same as the one on swords he had hung behind him."

"I see, and therefore you trained me?"

"Yes!"

"But why, why listen to this old man?"

"Because he is a man of great power and to not listen to a man like that is unwise."

And with that we turned in for the night.

The next morning, I found Coyote, the tent, and half of my food gone. But I was not mad; in fact, I was impressed he did all that in the night without distributing me.

Chapter 22

The Sparrow

"With my training with Coyote done, I turned my attention back to my search for the Stranger," Matrix said.

"So, this is the reason people call you the Wolf," the bartender said filling a drink and listening to Matrix's story.

"Yes, it was a name Coyote used for me," Matrix said. "From that day on I made it a part of my new identity."

Soon I was back on the road picking up the Stranger's trail. I was moving faster than before. My one hope was to get ahead of him and enact my revenge.

Even after my time with Coyote, I found the path fresh.

It was a month or so after I had left Coyote's when the trail of the Stranger went cold. I first started to fear when the next town I came to, which I believed should have been in ruins, was still standing.

Thinking it might be just a mistake, I moved on to the next town—nothing. After a week with no signs, I finally admitted to what I was thinking along: The trail went dead.

I spent days trying to figure out where I had lost his trail. With no clues on how to go forward, I did the only thing I could think of—back track.

This would normally be very difficult, due to the fact that since the Great Disaster and the World Civil War, all maps made in the old world are no longer useful. But I do not have that problem, thanks to my M.I.D.

The M.I.D has within it a G.P.S, or Global Positioning System. The system uses, according to what I read about it, a satellite in space to transmit a signal to my M.I.D of my location and what is around me.

Ever since leaving the Shadow Matrix, I had been following my moves with the G.P.S and recording the places I'd been. I had even made notes on where I saw signs of the Stranger's passing.

Within weeks, I had traveled all the way back to my beginning. This was, of course, not the first time I had been here. For some time now, I had returned to the Shadow Matrix to supply, unload unwanted unneeded items I did not need, or simply rest in true peace without worry.

It was then when I had the thought, maybe the Stranger had a similar place somewhere. A sanctuary, a place he goes to find peace. Thinking about this place, if he did have a place, it would most likely be in the Stranger's past. Backtracking the Stranger's path, starting from my father's village, and so I was off again back-tracking the Stranger's path.

I found myself moving faster than before. I didn't stop to investigate the signs of his destruction or to talk long to the people. Once I was sure I was on the right track, I quickly moved on.

But in my quiet thoughts, I started to wonder if I was ever going to find the

Stranger, and did I want to.

I was beginning to think the Stranger might just be out of my reach. He might even be dead.

I mean, how long could he go on before someone killed him? But I did not want to give up until I knew he was dead.

Waking from my thoughts, I quickly slammed on the breaks before driving over a cliff. Caching my breath, I let my nerves to calm down.

Getting out, I made my way over to the cliff. Walking to the edge, I peered over the cliff to see what was below.

Looking, I could see that the rock face was very steep. At the bottom of the cliff, I could see a large river flowing swiftly through the canyon. Even an experienced climber would have trouble on this cliff, and if someone were to fall from here it would surely kill them.

Getting back in my truck, I headed out again following the cliff edge. I was hoping to find a way around or over the canyon, but as I went it looked as if the canyon went on for days.

But all I cared about was just to keep on moving. I didn't even care anymore where I was going or if I would ever find the stranger. I just wanted to move on.

As I drove, I could see the canyon was growing wider on the other side. I could also hear the river below was growing in strength and speed.

Stopping suddenly, I got out in order to try to make sense of what I was seeing. In front of me the cliff side turned into a mountain. The other side of the canyon moved out to what looked liked another mountain which was forming on that edge too. But what was the strange part about this was there was another cliff between the two. But what really caught my eye was the small town sitting on the cliff between these two mountains.

My curiosity was on how a town could be in an area that seemed to be impassible. From where I was, there was no way to get to the other cliff. The only way I could see if there was a path going through the mountains. So, I went looking for the way in.

This wasn't a need to find the Stranger. In fact, I believed this town would be hard for anyone to find, even the Stranger. But I did believe I would find something here; I just didn't know what.

Following the mountain, I soon found it was quite large. I could see there were many caves in the mountain. But none went all the way through the mountain.

Just then on the south end of the mountain I found it, a canyon. It literally cut the mountain into pieces. Looking down the canyon, I could see my truck could easily fit though. But I decided to head back to one of the bigger caves to hide my truck and walk to the town.

Walking down the canyon, I could see the canyon was man-made, but I could not see why it was made.

It was slow going down the canyon. About two miles long, I could see there was a proper road at one time and even now was used often.

I spent two hours walking through the canyon before leaving it behind.

Outside the canyon, I could see the inside of the mountain was huge. Far larger than what I saw before.

It looked as if I was in a long dead volcano. Even I could see the evidence of the eruption that ripped opened the mountain.

The area in front of me was luscious with grass, around two acres large. To the left of me, I could see the townsfolk had farmland on the west side of the town. Livestock could be seen grazing close by.

Moving slowly, I headed towards the town, making sure I didn't make any hostile moves. I could already see a group of townspeople waiting for me on the edge of town.

On reaching the town, I found myself being met by what looked like everyone there. Only a few were armed and only with bow and arrows. But by the look of the people, it seemed they only used them for hunting, not for the fighting.

"Good evening," I said raising my hand in friendship. "I do not mean you any harm. I am only looking for food and shelter for the night. I will trade anything I have if you let me stay."

"Then I say welcome to you stranger," a young woman said stepping out from the group. "My name is Angelica, and I am the head of this town. We may not get many visitors here, but we will allow you to stay the night."

"Thank you," I said moving forward.

Angelica led the way followed by four elderly people. I followed them to a small hut, which was on the outer edge of the town.

It was a small but sturdy hut just big enough for one person. Inside there was one large room with a bed and a wood stove to one side, and in the back was the toilet. Putting my bag on the bed, I looked around the room and thanked my host.

"You are welcome, Mister," Angelica said.

"Matrix," I said, "You come call me Matrix."

"Matrix," Angelica said with a giggle. "That is a strange name."

"Well, not everyone can have a name like Angelica," I said, "or to be the leader of a whole town at your age."

She smiled at this, but remembering that we were not alone she quickly changed her tone.

"Well, I'm afraid it is a long story," she said looking at the four elders.

"Maybe if I am lucky, I will hear it before I leave," I said getting the idea.

"We enjoy group meals in our town. I will have someone show you the way when the evening meal is ready." And with that she and the four elders left.

I spent my time in hut first washing, using the bucket of warm water someone brought to my hut, and checking my weapons. I was busy cleaning and sharpening Dragon's Edge when I heard a knock on my door.

Going to the door, I found Angelica standing outside. Because of the mountain, night was already falling. Torches had been lit in the street.

The torchlight shone off her long blonde hair, and I found myself lost in her green eyes.

"Is there something wrong?" Angelica asked just standing in the doorway.

"No!" I said, "I just didn't think I would see you here."

"And why not?" she said put her hands on her slander hips.

"Well, I just thought you would have sent someone else for something so trivial," I said.

"What kind of leader would I be if I didn't do the 'trivial things' every now and then?" she said laughing.

Not knowing what to say, I just stood there. Smiling Angelica grabbed me by the arm and started pulling me out into the night air.

Outside she slowly led me through the town. As we walked, I found myself answering questions. She seemed to want to know everything.

But I also learned her parents were the founders of the town, around twelve years after the Great Disaster. But what I found more incredible was that she was born only four months after the Great Disaster.

As we all know, the first year was hard. Many pregnant women died, and those who survived lost the child. Even if both mother and child lived, many of them had problems in life. Either child died in birth, or the mother died, or both mother and child died.

Walking to the town hall, I saw the large structure that looked as if it had been build out of the mountain itself. Inside there was a large grand room, with several long tables set in the shape of a U. On both sides of the tables were benches.

Following Angelica, I found myself seated beside her and the members of her advisers. Looking around, I could see nearly everyone was focused on their plates and their own conversations. Only a few people would look in my direction, only to look away quickly. Angelica was the one person who almost never turned her eyes away from me.

Throughout the meal, the conversation was pleasant, and the food was plentiful. A feeling of friendship could be felt all around by most in the hall. Though I still felt a little hostility from some of the people.

This feeling was greatest in one man. He was seated on the other side and several seats down from us. Even at that distance, I could see his hatred for me, but I did not know why. The answer came when I excused myself from the table.

"Excuse me!" I said standing up. "It was a wonderful meal, but I must retire for the night."

"As you wish," Angelica said, but as she began to get up, she was stopped.

"I am sorry, Angelica, but there is something we need to speak about," said one of the council members.

"Of course," Angelica said, "but who will show Mr. Matrix back to his hut?"

"I will," said a man. The same one who I sensed didn't like me.

"Fine, Darryl," the council member said.

With this, I said good night to Angelica, the council members, and the towns-people before following Darryl.

He did not say a thing as we walked. It was as if he did not know what to say, or he didn't trust what he would say. Only on reaching my hut did he finally say something.

"Good night," he said.

"Good night," I said.

But then as I turned around to head inside, Darryl stopped me. "Be sure you leave in the morning," he said.

"What did you say?"

"I said be sure you leave in the morning."

"What is your problem with me?"

"You're my problem."

"What do you mean?"

"You come to our town and mess with our harmony."

"Your harmony?"

"Yes!" he said pointing at me. "You are coming in here and messing with everything and everyone."

"You mean Angelica, don't you?" I said getting him true message.

"Don't talk about her!" Darryl said pushing me up against the wall.

"Did I hit a nerve?" I said just standing there.

He didn't say a thing. He just stared at me. I could have of course taken him down easily, but I decided it would be better to do nothing.

"You should just leave, now!" And with that Darryl turning and walked off.

Heading into the hut, I lied down on the bed and went to sleep.

In the morning, I packed my thing and got ready to depart, and at the door with toast, butter, and some cheese was Darryl. I am sure Angelica would have come herself, but Darryl stopped her before she could. It showed his distrust of me, or was it in Angelica?

I ate as Darryl escorted me to the main entrains. The townspeople were out and about attending to their own business. Only a few stopped to say 'goodbye,' or 'have a safe journey.'

We made our way towards the canyon entrance. Up ahead, I could see several people there to see me off. Among them I could see Angelica there as well as the members of her council.

"This is quite the standoff," I said looking at all the people.

Angelica just smiled and held out her hand. Taking it in mine, I smiled back, looking deep in her green eyes.

"Don't forget to stop by if you happen to be in the neighborhood!" Angelica said blushing a little.

"I won't," I said nodding to her and looking at Darryl's face.

It was clear he was wishing I never ever came to be in the neighborhood again.

Chapter 23

The Bull

Back on the road, I found it hard to go forward. I felt like I had left something behind in that town. I knew what it was: Angelica. It wasn't long before I found myself returning to the town and to Angelica.

It was quite clear that Angelica was overjoyed to see me back, and Darryl was displeased to see me. I was welcomed to the town; only Darryl and a few others thought ill of me.

Other than the hostility between Darryl and me, my time in the town was wonderful. It wasn't long before I became comfortable there. Within a few weeks, I had begun to leave my weapons in the hut. Several weeks later, I had exchanged my armor for some regular clothes.

There were many things in the town for me to do, so I didn't get bored. Helping around the town I used as payment for staying in the town, and to keep me nearby. At every mealtime and all my free time there was Angelica by my side.

After about four mouths, it was like I had become part of the town. But not everyone thought that; Darryl still wanted me out. It was just a matter of time before he acted.

"Excuse me!" Darryl said one day at the evening meal.

"Yes, Darryl, is there something you need to tell us?" Angelica said seeing nothing in Darryl's actions.

It sometimes happened at the evening meal where the townspeople would tell everyone of joyous news. Like the birth of a new colt or sheep. Or to tell the town about plans to marry or about a baby on the way, but Darryl had something else on his mind.

"Yes! I would like to speak on the matter of Matrix," he said looking right at me. "He has been here for over four mouths now and has not yet told us of his plans. Is he staying or is he going? The choice must be made.

"If he plans to move on like he said, four mouths ago, then he must leave tomorrow. If he is to stay, then he must go thorough the requirements in order to join our community and stop leeching off us."

"Matrix has not been leeching off of us!" said a man by the name of Tom who had become a friend to me. "He's been helping around the town, helping us finishing projects all around the town. In many ways, he is already part of this community."

This statement was met with sounds of agreement.

"That may be so, but he isn't!" Darryl said with a grin. "Matrix is not part of our community. There are procedures he must go through in order to join this community."

"Darryl does have a point," Angelica said standing. "Matrix, you will have to give us an answer to this question."

"I do have an answer," I said staying in my seat with my eyes closed. "I have been thinking on this for some time now. I will do whatever it takes to be part of your community. Until then, will you excuse me?"

With that I stood up and left for my hut.

The next week, I went through the procedures to become a member of the community. In this time, I saw little of Angelica. Only in official meetings did I see her at all. At mealtimes, we sat separate.

Finally, the day came when my fate was decided. In the Great Hall, everyone gathered. Angelica and the council sat in fount of everyone and I sat before them.

The meeting went much like the first time. People on both sides of the discussion both had their say. There were many who spoke against me, but the loudest was Darryl.

But the loudest voice was for those for me than against me. It is no wonder why, when it came time for the council to decide, they said yes to my staying.

Darryl was outraged about the decision and stormed out of the hall. But I was not going to think about him now. There would be another time to think about that.

After the meeting, a grand feast was prepared in my honor. It was there the townsfolk congratulated me and made me feel more like a neighbor than a visitor. Even some of the people who were on Darryl's side congratulated me, which was a surprise.

At long last, Angelica and I were able to spend time together. The whole time at the feast she was there with me. And Darryl, I saw him once coming in to grab some food and drink before he headed out once more.

Months passed, and my time in there was the happiest I ever had, and my relationship with Angelica grew. It wasn't long before we were married, and our first child was born.

The marriage and the birth of our son even helped me to come to peace with Darryl. Even if it we would never be close friends, we could have agreed to a truce for the happiness of Angelica.

But like last time, my happiness was not to last. A year after my son was born, disaster struck.

I was on a trip to the south to the nearest town. We were going down there to do some trading. It was just me and two other men from the town, three horses, two of them pulling the cart with our supplies.

After two days of riding we finally came up to the town. It was in what looked like a crater that only had a path big enough for two horses to walk down at the same time.

But when we looked down at the town, what we saw shocked us. The town was being attacked by a band of heavily armed marauders. The townsfolk were putting up a fight, but I could see they were going to lose.

"We got to do something," Tom said.

"No! There is nothing we can do now," I said already turning away.

"How can you say that, Matrix?" Tim said pointing. "These people are our friends; we can't just leave them."

"If we are going to save our friends and family back home, we must," I said.

"You are saying they will head to our town next?" Tom asked.

"Yes, I am!" I said.

"How do you know that?" Tim asked.

"Because of the transport vehicles they had," I said pointing them out. "Enough for several towns of people and supplies, they are on a crusade and will not turn back until they are full. This means they will continue to move forward. Heading north and north means home."

"Ok!" Tom said, "So what do we do now? It's a two-day ride back north. How are we going to beat them there?"

"Well, time is on our side," I said looking at the wagon and the surrounding area.

"Time," Tim said, "what do you mean time?"

"How much time do we have?" Tom asked.

"They may have speed on their side, but they also have numbers, and that will slow them down," I said.

"What do you mean?" Tom asked.

"For us it is a two-day trip, but for them it might take them four to five days," I said. "And this is not including the time they will spent here. So, we should say we have somewhere around seven to nine days maybe ten. So, we have plenty of time to get back and get everyone out or to prepare to fight. But first I want to set a surprise for them."

For the next two hours, we worked digging a pit ten by ten. Putting what supplies we could on to the horses. In the pit, we put spikes made from the wood from the cart. We then covered the pit with whatever we had left and covered them with dirt.

After we were done, we headed for home. Behind us, I could see that the battle was over, but our war had just started.

Chapter 24

The Turtle

A day-and-a-half hard ride, my friends and I made it back home. We were tired, hungry, and filthy. We didn't sleep or eat. What sleep we got was as we rode and the others led.

On entering the town, we were quickly hit with many questions. The first, of course, was why we were back so soon.

The tale was told quickly, but what to do next took time.

A meeting was held in the great hall. Many people were talking all at once, trying to figure out what needed to be done. Some spoke of leaving, while others wanted to stay to fight for their homes, and many did not know what to do.

Finally, Angelica stood, and the crowd went quiet.

"Matrix," she said looking at me. "How much time do we have before they get here?"

"I would say about a week," I said thinking hard. "But thankfully we have the time to prepare. If we are to run, then we should go now. Gather everything that is important to us and find a safe place to hide. Once they come through this area, we then can return. But if we are to fight then we need to get to work now to fortify our defense."

"How do we do that?" Darryl said. "The only weapons we have are bows and arrows. How can we fight them?"

"Well, for one we do have the advantage," I said. "The canyon is the only way in or out of the town. Only one vehicle can move through the canyon at one time. We can bottle neck them in there. But we need better weapons."

"But where can we get that kind of weaponry in a week?" a woman asked.

"I know a place where there is a stash of weapons of the old world," I said. "If five men were to come with me, we can be back in two days. But if we are to go, we must go now."

"Very well then," Angelica said. "All those in favor of leaving our homes say aye!"

Only a few voices were heard.

"All those in favor to stand and fight say aye!" Angelica said.

As she did, a roar came, as most screamed at the same time.

"Very well then," Angelica said turning back to look at me. "Matrix, as you are the one with the ability to organize our defenses, I am placing you in charge of this. Do you accept this responsibility?"

"I do!"

After the meeting, I went right to work; stepping outside I looked around at the layout of the town. I needed to find the best way to defend the town and protect all the people.

As I did this, the townsfolk were standing behind me waiting for me to say or do something. Without turning around I began to speak. "I will need five volunteers to be ready to leave within the hour," I said. "Everyone else will stay here and ready our defense."

It was only then did everyone move off into town. As Darryl walked by me I stopped him.

"What is it Matrix?" Darryl asked.

"I need you to take charge of the townspeople while I am gone," I said.

"Ok!" he said standing by me. "What is it you need me to do?"

"First, I need you to block off the alleys in between the houses." I said pointing then out. "We need to make sure when they come they don't come at us from all sides."

"Right," he said. "Anything else?"

"Yes!" I said. "I also want three barricades built. One just in front of the town, one about halfway down, and one right here just before the stairs."

"How big?" Darryl asked.

"Five men can stand behind it and high enough so they can hide behind them."

"Fine," Darryl said already heading down the stairs. "I will have it done by time you get back."

"Darryl," I said stopping him before he was halfway down the stairs. "I know you and I will never be true friends, but it is good to know we can be allies."

Darryl nodded then continued down the stairs and moved on to start working.

"I see you two have come to an agreement," Angelica said standing beside me, with our child in her arms.

"For the time being, at least," I said looking down at my son.

"What is it you need from me?" Angelica asked, placing a hand on my check.

"Even with the weapons, there is still a chance people will get hurt," I said looking up the cliff side; I knew what a large cave it was. "That is why we need to put all the people who can't fight or won't fight up in the cave on the cliff. So, I need you and those who will help to go up there and make the cave livable for as many people as we can."

"I will," she said giving me a kiss before heading off.

Back at our home, I pulled out a box I had not opened in over a year now. Opening the box, I pulled out my armor, my guns, and my sword. Dressed in my armor, I sat down and inspected all my guns, and cleaned and sharpened my sword.

A knock on door told me it was time to go. Standing up I sheathed my sword and went to the door. Outside stood five men, all with packs ready to leave. Among them there was my friend Tom.

"We're ready to go," Tom said speaking for all.

"Follow me!" And with this we made our way out towards the outside world.

As we left the town, I could see the whole town was busy with preparations. Before heading into the canyon, I turned and looked back. There in the middle of the town, I could see Angelica. She was busy like everyone else helping move supplies up to the cave.

In one moment, she turned in my direction and waved. I waved back before moving on.

Everyone was gathered by the time I made it out of the canyon.

"So where to now?" Tom asked looking around.

"This way," I said heading toward a cave.

Inside was my Humvee, just as I had left it.

"Everyone in and pay attention, as I teach you all how to drive."

"Why?" one of the men asked as the others piled in.

"Because," I started, "there are two other vehicles like this in my sanctuary. The more weapons we can bring back the better we are."

And with this we were off. As we drove, I explained the controls and how to drive to every man.

By midday, we had made it to my sanctuary. To everyone else it looked only like a wall of rock. I could feel the others look of confusion.

Walking over to the mountain face, I began to feel around. Finding the rock I was looking for, I removed it from the wall. Beneath it there was a scanner. Taking my M.I.D out of my pocket, I held it up to the scanner.

Suddenly the mountain face split down the middle and opened wide. Looking down the opening, all one could see was darkness, but I knew what was down there.

Jumping back in the Hummer, I drove in slowly. As we did light flared into life, and the cave door began to close. In no time, we were out of the tunnel and into the Shadow Matrix.

The others were in awe about the size of this place, but I quickly got them to focus. Taking the lead, I led them downstairs to the armory. Once inside we got right to business.

"You two," I said, tossing several bags at two of the men. "Go to the mess down the hall and fill the bag."

They nodded and headed down the hall.

"You," I said, tossing more bags to the third man. "Go up to the infirmary and grab everything you see."

"Right," he said running to the stairs.

"Don't just stand there, you two," I said, looking at the last two. "Grab a bag and start filling. I want this armory empty."

We spent the rest of the day filling bags with food, medical supplies, guns, rockets, ammo, and explosives of all kinds. We also grabbed all the body armor we could find.

All three of the Hummers were now filled to bursting, and there was very little left in the Shadow Matrix. With the final bag in my hand, I stopped at the door to the armory. Looking around, I could see nothing on the racks. Only one thing was still there, and this was the helmet to my armor.

It was still there, just as ugly as before, but right at this moment, I did not care. Grabbing the helmet, I put it under my arm and closed the door behind me.

I found the rest of the guys upstairs by the Hummer. They had put out some food from the bags and were having a small meal. I put my bags and helmet in the back of my Hummer and then joined then.

After eating, we went up to the barracks and went to sleep. I was in the general's barrack, while the others were in the officer barracks.

The next morning, we were up early. After a quick breakfast, we prepared to leave. Checking to make sure everyone knew what they were doing, I set all their G.P.S.s so even if they lost me, they could find their way home.

Taking the lead, I swiped my M.I.D. on the scanner by the tunnel opening. I led the way out of the mountain, closing it as we drove home.

Chapter 25

The Hares

By midday, the town was in sight as we headed down the canyon. On the other side of it, we could see the whole town coming out to see us. It was a feeling of pride I felt when I saw them coming toward us with axes, clubs, and whatever else they could find to fight with if we were not friendly.

There was no time for a long hello. After all, the more time we wasted the closer the riders got. We had to start work now. So, gathering everyone together, I started to explain the plan.

Pulling out a big roll of paper out of my bag, I showed everyone my idea. On the paper was a crude drawing of the town and the crater we were in. Arrows and notes littered the map describing what and how we would defend our home.

The first thing I pointed to was the canyon itself. It was by far our first line of defense, for it was so narrow it was only big enough for one vehicle to pass though at one time. This meant it would take time to even enter the town. But it was also the best place to strike first.

My plan was to place prima cord on the canyon wall and set three different detonators. Once the first person or vehicle reached the exit, we detonate the first set, closing the way into the town. Then we set off the second one trapping them inside the canyon. Finally, we set off the third causing the canyon to collapse on top of all who are trapped inside.

Doing this may accomplish one of two things. Make them rethink attacking our town and just move on. Or force them to use their own explosive to clear the rubble to get to us.

Next, I pointed to the field in between the canyon's mouth and the first house, roughly one mile long. Here was where we would have our minefield. Many of the townsfolk were not too keen on having the minefield at all. But I told them the more that go down before they reach the town, the better our chances. They agreed!

Moving on, I told them if the canyon trap and the minefield did not stop their advance then it would be up to us to stop them. Therefore they worked so hard to build the barricades and closed off the opening in between the houses, forcing them to come straight at us.

I told them I wanted snipers on the roofs of the house armed each an M 40 Tactical Sniper Rifle. The sniper team's main job would be to thin out their numbers and if at all possible move them into the mines.

If they made it past the mines, it would be the job of the ground forces to keep them back. Men would be placed at each of the three barricades armed mostly with M 16 assault rifles. Side arms would only have to be used as back up.

If they passed the mines and the forward barricade becomes undefended-able, we will retreat to the second barricade. With the ways between the houses blocked off, they will be forced to come down one way.

If we can't stop them, there we will fall back to the last barricade. At this point, we will have all snipers get down from their positions and join the ground team.

If we cannot stop them from taking the town, we will move to the cave on top of the cliff. At the opening of the cave, the three Humvees will be acting as barricades.

The cave would also be where the women, children, and anyone else who cannot or will not fight will be. Guards will be posted there for the people's protection. That will be our last stand.

"That's it!" I said standing up. "This is the best plan we have to stop them. Do you have any questions?"

No one said a word. Whether it was because they were too shocked by the plan or because they thought it was a good one, I couldn't tell.

"Very well then," I said looking up at the midday sun. "It's midday now. I need twenty of you to come with me. Bring ten sets of long climbing robe and climbing gear with you. I will meet you on the cliff face."

Turning towards the cliff, I grabbed the bags full of explosives and made my way to the canyon.

"Darryl," I said stopping next to him. "Get a group of ten to gather and start digging holes for the minefield. Space them about ten feet apart and about five holes down and ten across."

"I'll take care of it," he said, before moving off to gather the shovels and men.

It wasn't long before the twenty men were up on the cliff rope and gear in hand.

Splitting them up in pairs, I sent ten to the other side of the canyon. Each group of ten would send five over the edge each with a bag of prima cord, rock spikes, and hammers to attach the prima cord to the wall.

I watched from the top of the cliff as the teams moved along their part of the wall, placing the prima cord along the wall. I was glad to see them using every crack and imperfection in the wall to cause the greatest damage.

Once the teams had finished placing the last of the prima cord, I went down the wall myself and placed the detonators. To do the job right, I would need six detonators set on three different setting.

With the detonators set in, I made one more check on the remote. I then instructed the lookout on how the remote worked. Before leaving, I pulled off a radio and handed it to the lookout. I told him all he needed to do was push a bottom and talk, and I would hear him.

Satisfied he understood and would tell the others what to do, I then headed back down the cliff.

At the bottom of the cliff, I saw a good fifty holes dug just as I had asked. As the sun set, I began to set, and buried the mines in our minefield.

Night had truly fallen by the time I had finished my task, but I was glad I had done it myself. I did not want any of the people to mishandle the placing of the bombs and risk blowing them up.

The last thing I did before heading to the Great Hall was to check the signs around the minefield. This sign would remind people about the mines and to stay away. While another set of signs would tell the lookouts the safe way around the field and up to the cliff. Those signs would be pulled before the attack began.

Satisfied, I headed to the great hall. Inside, I found the hall strangely quiet. People were talking in quiet whispers. Most of the talk was about the plan and defense. There were many men speaking of where they would like to be placed in the defense. Not wanting to be a part of these conversations, I grabbed a loaf of bread, a wedge of cheese, and a skin of wine before leaving the hall.

With food in hand, I made my way to the first barricade just outside the town. Sitting on the barricade, I ate quietly thinking. Looking up, I could see Angelica moving towards me.

"Is there something wrong?" she asked sitting beside me.

"Why do you ask?"

"Because you didn't stay in the hall."

"I just needed a quiet place to think, that's all."

"Thinking about what?"

"Mostly about who should use what weapon?" I said, picking up the largest gun on the ground. "Like this one, for instance."

"And what is it?" She put her head on my shoulder.

"This is a Barrett M82 Sniper Rifle," I said. "It has a .50 caliber bullet and a 10-shot magazine and can hit a target from 1830 meters. But if someone was to shoot from the top of the tower, a good twenty stories high, he could hit them just as they left the canyon. The only thing is they would need to be a marksman to do it right."

"So, what is the problem?" she asked, wrapping her arms around mind.

"I am the best marksman in the town, but if I am up there then someone else has to run things down here," I said, looking up at the tower.

"You are needed here on the ground, not in the tower, Matrix, and you know that," she said, stroking my cheek.

"Then who would be in the tower?" I asked, looking down at her.

"You know another person who is almost as good as you," she said, giving me a kiss. "All you need to do is ask him and I am sure he will help."

As I watched her go heading to our home, I know the words she said were true. So, with the Barrett in one hand and a bag of ammo in the other, I went looking for Darryl.

I found him on top the cliff side, positioning the Hummer into place in front of the cave. Thanks to the headlights of the Humvees, the job was easily done even at night.

"Darryl!" I cried out.

"What do you need, Matrix?" he asked, not looking at me but continuing to position the vehicles just right.

Looking at the positioning, I could see he had made a half circle with a small spot for people to get in and out.

"Looks good," I said, standing the Barrett on its end. "There is something we need to talk about."

With that said, I started down the trail. I know Darryl would follow, and sure enough he was at my side.

"What is it now?" he asked, as I sat down on the barricade near the hall.

"We need to talk about who fights where," I said, the Barrett leaning on the barricade. "The first person to think about is me, where I need to be."

"Well, that should be the easiest to do, at the head of the fight commanding it," he said, in a forceful tone.

"Yes, I thought so to but," I said, letting the word hang.

"But what," he asked.

"But this gun here could do the most damage to the enemy, but it needs a marksman behind it," I said.

"So, what?" he said. "You are still needed down here."

"Maybe," I said, "but I'm still the best shot we have here."

"Only in your head, maybe," he said, "I am just as good as you, if not better. So, give me the gun and tell me what to do."

With a smile, I handed over the Barrett and the bag and told him the plan.

"I would take it up the tower, now," I said. "There is also a radio in the bag. Always keep it on you. It is solar powered, so it won't die quickly. I, Angelica, and the watchmen also have one."

"Understood," he said putting the bag on his back and heading to the hall.

As Darryl moved off to the tower, I made my way home; there was one more thing I needed to do. Inside, I found my wife coming out of our son's room, her finger to her lips.

"Shhh," she said, "He just felt asleep."

Nodding, I followed her into the living area.

"There's something I need to talk to you about," I said sitting down on the couch.

"What's wrong?" she asked concerned.

"First off, I want to tell you that you and our son are the most precious things I have in my life," I said, holding her hand. "For that reason, I want you to go up to the caves when the fighting starts."

"What!" she exclaimed. "You want me to hide up there while are you waiting down here, fighting and dying? No way! How can you ask me this?"

"I need to know you are safe if I'm going to protect the town," I said, holding her close. "I can't lose you or our son so please, I need you to stay safe."

Something in my eyes must have told her the words I spoke were true, for she nodded.

"Fine," she said, "but only to defend yourself. I won't be a helpless woman in the cave, you hear me."

Knowing nothing I said would make a difference, I nodded.

"Then you will need this," I said, handing over a shotgun and body armor, as well as a radio. "Just stay safe for me."

Chapter 26

The Jackal

The days leading up to the battle were uneventful. Most of my time was spent in equipping and training the townspeople for battle. They learned very quickly, and soon we were ready for battle. Now there was only the waiting.

The town now had a war-like feel to it. Everywhere one looked was the sight of men and women ready to battle at any moment. Mothers kept their children close, while the men carried their weapons with them, always.

The days moved slowly by, and then the day finally came.

"I see smoke! I see smoke!" the voice over the radio cried.

"Stand by!" I said, already moving to the lookout point. "Darryl, Angelica, do you read?"

"Darryl here," Darryl said, "heading for the tower, now."

"I'm here too," Angelica's voice spoke over the radio. "I'm getting the women and children together and heading for the caves."

"Good," I said, running up the path. "Will report the enemies' movement as soon as I can, out."

On top the canyon, I moved low towards the lookout.

"Matrix, good to see you," Tom said, putting his binoculars down.

"What do we have?" I said, picking up the binoculars so I could see.

"They look to be only a few hours' away," Tom said. "But I don't know why they stopped there."

"Did you see anyone getting close to the canyon before?" I asked, look at him.

"One man did move off from the others," Tom said. "I saw him pulling binoculars out of his coat. At that point, I ducked down; I didn't want him to see me. I finally looked up; he was already heading back to the others."

"Good job!" I said. "It is a good chance they know our town is here. Thanks to your quick thinking, they won't know we are waiting for them. They will rest for now and attack at first light. Keep your eyes on them. With the sun almost down, you don't have to worry about the glare, but stay vigilant."

"Got it."

With this, I headed back to town.

I got back; everyone was asking about the enemy. I told them everything I knew, and they should get ready to fight.

"I know you're scared," I told the crowd, "but this is what we have been preparing for this whole time. Remember, we are not trying to obliterate them; we just want to make them regret coming. Make them lose their will to fight. If we stay alive, we win, understood."

"Yes, sir!" They cried, all at once.

"Good, to your position."

Then it was the waiting. Knowing it was going to be a long wait, I ordered everyone to sleep, in turns. We all needed to be alert when the time came.

"Matrix!" the lookout's voice came over the radio.

"What is it?" I asked, looking over the barricade.

"They're coming," he said.

"Ok, stay down and wait to blow the charges," I said. "Darryl, you awake."

"I'm awake," Darryl said, over the radio.

"I want you to give the command to blow the charges, seeing how you can see when they are at the exit better than me."

"On my command, then," Darryl said.

"Now."

With the command given, the first set of explosions went off. I watched as the rock wall began to fall, crushing the first men exiting the canyon. Seconds later, more explosions, the sounds of rocks falling and men screaming. Now we wait.

Moments later, the lookout came down. Just as he did, we heard more explosions.

"I am guessing they are not leaving, are they?" I said to the lookout.

"No," he said, "the last thing I saw, they were grabbing what looked like every explosive they have."

"So, they are going to blow their way in," I said thinking. "Good to see they are doing as I planned. Tell everyone to be prepared. It will take time to blow their way in, so stay frosty."

So, my command was passed along.

We all stayed at their posts; the sounds of the distant explosions kept everyone quiet and still. At midday, I went up to the canyon myself. I wanted to see where they were in the canyon.

Staying low to the ground, I made my way to the edge and looked over the cliff. A quick glance told me everything. They were halfway through the canyon, which meant they would most likely attack us tomorrow.

"How can you be sure of this," the men asked me on my return.

"Because no army attacks with worn out men," I said. "They will keep the last rock wall up tonight and blow it up tomorrow."

"So what do we do?" Tom asked.

"Nothing," I said

"Nothing?" Tom said. "But they are helpless; why shouldn't we attack now?"

"We have little weapons and a handful of grenades; we can't attack them now, and we need to wait," I said.

"We need to wait?" one of the men asked. "Wait for what?"

"Just wait," I said. "We can't rush into things."

I could still sense the others still wished to act now, but all knew what I said was true. So, we waited.

As night began to fall, so did the sound of the explosions. An hour later, the night air was quiet. Within the canyon smoke they could be seen and I knew they were camping for the night.

"Alright, you five come with me," I said, grabbing a bag and heading to the path.

The others followed without questioning me, but I was sure they were all wondering what we were doing. Within minutes we had made it to cliff side path. It was here where I laid out my plan.

"Alright," I said, speaking to everyone, "I am going up the path to check things out. You five will stay here, understood?" They all nodded. "Good," I said turning to Tom. "Tom, I need you to keep your radio on. When I give the word, I want you to send two men up my way, and take the other two to the other side, get it?"

He nodded.

"But what are we doing here?" one of the men asked.

To answer him, I opened the bag and handed each one grenade. They all looked down at the grenade in their hands and then up to me.

"We are going to strike them, first," I said, before going through the proper way to use a grenade.

"Now remember," I said, "you will pull the pin, drop the grenade over the edge, and walk away. Don't stay and watch, understand?"

With a nod, I turned and headed up the cliff.

On top of the cliff, I made my way over to the canyon edge. Peering down, I could see the invaders were indeed sleeping inside the canyon. Though there were many fires still burning, I could see no one on guard. They must think they were safe in the canyon and we didn't have the means to attack them.

As I scanned their camp, my eyes fell on the other end of the canyon, the part still backed by rock. I could see it was already set to go off in the morning.

"Tom," I said, over the radio, "come on up." Moments later, I had the two guys on my side in position. As for Tom's side, I had to communicate over the radio on their positions. In no time at all, I had everyone in position, and we were ready to attack. "Alright, everyone get ready," I said. "Drop!" I cried.

Pulling the pin of my grenade, I then put my hand over the edge and released the grenade; around me I saw the others had done as I had. As one, we all turned and started back.

The grenades went off; shortly after, the sounds of the explosions mixed with the sound of the screaming men and rocks falling.

As we made our way back to the barricade, my radio screamed a question from both Angelica and Darryl. Sitting down behind the barricade, I explained to them both what we had did.

Once I had finished explaining to them, I told the others to wake me before dawn and went to sleep.

Chapter 27

The Vulture

"Matrix," Tom said shaking me, "you awake?"

"Yes," I said, sitting up and looking over the barricade. "Any movement?"

"Nothing," Tom said.

"Good," I said, "but I want everyone on their toes." Just as I said this, a huge explosion rocked the town, and the rock wall was gone. "Here they come!" I cried out.

As the first man headed out of the canyon, he fell down dead. The only thing told us how he died was the gun shot seconds earlier. Darryl was doing his job.

At first, Darryl was the only one firing, his gun having the longest rang. But soon they were coming out too fast for him to stop them alone. At this point, the snipers on the roofs started firing.

An explosion went off at the edge of the minefield taking out two of the invaders. The others stopped for a moment before the constant fire from the snipers forced them to keep moving forward. As they moved forward, they began spreading themselves out to try to avoid the mines.

"Let them have it, guys!" I said to the men beside me.

After that the only sound was the sound of the three .50 cal. Browning Machine Guns firing at once. One maintained fire in the center while the other two focused on the edges.

After spending half our ammo, we only seemed to cut the enemy numbers by one quarter, and they were still coming. It seemed as if they did not care for their own lives or the lives of their comrades. I had only seen this type of devotion in holy wars.

Running low on ammo, I could see we were going to have to fall back soon. "Snipers, fall back!" I cried out.

We used up the last of our ammo to give; the snipers needed time to get to their second position, and as they did, I saw something new coming. A Military Stryker Infantry Carrier was coming down the canyon.

"Squeeze off your last round then fall back," I said to the others over the sounded of gunfire.

As the last rounds were fired, the Stryker rolled into the crater. The others around me fell back grabbing what weapons were around us and heading to the second barricade. As for me, I stayed to cover their retreat.

Knowing there wasn't much time, I reached down pulled out one of two M72 Rocket Launchers. Arming the launcher, I aimed it at the Stryker and fired. I had aimed the first rocket at the Stryker's weapons on top and the second at its wheels.

With the Stryker hopefully out of commission, I fell back to the second position. Everyone else was already there with M16 and Beretta pistols in hand. Mines going off and the sound of Darryl were now all we could hear, as we waited for the fight to come to us.

In moments, the enemy started to come around the houses at the end of the street. Without hesitation, we all opened fire at once cutting down the enemy. We watched as the enemy ducked down behind the first barricade.

"What are we going to do now?" Tom yelled.

"Don't worry, I got it handled," I said, pulling out a detonator out of my jacket.

Pushing a button on the detonator, the first barricade blew up, and the enemy was taken completely by surprise. Shrapnel hit even those who were not directly behind the barricade. In one blast, around twenty men went down.

"Was that thing set to blow all this time?" Tom asked, looking over the barricade.

"Yeah," I said opening fire once more.

"Do I even want to know if this one is ready to blow as well?" Tom asked, reloading his gun.

"You know, Tom, it is best not to ask questions you do not want to know the answers to!" I said, keeping my gaze forward.

"Oh, fuck me!" I heard Tom yell over the gunfire.

As the fighting went on, it seemed to grow more intense. The invaders seemed to never run out of men. They came in full force never stopping, all seeming ready to die for some unknown cause.

"We need to fall back," I said to those around me. "Grab all the weapons and ammo you can carry and fall back. Tom and I will cover you."

While Tom and I fought the oncoming onslaught, the others ran back to the final barricade. Once the others had made it, I had Tom go while I covered him before I headed back.

Though the invaders were at first reluctant to go near the barricade, they would have to if they were to reach us. When they finally got close to the barricade, I again pulled out the detonator and blew up the barricade.

Bodies went everywhere, but it didn't matter for there were always more to kill. It was only now I could see we were not winning this fight.

"Darryl," I called, on the radio.

"Yeah," he yelled back.

"How is it looking up there?" I asked over the radio. "Is there an end in sight?"

"If there is one, Matrix, I don't see one," he said.

"Shit, this is what I was afraid of," I said thinking quickly. "Ok, Darryl you need to start your way down now; we will cover you."

"No!" he said.

"No! What do you mean no?" I said, thinking I missed something.

"I mean I am staying right where I am," he said. "After all, I still have ten clips up here. I can still do better up here than down there."

"But if we leave our position, there will be no way for you to get out."

"I know."

"Darryl!"

"Go, Matrix, protect her!"

"Sniper team, fall back, now," I yelled up to the snipers who had set up positions on the second-floor roof of the Great Hall.

"We're staying too," one of the snipers yelled back.

"What!" I cried.

"We all decided," a second sniper called, "we're staying too."

"But it will be suicide!" I yelled, trying to make them all understand.

"We all know the sacrifice we are making, Matrix," Darryl said over the radio. "Please, let us give our lives for our friends, our family, our town, and for you."

Looking up at the snipers, I knew there was no more to say. They were all willing to give their lives for everything they had and loved. That kind of devotion is something to be praised, not discouraged.

"Ok, everyone else fall back to the cave," I said to the men around me. "The snipers may be staying, but they need our guns up in the cave. So, move out!"

As the others moved towards the cave, the line began to break. The enemy forces were coming on strong. Knowing there was nothing more I could do, I started my own way up.

Throwing my M16 down, I started towards the path drawing my 9s as I did. Shooting over my back kept their forces at bay, for a time, but I was quickly running low on ammo.

When my guns went dry, I turned and found myself only halfway to the cave. It was then the worst thing that could have happened, happened; my armor felled.

A bullet hit just above my right knee and pierced my armor. The shock caused my knee to buckle, and I fell to the ground.

In pain, I knelt there on all fours unable to think clearly. My mind racing, I seemed ready to just sit there and wait to die.

Then I could hear footsteps behind me and voices crying out my name; I surged back into action. Standing, I drew my sword and stood ready face whatever came my way.

As the first of the enemy came within reach, my sword slashed through his body. As the first body fell, I was already moving, cutting the arm off one man and cleaving another man's head.

The next few seconds were just of slashing, cutting, stabbing, and killing. I removed heads, arms, legs, hands, bodies, and anything else that was in sword length. Soon, a pile of lifeless bodies were all that remained.

"Aim," I heard a voices cry.

Looking down the path, I could see around twenty men standing in formation, weapons aimed and ready to fire. The man who had spoke was standing next to them and seemed to be in command.

The next word he spoke chilled my very blood in my body.

"Fire!"

I covered the best I could, but there was nothing I could do. In no time, I was hit with a volley of bullets all at once. Many of them bounced off the armor, but I know it was only a matter of time before it felled again.

It did, first on my left side, then on the right shoulder and left leg. By time the fourth bullet hit my left arm, I started to lose count.

Lost in the pain, I could feel my body growing heavy as I fell. Falling into darkness, the last thing I remember was a woman calling my name.

Chapter 28

The Cub

"What happened?" the bartender asked, putting a plate of food in front of Matrix.

"Hold on, my friend, all in time," Matrix said, taking a drink. "I didn't know what happened. All I knew was that I was in pain. My body hurt and my head felt like it was split in two."

It wasn't just that my body was in pain; I was also cold and wet. My mind was also foggy. I found it hard to think. I didn't know why I was in pain or why I was cold and wet.

Just as I tried to make my mind work, I felt a cool breeze on my face. It seemed weird I could feel the wind at all, but I couldn't think why that was weird.

Reaching up with my right hand, I tried to push the hair from my face and nearly knocked myself out with my own sword handled. Seeing the sword in my hand, my mind started to work, and I finally remember what had happened.

The attack and the battle played back in my mind. Rising quickly, I sat up. As I did, I felt pain shoot through my whole body.

Looking around, I saw my helmet beside me. I could see it was now in two pieces. It must have taken the impact of the fall and split in two.

Just as that thought came to me, I reached up to feel the top of my head. I could feel dried blood from a large cut. I was still in one piece thanks to that ugly helmet.

Picking it up, I made to stand. As I did, I could feel the pain from all my bullet wounds. Many of my wounds started to bleed once more.

Using my sword as a cane, I started my way up the path. I need to get up to the town. I needed find out what happened. It was slow going, but I had finally made it. Looking around I saw no one in the town.

Slowly making my way up to the path to the cave, I walked. Even before I reached the cave's mouth, I could smell the blood and death. Framed in the cave opening, I saw only bodies from both sides on the cave floor.

Stepping carefully, I moved into the cave stepping over the bodies of both friend and foe alike. As I did, I noticed the bodies were stripped of anything of value. Shoes, clothes, weapons, and little items were taken as well.

Going from body to body, I began the search for my wife and son. Looking around the cave in my search, I saw a woman's body. It wasn't my wife's body but my son's nursemaid. Her back was to me, and I could see she had been shot in the back.

Rolling her on to her back, I felt as if my heart was ripped from my chest. In her arms was my son, dead. It looked as if she had tried to protect him by shielding him with her own body. But the force of the bullet was able to pass through her body and out my son's head.

Gently, I removed my son from her strong embrace and held my son in my arms. As I held him, I allowed the sadness I felt over his death to burn and soon it turned into anger before I was red with hatred. Kissing him on his head, I laid my son down by his nursemaid before continuing my search for his mother.

Finishing my search of the cave, I discovered my wife was not here at all. With my search here done, I headed back down to the town in hopes of finding her there.

Down in the town, I saw the homes were in ruins. Looted for anything of value before burned to the ground, bodies were left where they fell, stripped bare.

As I searched the town, I found most of the bodies down here were the attackers and not the townspeople. That thought gave me hope, for it meant there were many still alive. That meant Angelica was possibly alive, too.

But now I couldn't think about where she was or what was happening to her. I had to focus on figuring out who these men were and where they had come from. But before I did anything, I needed to take care of the bodies.

After bandaging my wounds the best I could, I began the task of moving the bodies. Because I did not have the strength to dig a grave for every person, I decided to move the townspeople up to cave and bring the attackers down to the town.

Once in the town, I would then burn them, the attackers in one pile. As for the townspeople, I will simply close off the cave mouth sealing them inside. Thankfully the prima cord in the third barricade was still there. It was therefore easier for me to close the cave.

Once I had all the bodies of the attackers out of the cave and set the prima cord around the cave's mouth, I headed back to the town for one last thing. I had managed to take down all the snipers' bodies up to the cave. But there was one place I had not gone to yet—the top of the tower.

Taking my time, I moved my way up the stairs of the tower. Due to my wounds, I was forced to stop several times before continuing. At the top of the tower, I found Darryl on his back, dead.

Like the others, his weapon and anything else of value was taken. But by the look of the blood nearby, he managed to kill many before he fell.

"I am sorry, Darryl," I said, picking up his body. "I could not keep her safe, but I will find her."

With his body over my shoulder, I made my way slowly down the stairs, then up to the cave. By the time I made it up to the cave, the day was already gone.

Standing at the cave's opening, in silent reflection, "I'm sorry," I said to the mass grave before me. "I am sorry you all died. Maybe we should have run when we had the time. Maybe it was I who caused your death. It doesn't matter now; what does matter is to find those who were taken and get my revenge."

As the last of the light faded behind the mountain, I headed back down to the town. Only when I was halfway down the path did I detonate the explosives and seal the cave.

Back at the hall, I sat on the stairs redressing my wounds. Looking up, I just stared at the mound of bodies I piled in the middle of the town.

Standing, I moved up the stairs and headed into the hall. Sitting against the wall by the door, I ate a small meal of bread I found and one small rat I managed to catch.

Lying down, I tried to sleep, but the pain from my injury made it hard. Every time I moved, the pain would wake me. Unable to sleep, I got up and made ready to leave.

It took me little to no time for me to get ready. Not much was left over, and what there was wouldn't last me long.

With my supplies on my back, I made my way to the door. As I did a sharp pain hit me and I fell over. Reaching out, I put my hand to the wall to steady myself.

As I did, my hand felt cold metal beneath the dust. Brushing the dust away I found a medal plate with letters engraved on it. As I read it, I felt my breath leave me, for I had read it before.

The plate read James T. Morris Federal Correction Facility for the Criminal Insane. This was the place, the place the Stranger, or as known back then, the S.A Killer was sent to prison. This was the place he was to be sent and to be executed.

I could almost see it. Maybe close to two years after the Great Disaster when he decided it was time for him to leave. The place would have been left barren when he left. This is how Angelica's family found it, a good three years later, a five-year-old Angelica in her mother's arms.

"It doesn't matter anymore," I said, shaking my head. "He is as good as dead by now. But my wife may be alive, and I must try to find her."

Outside, I made my way to the huge pile of bodies with a torch in hand. Throwing the torch on the pile, I watched as it went up in flames before making my way south.

Chapter 29

The Eagle

"Wait you're telling me you went out wounded to search for the people who killed your son and destroyed your town," the bartender said, wide-eyed. "But you didn't even know where they were or where they went. How were you planning on finding them?"

"I didn't have much of a plan," Matrix said, taking a drink. "All I knew was which way they had come from and that was the way I was going to go.

But you're right," Matrix said. "In my condition, I couldn't make it five miles, and I didn't."

I found my mind beset by strange visions. Even now, I could not tell you what I saw. Many times I could see people over me speaking, but I could not hear or understand. Their faces all showed concern, but I did not know why.

I never had the time to ponder that question, or even who these people were. The strange visions assaulted my mind driving me to madness.

I went in and out of those strange visions. I couldn't tell you how long I was in this state. Like all I saw and felt was real but also fake.

I felt a wet cloth on my forehead and a person sitting beside me. The person stirred, and I saw a hand coming towards me. Without thinking, I reached out and grabbed the hand around the wrist. A woman screamed, and my hand released her wrist.

The woman stood up quickly and moved over to one of the walls.

"Where," I said coughing, "w-who are you? Where am I?"

"You are in our village," a man said from the door. "I am Daniel, and she is my daughter Ellen; you are safe here."

"How did—" I said, coughing again.

"Here," Ellen said, holding a cup of water to my lips.

Sitting up, I drank from the cup. The water stung my throat as it when down. Coughing again, Ellen took the cup away and helped me to lie back down.

"How did I get here?" I asked, again.

"I found you on the road," Daniel said, moving into the room and sitting by Ellen. "You were out cold and bleeding from many wounds. You also had a slight concussion and several broking ribs. You seemed to have been in battle."

"I was!" And I began to tell them both what happen.

"We had heard of an armed group moving from place to place, but we didn't know the stories were true," Daniel said rubbing his chin. "But to hear of someone who had fought them and survive is truly something."

"But, Father, his wounds are still bad," Ellen said. "The fever is just finally going down. How can you see this as a good thing?"

"It doesn't matter really," I said, closing my eyes. "All I need is time to heal, and then I will go and find my wife."

I was forced to spend a week in bed before I was even able to get up. Using a crutch Daniel had made for me.

The village was mostly small wooden homes, encircling a main square like a horseshoe. The hut I was in was close to the center of the top part of the horseshoe. A blacksmith forge was on the right side, and a school and tavern on the left.

The committee was a diverse group of people. Everyone here lived the simple life, working on his or her only interest. There was farmland outside where the village was growing their crops and the livestock were grazing. Life here was peaceful.

Over at the blacksmith forge, Daniel worked long and hard to fix the plates in my armor. While several of the village's seamstresses worked on stitching up both the cloth and Kevlar pieces of my armor.

A day after I woke up and five days after Daniel found me on the road, Daniel came into the hut and showed me the pieces of my armor. Taking out one of the plates, he showed me the large hole in it.

He also told me the plates had shown signs of weakness before I was shot. He had proved this by showing me another plate. This plate had no holes in it, but it was dented in many places.

"You have never taken the time to repair or replace these plates, have you?" he asked, placing the plates on the table.

"No," I said, "never knew how."

"I thought so," Daniel said. "But don't worry about it. I can use the pieces; I cannot only fix your armor but might even be able to make it stronger and lighter."

From that point on, Daniel had been hard at work repairing my armor. As he had, he was teaching me how to fix and maintain my own armored plates.

"If you don't learn how maintain your armor it will fail on you again," he would tell me.

So, I took the time to learn how to use a forge. Though I wouldn't be able to master the skills of a blacksmith, I could at least learn the basic skills; besides, working in the forge helped me to regain my strength.

As both my body healed and my armor was repaired, I looked about the town. The people were kind, caring, and seem to be resistant to violence.

After several weeks, my injuries were well enough that I could move freely. My armor as well was coming along; it was only a matter of time before I would leave again to find my wife and those who killed my son and friends.

"There is one thing we do need to speak of, my friend," Daniel said to me as we worked in the forge.

"What would that be?" I asked, wiping the sweat from my face.

"About your helmet and mask," he said, slowing me the ruined pieces of metal. "I could weld the pieces together, but it will not be as strong as it was before. Or we could remake the helmet and mask, and if so then we must come up with a design."

"In truth, I never liked that helmet," I said. "In the defense of my town was the first and only time I used it. Before that I thought the helmet would be too cumbersome for me to carry around. Plus, the mask was far too ugly to wear."

Standing up, I walked over and picked up the two pieces of the helmet.

"But it would be a good idea to have a means to protect my head from attacks," I said. "But I don't want to carry around a bulky helmet wherever I go either."

So, we started to come up with a design for my new helmet and mask. To make the helmet more portable, we decided to use a hood. The hood itself would be lined with extra pieces of Kevlar from one of the ruined Kevlar vests I had found after the battle.

Metal plates were then placed in between the Kevlar in the same way as my armor was made. The metal plates were made small so it would lay flat when it was not in uses.

As for the mask, I thought I needed something more personal, something that would scare my enemies. It was for this reason I decided on using the face of a snarling wolf.

Agreeing to the design, Daniel started by measuring my head and face before drawing up a design on paper. Several papers later, both Daniel and I had a good idea of what to make.

Due to the scale and difficulty in the mask alone, Daniel would have to do most of the work himself. So leaving the forge, I went out walking through the town.

"Greetings, oh, Young Wolf," a voice from behind me said.

Looking around, I found an old man sitting under a tree. His copper skin face was lined with age, and his long hair was pure white. In his hands was a long wooden staff with an eagle craved on the top.

"And you are, old man?" I asked.

"Did not Wise Coyote speak of me before you parted?" he asked, looking up at me.

It was then I could see that the old man was blind. "If you know Coyote then you must be Soaring Eagle?"

"I am Soaring Eagle," Eagle said, "and you are Wise Coyote's student Young Wolf."

"So why are you here?" I asked, moving closer.

"To show you the way," Eagle said.

"The way?" I asked. "What way is that?"

"The way you must follow," Eagle said. "The way to your Beloved Sparrow."

"You mean my wife?" I asked. "You know where my wife is? Where is she?"

"Your Beloved Sparrow is with the followers of the Circling Shark," he said.

"Who the Circling Shark?" I asked, "And where do I find him?"

"Follow the Eye of the Circling Shark," Eagle said. "The Eye will show you the path you must follow."

I tried to ask Eagle what he meant, or even where I was to start to look when I heard an eagle cry somewhere above me. Looking back down, I was shocked to find that Eagle had disappeared. It was almost as if Soaring Eagle had just flown away.

I found it hard to sleep that night. Eagle's words rang in my ears. I knew I could not take his words literally, and I knew I needed to figure out what this meant.

"But how," I said out loud.

My thought was interrupted by a loud bang. Looking out the window, I could see the fountain in the town square had been destroyed.

By the light of the fires I could see five men and one who had a grenade launcher in hand. The others had both pistols and clubs in hand, and on their shoulders was the same symbol as the ones who destroyed my town.

I watched as the men started going from house to house kicking down the doors and pulling out the people, gathering them into the center of town.

"Find every person and bring them here, now!" said the man with the grenade launcher.

Coming to my door, one of the men kicked the door in, and in the dark the man entered the room. Before the man could look around, my sword tore through his chest.

As his body fell out of the doorway, his friends were already moving to where he fell, but they suddenly stopped when they saw me.

"Who the hell are you?" their leader asked.

Without speaking, I moved out into the town, my sword crimson in my hand.

"Not talking, huh," the leader said. "Kill him!"

At his word, his three men came at me. The first came from the right. Ducking under his club, I brought my sword up into the man's head. By that time, the other two were almost on top of me.

Sidestepping, I removed my sword from the man's head and threw his corpse at his buddies. His corpse managed to trip up the first guy, but the second was able to dodge it. Throwing his club at me he then went for the pistol at his hip, but I was too quick. Catching the club in the air, I quickly threw it back breaking his hand. As he dropped the gun, I took my chance and stabbed him in the chest.

After finally removing himself from beneath the corpse, the last guy came charging. With both his club and his friend's club in hand, he came at me like a wild man. Ducking under the first club, I caught the second one with my sword. Knocking the club out of his hand, I quickly decapitated him.

"You are either the luckiest man alive or the dumbest," their leader said throwing down the launcher and drawing a sword. "Now, let's see how you do against me."

His sword was like one naval officers used to carry, and by the way he held it he knew how to use it. When our swords met, I knew for sure that he had been properly trained.

After several moves, I could see we were equal in skill and strength. This meant that only style of fighting would win this battle. Quickly he had managed to disarm me. With a quick thrust, he aimed for the center of my chest.

Before the point of the blade could penetrate my chest, I was able to catch the blade between my hands. Spinning around the blade, I was able to knock the blade from his hand and struck him under his nose, killing him.

Retrieving my sword, I cleaned off the blade before putting it away. I then started going through the men's stuff, taking what was useful and discarding what was not.

By the time I was finished and heading towards the forge, the villagers were beginning to move around. Checking on the injured, putting out fires, and generally doing what was needed.

"I'm sorry, for all this!" I said, seeing Daniel had followed me.

"You did what you thought you had to do, I'm sure," he said, standing in the entryway.

"Yes, I did," I said, changing into my newly repaired armor.

"So now you are going out to find them," he said, picking up my mask.

"These are the same men who attacked my town mohths ago," I said checking my weapons.

"But how will you find them?" He asked, handing me the mask.

"They came here in one of my vehicles," I said, taking the mask. "All my vehicles have tracking devices in them, so I just need to follow the signal to their base."

"Then what?" he asked, almost hesitantly.

"Then I am going to save my wife, free my friends, and make those who took them pay."

Chapter 30

The Shark

It wasn't long before I had the location of my other vehicles and was on my way. Within a day, I had located the base.

It looked as if it was once a school. It was two stores tall and had a shape like that of a V. Around the building was a fence line about fifteen feet tall, and guards walking portals.

"This is not going to be easy," I said, checking the back of the Humvee.

Thankfully, it was fully equipped. Inside, I found several assault rifles, shotguns, pistols, and several units of ammo. Taking one of the M16, a shotgun, and several rounds for both, as well as several clips for my 9mm pistols, I made my way towards the base.

Staying in the shadows, I moved around the fence line looking for a quiet means to enter. As I did, I found an area where for a moment the guard was lax. I just needed to get past the fences, but thanks to my armor, it wouldn't be a problem.

In an instant, I was up and over the fences. I only had a few moments before the guards returned. I needed to find a way into the building without being seen. Within seconds, I found my way, a small window at ground level, most likely leading to a boiler room. With my sword, I was able to break the locking mechanism and entered through the window.

The room inside was dark. Moving through the darkness, I managed to find a door. What I found on the other side of the door surprised me.

The room was lit with dozens of electric lamps all around the room. But what surprised me the most were the hundred or so people. From what I could see, it was a diverse group of people of both men and women and even several children.

Moving through the crowd, I found most of the people didn't see or notice me. As for those who did, they only looked away the moment they saw me. But they all had the same look on their faces, that of beaten and defeated people.

"Matrix, is that you?"

Looking around I saw Tom walking through the crowd.

"Tom?" I asked, grabbing his hand.

I had known Tom was not one of the dead but wasn't sure he still survived.

"It's good to see you again," Tom said. "When you went over the cliff, we all thought you had died."

"Almost," I said, looking around. "Are the others here, too?"

"Many are," he said, as we moved through the crowd. "Those of us who survived were gathered up, put on trucks, and brought here, but it wasn't long before many were taken elsewhere; we don't know where."

"And Angelica, is she here?" I said hoping I'd see her.

"She was taken," another said.

In no time, I found myself in the company of the others from the town.

"What do you mean, 'she was taken'? Taken were?" I asked, as I was reunited with everyone.

"I heard the men talking," said one of the women of the council. "They found her interesting being one of the few women who fought. So they separated her from us and took her to the upper floor, doing who knows what with her."

"So, she is still here?" I asked, almost too soft for anyone to hear.

"Yes, but there's no way to get to her," Tom said. "There is only the one way out."

As he said this, he pointed up at the stairs and a door at the top.

"Then that is the way out!" I said, already heading for the stairs.

"No!" Tom said, holding me back.

"You can't," the council woman said. "There are close to two hundred men up there; we can't get by all those men."

"Why don't we go the way you come in?" Tom asked.

"That won't work," I said, shaking my head. "The window is too small and guarded too well. It would take days to get everyone out that way. No, the only way out is to go up."

As I said this, I began to ascend the stairs to the door. Halfway up the stairs, I stopped and turned.

"Tom, make sure everyone stays here and stays calm," I said, looking up at the door, "I will be back for everyone later. After I find Angelica."

With that, I headed straight for the door. The door itself was made of sold steel and looked as if had stood for years. A loud bang rang as I knocked.

"What do you think you doing?" a man asked, opening a shutter. "Get back down there with the rest of the slaves. I said go—"

His words were lost, as I had put the barrel of my gun through the shutter.

"Don't yell or I'll shoot," I said through the door. "You run and I will shoot, you understand me?"

I watched as the man's eyes moved up and down.

"Good," I said, pulling back the hammer. "Now, open the door, slowly."

With a rattle of keys, the door opened. Reaching around, I stuck my right arm out a gun in hand.

"Now, back up!" I said, as I slid out the door.

As he moved back, his eyes went wide as I came around the door. His shocked look wasn't because I was armed. No, the shocked look on my face was the wolf mask I had put on before knocking.

"Turn around," I said, pointing to the wall.

I then hit him with the back of my gun, knocking him out. I then dragged him over to the chair by the door. By the chair, he had some food, a drink, and a large club and a MP5 submachine gun. Picking up the gun, I checked the weapon before calling down to Tom.

"What do need?" Tom asked; he too was shock when he saw me.

"Take this and keep everyone calm. I will be back," I said, handing over the gun.

"What about you?" he asked as I walked away.

"I am fine," I said without turning around. "You just keep them safe."

Moving quickly and quietly, I made my way to the stairs. On the second floor, I opened the door a crack. I could see only one man standing at a door, halfway down the hall.

In a flash, I went down hall. The man just had time to see me when with a quick grab and twist, I snapped the man's neck. Finding the key on him, I quickly unlocked the door and entered dragging the body inside.

The room was once a classroom, but the only thing I noticed was my wife. She was shackled by chains to the ceiling; her body was covered with cut and bruises. Her clothes were all ripped and torn and barely covered her body. A quick slice of my sword cut her from her bonds.

Removing my mask, I fell to my knees to embrace my wife, but as I touched her, she recoiled.

"Angelica," I said, reaching out to her again. "Angelica, it's me, Matrix!" Reaching out to her, I literally had to force her up off the ground and turn her to face me. "Angelica, it's me," I said, looking her in the eyes.

"Matrix," she asked, in a weak voice. "Is that really you?"

"Yes, it's me!" I said, placing her hands on the side of my face.

She stroked my face as she looked deep into my eyes.

"It is you!" she said, overjoyed.

Holding her close, I hugged and kissed her over and over. As I held her in my arms, I told her all that had happened, and fresh tears streamed down her face as I told of our son's fate. Wiping way her tears, I kissed her on the brow.

"It's okay," I said, "I'm going to get you and everyone else out of here."

Nodding, I helped her to her feet. Seeing the rags she was left in, I quickly removed my jacket, and I placed it over her shoulders before handing her my shotgun. Putting her arms into the sleeves, she took the gun.

Going to the door, I opened it slowly as I looked to see if the hall was clear. It was; not a soul was around. Slipping out the door, I made my way quietly to the stairs.

"Look out!" Angelica said, as she pushed me away.

The next thing I knew, I heard two gunshots and two bodies falling to the ground. Turning around, I pulled my M16 up, but dropped it went I saw Angelica on the floor.

"Angelica," I said, kneeing beside her.

Bending over her, I looked over her wounds, but I knew it was too late; she was dying. Lifting her up, I put her on my knee and I held her close. With tears in my eyes, I looked on the face of my wife.

"There's nothing you can do, is there?" she asked, her hand on my cheek and tears in her eyes.

"I'm sorry, my love!" I said holding her closer.

"It's okay!" she said lovely. "You did everything you could, and besides I got to see you once more before I died."

Reaching up I tried to hold her hand, but her hand fell from my cheek and I knew she was gone. Closing her eyes, I howled my grief into the skies.

Chapter 31

The Crow

My mournful scream turned into a howl of rage and anger. With the both the gunshots and my howls of grief, I shouldn't have been surprised that I heard footsteps coming up behind me. I could tell by the sound it was four men coming up the stairs.

"What's going on up here!" one of the men asked. "Who are you, and what is that whore doing out of her cell?"

I just sat there holding my wife in my arms as the man who spoke walked up to me.

"Didn't you hear me?" he said, standing right behind me. "I asked you, who you are and what is that bitch doing—"

He wasn't about to finish his thought for I had put the shotgun barrel to the man's face.

"I'm Matrix, and she's my wife!" I said, pulling the trigger.

The man was blown completely off his feet, his face blown off. The other men's slow reaction gave me the time to fire three shots killing them all.

Knowing the sounds would bring more man, I made ready to move. Dropping the shotgun, I once more placed the wolf mask over my face. Just as I put my hood over my head, a man came up the opposite stairs. Moving quickly, I raised my rifle and pelted the man in a hail of bullets.

More men came from behind me. Spinning around, I fired into the men a hail of bullets into the men's ranks. Ejecting the magazine, I quickly reloaded my rifle. Taking one last look at my wife's body, I headed for the stairs.

Halfway down the stairs, I was ambushed by a group of men. Without out hesitation, the men fired up at me. I did not even flinch, just stood there as the bullets just bounced off my armor, barely even feeling bullets. Raising my rifle in a lazy movement, I showered the men in gunfire.

Voices and screams warned me more men were moving across the second floor. Spinning around, I fired just as the men burst through the door.

On the first floor, I made my way slowly as I went to every room killing all I found. Going room to room I saw they had transformed the old classroom into sleeping quarters, meeting rooms, and other rooms; I couldn't really tell what they were used for. As I searched, I seemed to meet very few men, and of those I did fight, many of them turned and ran away.

At first I thought it was the mask that scared them off. But as my rage began to calm a little, I started to think they may be planning something. If I were right, then this might mean ambush.

My thoughts were interrupted when a hail of bullets assaulted me after kicking in a door. Moving to the side of the doorway, I took a moment to check for injuries. Thankfully my armors seemed to have saved my life. A quick look around the corner told me there were five men in the room each with an automatic rifle in hand, and behind makeshift barricades.

I soon found myself exchanging fire with those in the room. Seeing no end to this, I decided to make my move. Waiting for the right moment, I moved from one side of the doorway to the next shooting wildly into the room.

On the other side of the door, I waited listening for any sounds. There were no shots fired back in return. But I could hear sounds of moaning coming from inside.

With a pistol in both hands, I slowly made my way into the room. Looking around I could see all the barricades were destroyed and four of the men were dead. As for the moaning, it was coming from a single man lying in a pile of rubble.

Moving over to him, I could see it wasn't just the rubble that was hindering him. I saw his wounds were not just stopping him but killing him. I stood over him and watched as the man reached in vain for a revolver. Stooping down, I picked up the revolver. I emptied the weapon before putting it in my belt.

"Well, what are you waiting for? Kill me!" the man said, his words turning into a scream.

"Tell me where everyone is at!" I said, my voices echoing though my mask. "I know there are more of you than I had seen. After all, there were several hundreds who attacked my town."

"Why should I tell you anything?" he asked.

"Because if you don't, I will let you live," as I said this, I turned and started to move away.

"No!" he said, crying out in pain.

"So, are you going to tell me where your friends are?" I asked.

"Only if you promise to help end my misery." Nodding my head, I moved close so to better to hear the man's dieing words.

"Down this hall, you will find a lager room; everyone is holding up there."

"How many men?"

"Around two hundred."

"How many ways in?"

"Four, two inside and two out, but it's no use; all the entrances will be blocked and guarded by now. There will be no way in."

"We'll see!" I said, before turning around to leave.

"Wait!" the man screamed. "You said you would help me."

Turning, I pulled the revolver out from my belt and loaded one bullet. I then dropped the revolver just within his reach before walking away. As I made my way to the door, there was a loud gunshot. Without looking around, I moved into the hall. Now knowing what to expect, I made my way to spring the trap.

The first thing I did was not go rushing in. I took the time to look over my options. Looking over the four doors, I began to come up with a plan.

Taking some explosives I found in one of the rooms, I went about setting the doors to blow. With a remote detonator in hand, I readied myself to attack.

Blowing the doors, I watched as the door blew into pieces. The shrapnel from the door hit the men closest. While the others farther back were stunned by the explosion. It was in this confusion I made my move, but not through any of the four doors.

In my search, I found another way in—a sky light on roof. With a rope and harness, I jumped down into the middle of the mob. With pistols in hand, I emptied a clip each as I descended the rope with the harness slowing my fall.

When I hit the ground, I smashed a button on the harness releasing the rope. Reloading my pistols, I began firing into the crowd. But the crowd couldn't do the same, not without shooting their friends.

It wasn't long before my ammo was gone, and I was taking the weapons of those around me or forcing them to shoot each other. I even killed many with my bare hands.

I would like to say I survived this fight without a scratch, but that would be a lie. A few minutes had passed and already I could feel my armor beginning to fail. As for now my armor was still whole, but it wasn't going to stay this way.

Taking two H&K Sub-Machine guns, I begin clearing a path to one of the barricades by the doors. Just as I made it to the barricade, I managed to grab to new pair of Sub-Machine guns. Jumping over the barricade, I quickly turned and emptied both weapons into the crowd.

My back to the barricade, I looked around me and soon noticed there was not a single gun, clip, or bullet near me. The only weapon I had was my sword. With my sword in front of me, I sat and tried to come up with a plan. As I sat, I listened to the men as they moved about speaking in a low tone.

"You three," one of the men said, "gather the guns. The rest of you cover them."

"What's the point?" another man asked. "There are only twenty of us left!"

"Quiet, you fool," said the first man, who must be their leader, "Just do as I say, *now*!"

Sitting there on the ground, I found myself laughing. Out of two hundred men, only twenty still survived. But it did not change my position; I was still trapped with only a sword and they had guns. I needed a distraction or a diversion so I could get the time to get close with a sword.

Listening to the commotion behind me, I could hear the men sounding scared. If so then I just might have a chance to take them all down.

"Which one of you is the leader?" I asked, yelling over my shoulder.

"I am!" said their leader. "What is it do you want?"

"To talk of surrender," I said, not moving.

"Then surrender and be done with it!" he said, yelling the words.

"It is not my surrender; I am talking about your surrender!" I yelled back.

"Why should we surrender?" he laughed. "There are more of us than there are of you."

"Yes, you do have me at twenty to one," I said mockingly. "But those are better odds than two hundred to one."

"What would be your proposal?" he asked.

"Why don't we do this face to face?" I said, removing my mask. "Give me your word you won't shoot, and I will stand and face you, man to man."

"You have it!" he said. "But my men will be ready to fire on my order."

Slowly, I stood up and made my way around the barricade. With sword sheathed in my left hand and out to side, I turned and faced my enemy. Twenty guns in two lines were trained on me while the leader stood to the right of then. I could see in the face of each of the men, they were indeed frightened by me.

"So, what is it that you want?" Their leader asked.

"My deal is you let me and all your slaves downstairs go and you will all live," I said, watching their leader's reaction. "Or I will kill you all and free your slaves myself."

"Or you can join us and work for me and keep all our slaves, or you can become a slave yourself," he replied.

"I will never serve you willingly or as a slave!" I said.

"Then we will just kill you!"

"Be smart!" I said. "Let us go and you live, or keep fighting me and you will die."

"By you?" he asked

"By me or by your slaves, it matters not to me."

"What do you mean by our slaves?" he asked. "They do whatever we tell then."

"Yes, but that was when you had numbers," I said. "But now there are more of them than you. It would be easy for them to overwhelm you."

"You need not worry about this; I can replace the men you kill in no time at all," he said confidently.

"Even so," I said, "it will still take some time to replace your men. You should be smart and surrender now or die where you stand."

"I have heard enough," the leader said. "If you will not surrender to me, now I will have no choice but to kill you."

"Fine," I said, "then I will kill you all!"

As I said this, their leader ordered his men get ready to fire, but before the command to fire was given, I was off like a flash. Only the man whose chest I pierced knew what happened and only briefly. Before the others could react, I spun around ripping my sword out from the man's chest and removed another man's head.

For the next several moments, it was just a blur of movement, just a constant motion of hacking, stabbing, and slashing. Before long I was standing in front of a pile bodies. Many of the bodies were missing arms, legs, heads, and even some were completely sliced in two.

Only their leader survived this massacre. When the fight began, he cowardly backed off to the left side wall where he stood petrified. Now that all his men were dead, I turned to face him. With my sword held out, I slowly moved towards him.

Seeing me getting closer, the leader began searching for a weapon. Looking down, he found an old Colt revolver. Picking the weapon up, he pointed it at me and pulled on the trigger. Click, the weapon did not fire. Five more clicks told us both the weapon was empty.

The odor of urine filled the air, as the man dropped the gun and fell on his knees. There was nothing else he could do. I was too close, and the other weapons were behind me. If he tried for them or even tried for the doors, I would cut him off and cut him down.

Standing in front of the man, I placed my sword point under his chin. With my sword, I forced the man to get on his feet.

"With your death, my wife and son will be avenged," I said, my sword poking the man's throat.

"Is that what this is about, revenge?" he asked, bewildered.

"Yes," I said, "your men killed my son in a town several days south of here. As for my wife, she died in this very building on your second floor."

"You mean that whore," he started to say, but a sharp point of my sword stopped him.

"Don't you ever call her a whore," I said. "She was my wife; you will not talk about her like that."

"So, you will kill me then what," he asked.

"Then nothing," I said, "I will go my own way."

"If you think you can live happily after this, you're wrong."

"What do you mean?"

"I mean if you think killing me will end this, you're wrong," he said, a bit of courage entering his voice. "You may kill me, but you will die soon enough."

"How?" I asked, thinking this was just some way to stall for time.

"Not by me or by any whom I command," he said, his face growing into a smile, "but by the Sovereign."

"Who is the Sovereign?"

"Our lord and master, the Sovereign sees and knows all. It was he who commands us to attack every town and village we see, and we always do as the Sovereign commands. As all do who stares into the Sovereign's eye."

As he spoke his last word, he pulled out a necklace from beneath his shirt. On the end of the chain was a gold and silver pendent with and red gem in the center. The shape of the pendent was the same one I saw before. The shark's jaws shaped like an eye, the red gem acting as its iris.

"I don't care who your master is," I said, looking the man in the eyes. "If he comes near me, I will kill him just as easy as this."

With this I decapitated this unlucky lieutenant of the Sovereign.

Chapter 32

The Hyena

Bending over the man's body, I cleaned my sword on his shirt before putting it away. I then grabbed the man's amulet and put it in a pocket.

Leaving this gruesome scene, I made my way back to the old boiler room where my friend and the other slaves were. As I came into the hall, I found the guard I knocked out was still where I left him. I watched as the man woke up and looked around. Seeing me, he grabbed the club beside him and charged at me. With a quick twist to the right, I cut the man in two.

Going up to the door, I knocked on the door. It wasn't long before Tom answered and opened the door.

"Matrix, oh, thank God it's you," he said, looking around. "Where is Angelica?"

"I'm afraid I failed again to save those who I care for, my friend," I said, mournfully.

"You mean she's," Tom said, the words too hard say.

"Yes, but it is not the time to mourn," I said, trying to get Tom to focus on what needed to be done right now.

"I need you to get everyone outside as quickly as you can," I said, adding an air of command in my voice. "You don't have to keep them together. Just tell them any supplies we find here will be distributed out to all who stay. I'll get started upstairs and work my way down."

"Ok, I am on it," Tom said, already heading down the stairs.

I know he wanted to know how Angelica died, and I knew I would have to tell him and the townspeople too, but there were other things to do now.

The search of the base for useable things went quickly, thanks in part to several men who assisted me with it. One of the men even asked if I wanted them to remove my wife's body from the second floor, but I told them no. It was a job I would do last.

Everything useful was taken out of the base—food, water, weapons, clothes, tools, gas, as well as many other things. These things were then laid in their own pile and distributed out to the people who stayed.

Within an hour's time, the whole building had been ransacked, and everything of use had been given out to the group. This then left only two things to do: destroy this place, and retrieve my wife's body.

On the second floor, I knelt at my wife's body. Picking up her right hand, I kissed it before removing her ring. The ring was once my mother's. I looped Angelica's and my ring together on a piece of leather and tied it around my neck.

I then started to wrap my wife in a white sheet I had found. With her body wrapped up, I then slowly made my way downstairs.

Once outside, I placed her body in the back of my Hummer feet first. As I moved away, the other townspeople had made their way over to pay their respects.

185

Turning back to the building, I grabbed a torch that was in the ground and tossed it in the doorway. The fire quickly lit the gas I used to start the fire. Papers, wood, other flammable items were used to keep the fire alive and moving throughout the building. In no time at all, we could see that the fire had made it to the second floor blowing out the windows.

With the building ablaze, the people began to go their separate ways, but not all left on foot. The servants to the Sovereign had many vehicles, horses, and even donkeys which people took as their own. The townspeople and I as one of the largest groups were of course taking three vehicles: my Hummer, a second Hummer, and one of the large troop transport vehicles.

With the vehicles packed up and everyone loaded up, we started our way east with me leading the pack. Driving until the light began to fade.

As we ate our evening meal, we discussed what to do next. I also explained what happen to Angelica. They were all shocked but not truly surprised how she died. They were also surprised to hear how I had killed all the men.

The next day we were off a little after dawn. We needed to find a place to bury Angelica and soon. As we drove, my mind was left to wander. Thinking of only one thing: how to find and kill the Sovereign.

Almost half the day had gone by and we still hadn't found a place to bury my wife. I was about to pull over for the evening meal when I saw a tall tree on top of a hill.

Within a few minutes, we were all parked at the bottom of the hill. Walking to the back of the Hummer, I grabbed a shovel and started up the hill. At the top, I noticed the tree was an oak tree.

Raising my shovel, I began to dig just between two large roots. Within moments, Tom was by my side digging as well as several of the other men. Everyone else, I could see they were at the bottom of the hill setting up camp and starting the fires. It wasn't long before the grave had been completely dug.

With the grave finished, I dropped my shovel and made my way back down the hill. As I slowly made my way down, the others were slowly making their way up to the grave.

Going to the back of the Hummer, I found myself looking down at my wife's body. Cradling her head, I slowly undid the wrapping around her face. Looking at her I saw she looked as beautiful as ever. Kissing her on the forehead, I quickly wrapped her face up before carrying her up the hill.

At the grave, I saw the people were standing to either side, many eyes hidden by tears. Walking between them, I could hear many payers being said, as well as silent curses under the men's breaths.

At the grave, I slowly lowered wife's body down placing her head at the foot of the tree. One of the older women in the group then started speaking. She spoke of many things, of life, and death, and rebirth. When she was done, others stood forward and said whatever they wished. They spoke mostly of the memory of Angelica, both sad and happy.

When everyone had said their peace, Tom and I started shoveling the dirt over my wife. Others wanted to take my place, saying that it wasn't right for me to be doing this. But I said it was just something I had to do.

When the grave was finally covered, the women and children came by and placed flowers they found next to the grave before heading back down the hill. The men too made their way slowly down leaving me alone on the hill.

Stepping around the grave, I made my way to the trunk of the tree. There I took out my knife and began to carve a massage into the bark.

It read:

HERE LIES ANGELICA ANN MATRIX
WIFE AND MOTHER
MAY SHE REST IN PLACE

At the bottom of the hill, the townspeople were already enjoying themselves, telling stories, crying, and laughing at all the good times and bad. Walking through the crowd, everyone would shake my hand or embrace me.

As the light began to fade, I stood up so all could see me and signaled for silence. Everyone quickly stopped what they were doing to look my way and waited for me to speak.

"First I would like to thank you all," I said, looking around. "I am glad to have met each one of you. But now, I am afraid I must leave." At this statement, everyone began to protest all at once. I quickly raised my hands for quiet before starting again.

"As I said I am leaving, for there is something I have not told you. When I killed the leader of the men who attacked us and held you prisoners, he told me he was just a servant to another master. What is more, this master, this Sovereign, will be coming after me for killing his men. Therefore, I'm leaving, not just two protect you all, but to kill the Sovereign."

"Then we will come with you," a man cried out.

Other voices soon joined in until everyone was crying out.

"No!" I said calmly. "If you come with me then more of you will die. If I go alone then I am the only one in danger, and I will have a better chance to get close enough to kill him."

"If you won't take us all, then at least take some of the men to go with you," a woman said.

"No!" I said. "I will be going alone; you need everyone else here to help you to find a new place to live. I am the only one who can leave without distorting the group."

More arguments began, but before I could try to regain order, another stepped up to speak. As Tom stood in front of the group, everyone went quiet.

"Matrix is right," Tom said. "It is he and he alone who needs to go. After all he is the only one who has tried to do what is necessary to protect us, and he did these by telling us only the truth. When we first heard we could be attacked, he told us our options: fight or run. It was us who decided to fight, and it was us who asked Matrix to train and lead us in the battle. And when the battle was lost, he came back from death to save us all.

"He has lost everything, both his wife and his son are dead, and though we all feel their loss, it is for him to take vengeance. We couldn't stop him even if we wanted to. We should be glad he took the time to tell us what he is doing. He could have just left in the middle of the night, and we would not know why. We might even have hated him for leaving without a word, but he didn't. We need to put our trust in Matrix once again and let him go and wish him good luck."

After Tom's speech, the townspeople seemed to change their minds. They now knew that I needed to do this, not just for myself but for them.

Grasping Tom's hand, I pulled him in close so I could whisper something in his ear. "Thanks, Tom," I said quietly. "You are a good friend, but now you are going to have to be an even better leader. For now you oversee everyone here. You must guide them to safety."

Walking away, I jumped into my Humvee, turned west, and drove away. Without looking back, I headed into the sunset.

Chapter 33

The Squirrel

"This was about six months now," Matrix said, putting down his cup. "I was hoping I would have found another one of the Sovereign's cells by now, but they are harder to find than I had first thought. It seems as if no one knows of them, or is too scared to talk."

"So, you have just been wandering the land. Hoping to run into them?" the bartender asked.

"That was the plan," Matrix said. "But sometimes you just need to talk to the right person to find the info you need. Like what I heard three days ago."

"You learned about one of the Sovereign's cells?" the bartender asked.

"Yes!" Matrix said. "I heard there was one in this area, and I feel I am close."

"Closer than you think," the bartender said, pulling out a shotgun from beneath the bar.

At the same time, the men at the tables also pulled out guns and pointed them at Matrix's back. Matrix just smiled, as if this was nothing to him.

"So, you work for the Sovereign!" Matrix said, looking down the shotgun's barrel.

"You could say that," the bartender said, pulling out an amulet of the Sovereign's Eye."

"A lieutenant of the Sovereign," Matrix said, "acting as small-time bartender of a shitty bar."

"You didn't suspect a thing, did you?" the lieutenant said smiling.

"Is this what you think?" Matrix said.

In a blink of an eye, Matrix grabbed the shotgun and elbowed the lieutenant in the throat. He then used the shotgun to kill the other men in the room. Turning around Matrix pointed the gun in the lieutenant's face. A click told them both the weapon was empty. Matrix then smacked the man across the face with the gun.

Before the lieutenant could move, Matrix was on top of him, a pistol on the lieutenant's face. With the other hand, Matrix ripped off the amulet off the lieutenant's neck. Pocketing the amulet, Matrix bent down over the lieutenant.

"Now then, let us talk," Matrix said. "I gave you my life story, why don't you give me the Sovereign's?"

"I don't know anything about the Sovereign," the lieutenant said.

"Don't lie to me," Matrix said pushing hard on the gun. "You must know something about the man."

"I don't know anything I swear," the lieutenant screamed, as the gun was shoved into his cheek.

"Ok, how about something simple," Matrix said, removing the gun. "Where can I find the Sovereign?"

"I don't know," the lieutenant said.

"What do you mean you don't know?"

"I mean I do not know where the Sovereign is."

"Well, if you don't know where he is then who does?"

"No one knows," the lieutenant said, laughing, "at least, not here. We are not that important."

"Then you're useless," Matrix said, getting off the lieutenant. "How can you work for this man and not know anything about him?"

"I know all I need to know about him."

"And what is that?"

"He is strong, and he will kill anyone he wants."

"Then you're more of an idiot than I thought," Matrix said, walking away.

"Is that what you think?" the lieutenant said, picking up a cleaver to throw.

Matrix turned and fired three times into the man's head. The lieutenant fell to the bar, the cleaver striking the wood by his head. With the lieutenant dead, Matrix grabbed his bags and threw them on a table.

A sound from behind Matrix made him turn around quickly, guns drawn. Looking down the barrel of the guns, his hand in the air was Steven the lieutenant's slave boy.

"Oh, it's you," Matrix said, turning away from the boy.

"Y-you mean you're n-not going to k-kill me?" Steven asked.

"I only kill those who stand in my way," Matrix answered. "Are you going to stand against me?"

"N-no sir, I w-wont," he said, lowering his hands.

"Good," Matrix said, opening the small bag.

"Ah, sir, m-may I ask how you knew my master worked for the S-Sovereign?"

"Eagle told me," Matrix said, turning to the boy.

"You mean that old blind man w-who told you where you w-wife was?"

"The very same," Matrix chuckled. "He told me, 'To the west you should go for the Sly Chameleon lies in waits in view but hiding from sight for thou foolish to come within reach. Taking all, he can please his master The Circling Shark.'"

"So, you believed my master was working for the S-Sovereign because of the bar sign?" Steven said, dumfounded.

"No, at least not just because for the sign, but the chameleon pins your master wore," Matrix said, pointing to a small chameleon shape pin on the dead lieutenant's shirt."

Not knowing if Matrix was serious about the pin or if it was a joke, Steven changed the subjected by asking, "So what are you going to do now?"

"Me, I am going to leave and find the next of the Sovereign's cells and destroy them, as I did this one," Matrix said pulling out a Benelli M3 shotgun.

"B-but you can't," Steven said.

"And why not," Matrix asked.

"B-because my m-master had all his m-men waiting for you to l-leave," Steven said, "o-over one hundred m-men."

"What of the others?" Matrix asked pulling out a M16 Assault Rifle.

"Y-you mean the slaves?" Steven asked.

Matrix nodded.

"M-my master didn't want them shot by mistake, so he put them in the barn," Steven said.

"Your boss didn't want to lose his stock of slaves, did he?"

"S-so what are you g-going to do now, s-sir?"

"Is there a back door here?"

"N-no," Steven said.

"What about a cellar or some place far from the door where you can be safe?"

"Y-yes, a c-cellar in the back," he said.

"Good," Matrix said. "Take the girls and get in the cellar and stay there until everything is over."

"Y-yes sir," Steven said, as he and the girls moved back to the cellar.

Now they were all out of the way, Matrix began to prepare for the fight ahead. He checked both the shotgun and M16 before loading both weapons. Removing his jacket, he then pulled two belts out of the bag. One of the belts had shotgun shells on it, and the other had pockets with M16 clips in them. Throwing the belts over his head they laid across his chest.

Putting on his jacket back on, Matrix then slung the shotgun on his back. He then clipped the M16 under his arm, so it was easy to reach. Next, Matrix checked both 9mm before reloading and chambering the first round.

Holstering the weapons, Matrix drew his sword. He cleaned the blade and sharpened the edge before sheathing the blade. With all his weapons in order, Matrix then checked the fit of his armor and insured there were no holes or tears in each armor pieces.

Finally, Matrix removed the wolf mask. Looking over the mask, Matrix found himself staring into the eyes of the wolf. With his mind focused on what he must do, Matrix donned the mask. After fixing the hood over his head, Matrix was then ready to fight and kill.

Zipping up his bag, he picked up both bags and made his way to the door. Kicking it open, Matrix stepped out into the high noon sun. Around him, he could see the men Steven had warned him about.

As Matrix investigated the faces of the men, he could see each one of them was terrified. Many of them were carrying rifles while others had pistols, and Matrix saw most of those weapons were shaking.

Under the mask, Matrix smiled at the fear he held over the Sovereign's own men. Before the men could get over their fear, Matrix threw down his bags and raised the M16 and fired into it into the crowd.

CPSIA information can be obtained
at www.ICGtesting.com
Printed in the USA
BVHW040520060122
624405BV00002B/5